Next Steps

Next Steps

Elaine Durbach

Copyright © 2024 Elaine Durbach

All rights reserved. Except as permitted under the U.S. Copyright Act of 1976, no part of this publication may be reproduced, distributed, or transmitted in any form or by any means, or stored in a database or retrieval system, without the prior written permission of the author.

www.elainedurbach.com

Author: Elaine Durbach
Cover Design: Abigail Rothman
Book Layout Design: Linda Lombri, *Lombri Writes!*

This book is a work of fiction. The characters, incidents, and dialogue are drawn from the author's imagination unless otherwise specified in the text. Any other resemblance to events or persons living or dead is coincidental.

Next Steps

ISBN-13: 979-8-9858831-1-4 (paperback)
ISBN-13: 070-8-9858831-4-5 (ebook)

Dedication

This book was not in my plans. *Roundabout* and *LAF – Life After Felix* completed the story I wanted to tell about Sally Paddington. But then I kept learning online about older people, women and men in their sixties and beyond, who were finding love and achieving greater happiness than ever before in their lives, and I knew that was true of Sally. So, this book is dedicated, not just to beloved friends met in person, but also to this fellowship formed online, to the people who have expanded my notions of love and life.

Acknowledgements

Thank you to those who read my early drafts and put up with — even encouraged — my waxing on about another Sally Paddington saga. Especially, thanks to those who read version after version—Lisa Trusiani, Helene Thorup-Hayes, Ashley Case, and Birgit Matzerath. This was a particularly challenging task, providing guidance on how to keep readers of the earlier books engaged while ensuring new readers could follow the story. They did their best; whether I've succeeded or not, you all will have to decide.

For their professional skills, as with the previous two books, thank you to Abby Kanter, for her hawk-eyed editing, to Linda Lombri, for giving the manuscript a real-book form, and to Abby Rothman, for providing *Next Steps* with its outer face.

Thank you too to my fellow writers from the Montclair Write Group, and to my advisors-on-Zoom, Elena Taylor, Keri-Rae Barnum, and Sandy Vaile O'Grady, among others, for their extraordinarily generous advice. Writing can be such an isolated activity, but these in-person and online communities have kept loneliness at bay.

As ever and forever, most of all, thank you to my multi-talented husband, Marshall Norstein, and to our wise and loving son, Gabe, for helping make my life so happy, even when I'm agonizing over this writing process. I wish this book could be a bestseller so I could treat you like the princes you are!

~ *1* ~

Peering out from the wings as I'm about to walk out on stage, I spot a bright blur of color at the back of the auditorium. Just a glimpse, as a beam of light catches the tie-dyed T-shirt in that dark sea of elegance, enough to know it's Sam Parker.

Relief floods through me, instantly followed by anger. The contrast is dizzying, like a flash of *deja vu*, but I haven't known Sam long enough for *deja* anything.

It shouldn't matter that he's turned up. For these past few weeks, he seemed to think I was wonderful; now he no longer does, but so what? I straighten my back, lift my chin. I'm ready for this, I really am.

No, I'm not.

My friend Mary—Professor Burns—is winding up her introduction. She claims I dreamt up the idea for this gathering of dance greats and convinced her it should be held right here in Cape Town, our home city, where my own dancing began. I shake my head, but she isn't looking my way.

"Sally Paddington insisted amazing people would come to Cape Town," Mary says. "Amazing people have come—you, the innovators and inspirers of the dance world, joining with our wonderful local community. Together, we can transform lives in this city, and this country, and around the world."

I did say all that, and I did agree to give this talk—but that was a year ago, before . . .

"Helping others to experience the joy of dance, that has been Sally's greatest passion," she says. It's true, or it was. Mary's cadence rises: "Of late, her focus has been on those tragically restricted by physical limitations. In fact, she is working on a book on the subject, a follow-up to her classic, *New Steps*."

I had no idea she was going to mention the book. "This one, *Next Steps*, is based on her experience with disabled dancers around the world and on research by her late partner, Dr. Felix Barnard."

Who the hell am I to be writing this book, now, without Felix? I want to flee.

But she gestures in my direction. "Let her tell you about it herself. Here, for our finale and to show us those next steps, our very own Sally Paddington!"

The applause drags me forward into the light. Feel as naked as a featherless chick, definitely not ready to fly. Look down, but my discomfort isn't erased by my dress.

What possessed me to wear pink? Bought it last week with Sam in tow, inspired by him and his rainbow shirts and the feeling that life was beginning to return to normal. But then he

Next Steps

did his vanishing act, just as Felix did.

Nonsense, woman! I didn't choose to die, and Sam didn't dump you.

Hush! I have to focus.

My mind has gone blank. Teeter to the lectern and stretch up to the mic, feeling too short despite my ridiculously high heels. They're about as effective at making me look tall as the shoulder pads men wear in their suits to look broad-shouldered. Fortunately, with the lights shining right at me, I can see only the first few rows, women and men of all ages and shades. They are smiling and clapping. A few are standing. At least, now I can't see the rainbow shirt at the back.

The first slide pops up with the question: "Why dance?"

You've got this, Copper Girl.

I thought I did . . .

~ ~ ~ ~

It's after midnight. Still debating whether I should call my friend Bob Halpert.

Got home late from the conference after-party, utterly drained, ready to collapse into bed. Saw the light blinking on my phone and pressed the button reluctantly. A sonorous voice with a heavy Afrikaans accent boomed: "Miss Paddington? Please call Sergeant Roelofse at the Muizenberg Police Station as soon as you get this message. It is in connection with your friend, Mr. Samuel Parker."

Sam? Why did they call me? My first thought was that he got arrested for smoking pot on the beach with his new friends, the silly man. Is that why he rushed away instead of coming to the after-party like everyone else? Tried to warn him that neither his age nor his honest face nor his American accent would protect him, that the cops here in South Africa are still stricter than those in the States, especially with a foreigner who dresses like a hippy.

But perhaps he broke some other law. I don't really know Sam very well, though it feels as if we've known each other for more than these six or seven weeks.

With a jolt, I remembered the police can call for other reasons. Dialed and asked for the sergeant. That deep voice: "Roelofse here. *Ja*, Miss Paddington? I called you two hours ago. When you didn't phone back, Mr. Parker gave me another number to try."

"Is he okay? Is he hurt?"

"No, he's not hurt much."

Not much? "Is he in trouble? Is he under arrest?"

"No. He looked like he is intoxicated. He was asking an officer to help him. He couldn't find his way home, and he couldn't remember where was his home—or his hotel."

"Who did you phone then?"

"He said we should call Reverend Halpert, the minister in Kalk Bay. You know him? He came to get Mr. Parker."

"Yes, Reverend Halpert is a friend. Thank you."

Whatever happened to Sam, it was a wise choice to call Bob Halpert. He is clueless with pets and plants—overfeeds both—but when it comes to people, he is a true shepherd. But it's way past Bob's bedtime. Too late to call him.

Now that my fear has subsided, I'm even more perplexed. When we met, on the flight to New York back in December, he told me he comes to Cape Town often for his work and has

Next Steps

made a wide array of friends. Was Sam partying with people who led him astray? He could have been at some posh villa up on the mountainside, or down at the harbor with a bunch of fishermen, and then . . . ?

It's another of the ways he resembles Felix. When my beloved and I were together back in our youth, and again when we reunited here in Cape Town, living in this little cottage in Kalk Bay, he regularly brought home decidedly dubious characters. I always loved that openness in him—especially given how divided we still are in South Africa. I've admired it in Sam too. But it can be dangerous.

The cats are curled up on the duvet, and I yield the center to them, crawling into my old place on the right-hand side of the bed. Leave the left, Felix's side, empty—as it's been these past eleven months.

~ 2 ~

Saturday morning. Surface from sleep earlier than usual. It feels like forever since I last heard Felix for real, yet still my ears prick up, expecting him to call from the kitchen, "Coffee's ready, sleepy head. Come and get it." Silence. Grateful that I still hear him in my head. A real-life poltergeist—or should I say, real-death poltergeist? —or just the imprint on my soul of long, long acquaintance?

I'm such a hypocrite! And Sam Parker knows it better than anyone. How can I talk about others overcoming massive obstacles when I can't dance myself?

I kick the blankets aside, to the cats' disgust. Angry with myself for agreeing to give the talk, and angry with Sam. But how do you just drop a friendship? I refuse to care anymore. He's leaving next week, going back to his home in Oregon. No idea when—or if—he's ever coming back, and I don't care. Free to hunker down again in the safety of my little cave, with my memories.

Next Steps

Bullshit, Copper Girl.
I don't like being abandoned. You know that.
Oh, give me a break. And this is a new year, a chance for new beginnings.
It doesn't work that way. The heart isn't on a schedule. Not that my heart was involved with him. He was just a friend—and not even that in the end.
You didn't need to be a bitch.
Me, a bitch? You're always telling me to move on. Well, I am moving on—from Sam Parker. And apparently, he's already moved on from me.
Then why did he attend your talk last night? And why did he give your number to the police?
Oh yeah, that. The police.

~ ~ ~ ~

My companions are prowling back and forth across me, their mews growing more insistent, Mergatroid, in her tabby splendor, and her son, Skelm, glowing orange in the morning light. They won't let me delay breakfast any longer. Stagger out of bed and go feed them. Then—even before I drink my coffee—call Reverend Bob.

He's one of those people who rise with the sun, full of cheer and plans for the day. I'm not. It helped when Felix was around. Without him, yeah, mornings are a battle.

When Bob answers, I brace for his usual bright greeting. Instead, hear a hushed "Aha, Sally . . ."

"Is Sam Parker with you? Is he all right?"

"That depends on what you deem 'all right.' He was mugged last night. His shoulder bag was stolen, along with his wallet and his passport. He was very shaken. How did you know he was here?"

"The police. I was out but they left a message. The sergeant said he was drunk and lost. That didn't sound like Sam."

"Hmmm, yes, not what one would expect from your Yankee pal."

"Not a Yankee and not my pal. If he's safe with you, fine. I'll leave you two in peace."

He butts in, still sotto voce: "No, wait. I think you and he need to speak to each other."

"Then put him on the line."

"It would be better face to face. Have you had breakfast? There's fresh coffee. How soon can you get here?"

Bob lives just a few doors away. I splash my face, haul on jeans and a T-shirt. Catch sight of myself in the hallway mirror. I look like Einstein! Duck back in to brush my hair and put on lipstick, not to impress Sam Parker, but so Bob doesn't get more perturbed than he sounds already.

As I walk up the cobbled street, beyond bird calls and cars, I hear Felix: *Be nice, Sal.*

Too late. Sam hates me.

He doesn't hate you. But have a little mercy.

Mercy? I'm the one who got hurt.

Bob is hovering at his open door, sunshine glistening on his domed head. He looks angelic, while I feel decidedly not. He ushers me in but holds up a hand to stall me before we enter the dining room. He whispers, "If something between you brought on last night's excess, use this chance to clear the air. Sam's leaving very soon to go home. Wouldn't it be better

Next Steps

to part on good terms?"

The American stands in greeting, but without meeting my eyes. He winces as he eases back into his chair. His usually rosy cheeks are pallid. There's a graze on his cheekbone and gray stubble around his jaw. Even his habitual gaudy T-shirt, probably the one that caught my eye last night, is decidedly the worse for whatever went on afterward.

He passes me the basket of scones and pours guava juice into my glass. For a moment, that gallantry eases my wariness. Then he mutters, "Excuse me," and darts out of the room. The bathroom door thuds shut.

I mention that Sam seems to be in pain, in addition to his hangover. "Ah, that would be the bed in my guest room," Bob says. "The mattress has seen better days."

We sit in silence, toying with our food. Then Bob whispers, "This doesn't seem to be going as I hoped. The last time I saw you two, you looked as carefree as teenagers, very happy in one another's company."

"I thought we were."

"Could you fill me in? Of course, if it's none of my business, just tell me to get lost."

Consider doing that, but the hurt has been simmering all week; I want to complain. "Sam changed his mind about me. He thinks I'm cold."

Bob recoils. "Oh Sally, surely not! Why would he think such a thing?"

Try to make light of it. "We had a misunderstanding. Doesn't everyone at some point?" But Bob is shaking his head. He curls his fingers, an "out with it" gesture.

"Well, okay. This is what I remember. Last Saturday we had dinner at that new Cuban restaurant." He nods encouragingly. "Afterward, the band started playing something slow. Sam reached for my hand to pull me up to dance. I stood up—but then . . . "

"Then . . . ?"

"I pushed him away. I couldn't do it."

"Pushed? Oh, dear. That was the first physical contact?"

Think for a moment. "No. We've walked arm in arm, kissed on the cheek, if that's what you mean."

"You don't find him attractive? I think he's quite a pleasant-looking chap, but I don't know what appeals to women."

"He has a nice smile," I say, though it hasn't been in evidence this morning. "I just didn't want to dance with him. Too close, too intimate. I said, 'Don't!' or something like that."

"A little harsh! You women don't understand how much courage it takes for men to make the first move, even with another man." He looks down with a little smile. We've only recently begun to talk about his own romantic forays.

"I didn't mean to be harsh," I say.

"And that's when he said you were cold?" Bob shakes his head, as if trying to picture the scene.

"Not cold. More that I give mixed signals. Felix says I was a bitch."

"Felix? You mean he used to say . . . But Felix didn't ever say that. He would tell me how afraid he was of hurting you, that you were so empathetic and soft-hearted."

"Whatever. A shutter came down. Sam switched off.

Next Steps

When he brought me home, he just turned and walked away. No phone calls, nothing since. I hadn't seen him until last night, in the distance, at my talk. I don't know why he bothered to come."

"Perhaps because he cares for you?" Bob pauses and gives me a sideways look from under his wispy, white eyebrows. "Sally, have you told him about Felix?"

That seems like a non sequitur. "Of course. Why? Well, not in detail. When we met on the plane, he told me he was a widower. I said I'd lost my partner too, that I was kind of a widow. So, he knew."

"That's all you said?" The bathroom door opens, and we hear a voice in the other room, Sam making a phone call. Bob whispers, "You didn't tell him when you lost Felix, that it's only been a year?"

That fact tightens my chest. The anniversary of that hideous night is approaching. I've been trying not to think about it. I say, "I didn't want to bring my grief into this simple, happy companionship."

"But the grief is still there. Did Sam tell you about his late wife?" Bob's voice is still hushed.

"Yes. But it's different for him; they had thirty years together. Mainly, we've talked about our work, about his two daughters and his grandchildren in America." Bob nods, encouraging me to keep going. "You know they live in Portland? Not far from Felix's daughter, Joanie, and her husband, Eric, and their little Freddie. I told him how sick the baby has been, and that I was on my way to see them when we met on the plane."

"You didn't talk about Felix?"

"I said we weren't actually married, but that I love his kids as if they were my own." Bob knows how close we are.

"But you didn't say how recently you lost him?"

Shake my head. Can't explain how talking about Felix endangers my brittle pretense of serenity. Instead, just say, "Can we change the subject?" Bob frowns at me, worrying, just the way I don't want him to.

Sam comes back into the room. He looks like a contrite boy. "Reverend Bob, may I prevail on your hospitality again tonight? Evidently, I can't get my credit card replaced before Monday, and the hotel isn't willing to have me book in again without it. They say they've been scammed too many times."

Bob, of course, assures Sam he can stay. I ask what happened. Sam hesitates. Bob asks his permission and takes over. "Sam, you were intending to stay with one of your new friends for this last weekend, weren't you, so you checked out of your hotel? Apparently, Sam's host expected him to share his rather awful views on race and wealth."

Sam nods and takes up the tale. "We began arguing. My fault, perhaps. I was in a rather bad mood. Things got heated. He called me a communist and a foreign agitator."

"And then kicked you out, bags and all?" Bob asks.

"Yup, into the street. That's when I got mugged. Must admit, I'd downed more beer than I usually do. Must have looked like an easy mark. Got bashed on the head. And lost. And picked up by the police."

Fate shouldn't be decided by a piece of furniture, but that's what seems to be happening—if this is fate. No sooner has

Next Steps

Bob told Sam he can stay with him than he withdraws the invitation. "You're walking like an old man this morning. It's that awful guest room bed. I can't let you cripple yourself."

Sam shrugs. "Yup, it does sag, but you know what they say about beggars and choosing. I'm in a pickle."

Bob waves his hands. "No, no. We'll find you somewhere else to stay. Sally, you have a fine guest bed, don't you? Slept in it a few times when Felix and I talked until late and consumed too much whisky."

Sam interrupts. "Oh no, I wouldn't impose on Sally." His cheeks have gone blotchy. I don't think I've ever seen that happen before, the blood rise like a tide. "That's out of the question. I'll find another solution."

"Nonsense!" Bob exclaims and juts his chin at me, eyebrows raised.

Reluctantly, I grunt, "You can use my guest room, Sam."

As he ushers us out, Bob says cheerily, "Perhaps, this being your Sabbath, you could go to the synagogue in Muizenberg."

Sam is Jewish too? In all this time, we've never discussed religion. He and I exchange puzzled shrugs and head down the street. Bob must really think we need divine help.

~ 3 ~

There's so much that Sam and I don't know about each other.

On the plane, we shared his excellent chocolate and laughed together over an animated comedy. In the way of seat-mate strangers, we discussed all our where, what, why, and discovered we were both planning to catch a connecting flight to Portland—though in the end, I didn't take that flight.

I didn't want to talk about Felix, to risk tears which still tended to well up at the least excuse. Talked more readily about my to-and-froing between South Africa, where I was born, and America, where I spent most of my adulthood. Sam told me about his own travels, how he has developed close professional ties in Cape Town, though he didn't go into detail.

When we parted, Sam gave me his card. I noted only what I'd asked him to write, the name of the store where he bought the chocolate.

Next Steps

My friend Libby noticed more than I did. She met me at Kennedy Airport to grab some precious catch-up time while I waited for my connecting flight, and she saw Sam emerge from customs right behind me. Apparently, he waved, but I didn't see that. "I hope he wasn't hurt," she said. "He looked like a wistful puppy, watching you walk away."

My interest was decidedly unromantic; I was more interested in Sam's tax expertise than his expression, given that he said he was a lawyer-turned-accountant, and I could really do with some tax help. He didn't look like an accountant, with his tie-dyed T-shirt and ragged haircut (the work, so he said, of a grandson), but he seemed trustworthy, maybe because of those sad, brown eyes.

It was Bob Halpert who persuaded Sam to ask me out a few weeks later. I'd returned home to Cape Town, and Sam was back just as quickly on yet another business trip. The two men met on my doorstep when I was out. Apparently, it was the American's second attempt. I doubt he'd have come by again, but Bob was determined to connect us. My pastor pal knew how my loneliness had recently led me astray, into the arms of Felix's brother Humphrey. "This Sam fellow seems like a much better proposition," he told me.

Much to Bob's delight, Sam and I did link up. Libby was thrilled too. I had told her all about my little liaison with Humphrey, and she disapproved even more than the minister. When I insisted I wasn't attracted to Sam, she waved that aside. "Give him a chance," she insisted. "I think he's rather cute. And I bet he came back to Cape Town extra quickly to see you." I doubt it, but that's Libby—always dreaming up happily-ever-after scenarios for me.

Sam soon put an end to my hopes of gleaning tax advice. Turns out he is a forensic accountant, helping nonprofits battle fraud and theft. A whole lot more interesting than my initial impression, but no use to me. The man also works with an affordable-housing organization and serves on various boards. All in all, one of the good guys.

As for the attraction part, with the passage of time his haircut had improved. On date number three or four, sitting across a dinner table, I noticed his dimples. Not a remarkable face, feature by feature, but oddly charming in its mobility, the way his lower lip curves up in the middle when he's stressing a point or trying not to laugh. Then those dimples deepen. Loved also—well, liked—that he delighted in the ordinary things, like unfamiliar flavors, or quirky coincidences.

"Just what you need," Bob decreed. "It would do you good to have some simple, uncomplicated fun with a jolly fellow like Sam. And, if I'm not mistaken, you're just what he needs. Show him around our lovely city."

So, I did. But that was then. I'm dreading a weekend with this no-longer-jolly, no-longer-admiring fellow.

~ ~ ~ ~

Sam flexes and stretches his sore back while I search my pockets for my ever-elusive front door key. "I don't want to be in your way," he says. "I can make myself useful. You mentioned some repairs that need doing. Or, if you like, I could read over your manuscript, do some proofreading? Whatever keeps me out of your hair."

I nearly hiss, the way Mergatroid does when a strange cat

Next Steps

comes too close. I don't want his help with the book. He has been encouraging without having seen any of it, and he has mentioned people in the States who might help with marketing and publicity. But for all his multiple skills, he knows nothing about dance or therapy or whether I'm qualified to write it. Also, I don't want him reading about Felix and asking more about him. I don't want him doing my repairs either.

This feels so weird. Through the weeks of our friendship, I never invited Sam into my home. The last man who came in, other than Reverend Bob, was Humphrey. Embarrassing memory. I had invited him to stay over, lit up by the chemistry between us—and then changed my mind. We made peace, and now we have a rather wonderful, almost-sibling relationship. I'm immensely grateful. But if Humphrey saw me ushering Sam into my home so soon after I pushed him away, that sweet filial connection would be dead.

Deader than me?

Ugh, that's not funny.

Humphrey's ego could do with a bit of deflation.

You're a typical big brother.

Sam, on the other hand . . .

Don't start with Sam again, please, Felix. He's leaving anyway.

You know Sam would stay on, at least for a while longer, if you asked.

If I fling myself at his feet, rending my robes?

No rending required, just a bit more warmth.

Thinking busy hands might stop awkward conversation with the living as well as the dead, I reluctantly dig out my toolbox. Hand Sam a hammer and show him where the trellis on the patio is coming apart. While he hammers, I set about sanding and revarnishing the window shutters. The salt air does a number on the wood, and I've been meaning to refinish them for ages. Would have hired someone to do it, but money is so tight these days, nonessentials stay on my "soon" list.

We work in virtual silence most of the day, each lost in our own thoughts. Not a Sabbath rest, but a good way to keep things neutral. He is calmly methodical. I like that.

In the evening, we order take-out from the fish restaurant near the harbor. *Casablanca* is on TV, and we watch, seated side by side on the couch. It's the only way we can both see the screen without a glare. I doze off at one point, and wake leaning against him. He is awake, sitting very still. Embarrassed, I ask if I snored. "Yes, but like a well-fed kitten," he says.

We gather our belongings and depart to our respective beds. I must admit, it feels nice to have another human in the house.

~ ~ ~ ~

I've surfaced slowly, feeling better rested than in ages. Evidently, Sam didn't sleep as well. I hear him showering. When I pad into the kitchen, wrapped in Felix's scratchy wool robe, he is seated at the table, paging through my first book, *New Steps*, written years ago, just before my marriage to Charles foundered.

"You know most of this dance talk is mystifying to me, but it's a fascinating book," Sam says. "It's wonderful how you've pursued this passion all your life."

"It's a very narrow focus compared to how you've lived."

Next Steps

He shakes his head with a sheepish grin. "I'm a jack-of-all-trades, not expert at anything."

"That's nonsense! You're clearly good at your forensic accounting, and that seems to draw on economics and law, and . . ."

"Exactly, one thing after the other," he says. "Too curious for my own good. If I hadn't met and married my wife and been steered into the family firm, I'd probably have lost my way down even more trails."

As we talk, I'm taking out bread and eggs and cereal, asking Sam with hand signs what he wants. He nods or shakes, and then starts helping, slicing bread and slipping it into the toaster. I'm curious about his wife, Margo, but it doesn't seem the moment to probe further. He asks about my vision in *New Steps* and what led me to write it.

"Amazing how approaches differ from one culture to another," he says. "Was your Felix also involved in dance? Did he help with this book too?"

Forgot that Mary mentioned our co-authorship last night. Immediately tighten. I've told him so little about Felix or his expertise. Preferred to talk about Cape Town and my childhood, and his. I've shown him the oak-shaded house where I grew up, and the public swimming pool where I learned to swim, and where Spotty, the dog-shaped ice-cream joint we'd frequent on the way to the beach, used to stand. Now, there is just a mini version, but the memory brought a stream of anecdotes that he seemed to love. Told me a few about his own childhood, and how he would take his little sister to get ice cream, balancing on the crossbar of his bicycle. Parked and sat watching the surfers at Muizenberg. I told him how the boy next door taught me to surf with a belly board.

Said almost nothing about my sweetheart, how Felix and I met and fell in love in college. Why we fought and parted—not something I ever like to remember. How we finally landed up together again, what a blissful homecoming it was.

"Could you teach me to surf?" Sam asks now. "I saw you have some boards in the garage." Darn! The guy is in his sixties, a couple of years younger than me. I don't know if he swims well enough. But happy to have changed subjects, and the weather is perfect. If only I wasn't so pale and freckled. He is tanned, or just naturally brown, as I never was.

"Redheads don't tan," my mother would say, slathering me in lotion. If she were alive now, she'd have me using SPF-70, appalled that I haven't made more effort to prevent wrinkles.

As I signal to turn right from Main Road toward the beach, Sam points to the left, to the sedate, cream-colored building halfway up the block. "Is that the synagogue Bob mentioned?" he asks. I switch signals and turn left instead, grateful no one is on my bumper.

Imma and Pops loved that shul. It was where they first attended services after we arrived as immigrants in Cape Town. They were Polish speakers who had tried to settle in what was Palestine and became Israel, before they changed their minds and headed to South Africa. I, their only child, spoke Hebrew and Polish, and quickly learned English and, at school, Afrikaans and then French.

Sam is impressed when I tell him that, declaring himself awful at languages.

Next Steps

"Next time I come, perhaps we can go to a Friday night service," he says. Despite myself, I'm pleased that he is thinking of the future. Feel my parents smiling too. Their *meydele* is with a *mensch*. On the other hand, they thought Charles was one too, and I never gave them cause to think otherwise.

~ ~ ~ ~

The sea is rough and cold until we get used to it. The waves swamp Sam over and over, but he comes up grinning each time, still clutching his board, and persists until he manages to launch himself at just the right moment. He stays aloft, carried along like a cork, yodeling in glee all the way to the beach. Comes wading back for more.

We return home salty and sticky, with matted hair, eager to shower. I tell him to go first. As I come out of my bedroom, still in my swimsuit, slightly chilled, Sam emerges from the bathroom with a towel around his waist. We try to edge past each other, but move in the same direction and stop. We are almost breast to chest in the semi-darkness of the passage. I laugh nervously, aware of the heat from him and the drops of water still glistening in his chest hair, of his eyes seeking mine. I look up at him, wanting to lean toward his warmth.

He whispers, "I wish I wasn't leaving tomorrow night."

Click! Don't want to feel his warmth or anything else. Want to be alone, as I was before he came along, perfectly comfortable—or getting by at least. Step past him into the bathroom.

~ ~ ~ ~

I have a perfect excuse to get away, a dance recital in a poverty-stricken area out on the Cape Flats. Not a place for pleasure-seeking visitors. The invitation came last week from one of the teachers at the conference. I tell Sam he'll have the house to himself.

Estella is one of Mary's past students, a beautiful woman with smoothly straightened, gold-streaked hair that is almost the same color as her skin. She lives in Mitchells Plain, and teaches in the morning at a school there, but in the afternoon, she works with disabled children in a squatter camp, among the poorest of the poor. She said she'd observed some of my classes in the past, has read my first book, and would love me to see her kids. Reluctantly promised I'd come. Now I'm glad I did.

Sam rubs his hair. He says, "Would you mind if I tag along? I've seen very little of that side of the city."

Annoyed, trapped like I was at Reverend Bob's, I mutter, "If you want to." How can I say no?

~ ~ ~ ~

I have an approximate address, not enough to find on my phone or a printed map. "Just ask people," Estella had said. That works. As soon as we turn off the tarred road, a man points us in the right direction. It takes a few more inquiries, but everyone seems to know where the Sonskyn Hall is, and they help willingly. One man offers to get in the car and direct us, but at that point, our destination is within sight. The prefab structure is much larger than those around it, but hardly sturdier.

We park against a barbed wire fence, between a rust-pocked van and a cart hitched to a gray donkey. A teenager lolling by the fence offers to watch over my car for a rand. Sam

Next Steps

says he will pay him a second rand if all is well when we come out, and offers his hand to shake on the deal. The kid gives him a high-five instead. We step gingerly through sand to reach the metal ramp to the door.

Inside, it is muggy warm. The air smells of metal and sweat. The children are already assembled, some on crutches, some in wheelchairs, or with legs in braces. It can't have been easy for them to make their way here. Some kids look around eagerly. Others duck their heads into their shoulders, their faces twisted with effort or anxiety. But all are dressed for the occasion, the girls with net tutus and sparkly headbands, the boys with shiny taffeta cummerbunds and bow ties. We are the only white faces in sight, but no one seems to care.

A child with a listing, tiptoe gait shows us to our seats with the other adults, perched along plank benches. The tag stuck to her dress reads "Fausia." With an anxious smile directed at our feet, she offers us a photocopied sheet. "Is the program. Is free," she says.

The music, provided by a pianist and a guitar player, takes us on a rollicking world tour, from Scottish reels to Polish mazurkas and Greek sirtakis. Estella has her students moving however they can. A few lumber around the room past us applauding spectators. Others spin their wheelchairs or simply rock and wave their arms. As limited as they are, they are one with the music.

Little Fausia stands by the piano, watching wistfully. Afternoon light through the high, cracked window catches in the haze of hair escaping from her braids, like a halo around her heart-shaped face.

With the final piece of music, Estella invites the adults to join in. Most do, including Sam. I don't, but she insists I come forward at the end. "This is my guru," she says. "Through her work, she showed me hope where I saw only despair. The children prove her right every day."

In the car on the way home, Sam is silent for a long time. Then he asks, "Why wasn't that child dancing, the one with the programs? There was something so sad about her." I am taken aback. She has been on my mind too, that little face lost in dreams. I shrug. He exclaims: "And why are they in that shed? I talked to your pal, Estella, for a while, but I don't understand. It didn't even have chairs or ventilation. These are things that could so easily be improved."

"That's American thinking," I say. "All it takes is money, which they don't have."

"Or initiative," he says, "some determination."

"The people there are accustomed to making do, to surviving what seems impossible to change. That takes all their ingenuity."

"I get that," Sam says. "And they seem like wonderful folk. But most things can be improved if you believe they can. Are you going to work with them?"

"I don't know." Not ready to think ahead like that.

Sam says, "I'm sorry if I'm being high-handed. I don't mean to sound like a know-it-all."

"You don't." I am ashamed of my sharpness. "It's just that we're not dynamic the way Americans are."

He shakes his head. "I've seen plenty of dynamism here. And your presentation on Friday night was enough to light a

Next Steps

fire under anyone."

It's his first mention of my talk. I want to ask why he came, and why he stayed away from me in the days before. Before I can summon the words, he blurts out: "Sally, why don't you dance? Not with me, but not even with those kids?"

I keep my eyes on the road, hands clenched on the steering wheel. "Why do you wear tie-dyed T-shirts every day?"

"I'll answer you when you answer me," he says.

I don't know if he is smiling. I am not. Neither says another word the rest of the drive home.

Sam insists on making supper, a pie concocted from whatever he finds in my refrigerator, topped with grated cheese. While it's baking, he offers to finish the repair job he started on the trellis. When that is done, he helps me rehang four of the shutters I varnished. They are very heavy. Either he is surprisingly strong, or he is trying to prove something. He lifts each into place and holds it, so I can screw the hinges to the frames.

As he rinses his hands under the garden hose, he says, "You're pretty handy with tools. My wife wouldn't touch them. She stuck strictly to what she called 'women's work'—cooking. Wouldn't let me near the kitchen."

"Did she cook well?"

"Very!" He is silent a beat and then adds, "But never to her satisfaction. No matter how much I praised her, or anyone else did, Margo was always unhappy with the results. Her whole family was like that, as if admitting you were pleased with an achievement would invite disaster."

I'm horrified. "Was she like that with your daughters?"

"I tried to stop her. I think people thrive far more with encouragement than criticism." I tell him that is my philosophy as a teacher. He smiles at me for the first time in hours. "I thought it would be."

The pie is odd but quite tasty. He insists on washing the dishes afterward. I dry and put them away. As I slip the last plate into the cupboard, the words spill out of my mouth: "This is just how Felix and I divvied up tasks."

"Who was tidier, you or him?"

"He was messy." To my horror, my chin starts to wobble. Try to be chirpy to stop the descent into tears. "His daughter, you know, the one in Portland, is even worse. Genetics?" But already my breath is breaking up. All around me I can feel traces of the old chaos, the tumbling piles of science journals, the shells and rocks and bark Felix would find on the beach or up on the mountain, his latest hat find, whatever sweater he had just shed. All that chaos that isn't here anymore.

"It still upsets you?" Sam asks.

"I miss his untidiness. I miss everything."

Sam reaches out a tentative hand. "It's okay, Sally. It can take years to adjust."

"It's only been one year, not quite."

Sam lurches back as if I've slapped him. He frowns, his head turned to one side. "You never said . . . I had no idea. I assumed it was like with Margo, that it had been a while. Oh, heavens, I'm an idiot! That's why you . . . Oh, Sally, I am so, so sorry."

"No need to apologize," I mumble.

We agree to watch a video, one of the array of old favorites

Next Steps

Felix and I accumulated. I suggest *The Pink Panther*, knowing Sam's taste for slapstick, but he plucks out *Dirty Dancing*. Says it is one of his daughters' favorites, but he's never seen it and guesses—correctly—that I love it. I put it on, and we sit down on the couch again. The cats try to settle between us, but I shoo them off. He has told me he loves cats but is allergic to them.

Right in the middle of the climactic scene, as Baby launches herself toward Johnny, Sam pauses the movie. She is suspended in midair. I think he doesn't want to watch their embrace, forgetting that he doesn't know what's coming.

He says, "I can understand why you didn't want to dance with me last Saturday. You're not ready to be held by a different man. But I don't understand why you didn't tell me, why you didn't say how recently you lost Felix. I thought we trusted each other." He is frowning, though not at me, focusing instead on some point on the rug, as if he doesn't want our eyes to meet—for fear I might see his anger?

What about my anger at the way he cut contact? At the way he is jetting off again?

We sit side by side in silence, staring at the frozen image on the screen. Finally, Sam murmurs something about having a lot to arrange the next day, and says good night. I stay seated. Don't get up until I hear him finish in the bathroom and close his door. The cats don't claim their usual place on the bed. They must be in his room. I close my door. Minutes later I hear muffled sneezes, and then his door opens and shuts. Consider opening my door for them, and don't.

~ 4 ~

What has happened? Two and a half days ago I couldn't wait for this man to depart, to be left in peace. And now I'm slouched on a bench up here on the mountain, bereft, fed up with myself and everyone else.

Perhaps if I could have ignored Sam all day, his leaving would have been less wrenching, but he made that impossible. First thing this morning he asked if he could use my phone. With all he had to accomplish, it was foolhardy to think he could still make his flight this evening. Grudgingly told him it was fine if he needed to stay another night or two.

"That's kind," he said. "But I'm pretty sure I can make this work."

Didn't want to hear the inevitable frustration of call after call. Withdrew to the attic and tried to immerse myself in polishing my most recent chapters. But around 11 o'clock Sam climbed the stairs and knocked on the doorframe, looking sheepish. His cheeks were a telltale pink.

Next Steps

"I'm packed, ready to go, but I have a huge favor to ask: Do you think you could drive me to the city center? I thought I could have my documents delivered to the airport, but they insist I pick them up in person, and I don't have a way to pay for a taxi."

Offered him my car, but of course he lost his international license along with everything else. Felix would have taken the chance and driven without one; not this guy. I wouldn't either. So, I chauffeured him.

Put in a jazz tape I knew he liked, and we drove in virtual silence. At the various stops, I waited in the car, parked or circling the block. By early afternoon, he was done. I still don't understand how he got everything he wanted from a bureaucracy notoriously impervious to urgency, but he had a new credit card, a temporary passport, and a plane ticket.

I asked what skill it took, the lawyer in him, or the accountant, or the teacher. He replied, "As I mentioned, I like solving puzzles."

We were stuck in traffic, still miles from Kalk Bay, when Sam said, "Thank you, Sally, and not just for driving today, and your hospitality this weekend."

I glanced at him. "Then for what else?"

"For the very special times we had—or that I had."

I wanted to say, "They were special for me too," but I didn't. Instead, I blurted out, "If they were so special, why did you turn your back on me all last week?"

He swung around. "Why did I *what*?"

I flapped one hand at him and put it back on the steering wheel. "Forget it." I couldn't start explaining all I wanted to say. Turned the music up and we drove in silence. I was starting to get anxious about his timing. He never even glanced at his watch.

We turned into the driveway just as Sam's taxi driver buddy pulled up outside. A large, heavyset policeman with a walrus mustache was knocking on the front door. When he saw us, he called out, "Hello, Miss Paddington?" I recognized the voice at once, Sgt. Roelofse from Friday night. "Hello, Mr. Parker."

With a proud flourish, he presented Sam with his stolen wallet and his old passport and ticket. I started to sputter in frustration, but Sam simply thanked him. He added, "You guys are good!"

"Maybe your American law enforcement doesn't bother, but here we take our job seriously," Roelofse barked. "We nabbed these blokes in the act, trying their luck with another tourist." Sam asked if he could express his appreciation with a donation to a police charity. The policeman squared his shoulders and refused.

As he stalked back to his vehicle, Sam signaled to the taxi driver to give him a minute. I waited while he went inside to get his suitcase. He came back out and stopped in front of me. "Seems I keep misreading people. I've made a lot of missteps these past few weeks."

"That's the part that bothers you right now, misreading people?"

"Yes. Pretty dumb stuff," he said. "I don't understand what's been happening."

I started to answer, but the taxi driver tooted his horn. Sam

Next Steps

reached out his hand. I shook it and turned away. Didn't wait for him to get into the car. Shoved my hands in my pockets and climbed the steps to the road above Kalk Bay.

~ ~ ~ ~

Finally calming down. From up here, looking down over the crazy quilt of roof tops, perhaps I can do some puzzle-solving of my own. It's still bright, the sun just above the crest of the mountain, but fingers of dark cloud are spreading over the ocean. Within minutes the sun will dip and the slope will be in shadow.

Last Monday, a week ago, the conference had just begun. Sam hadn't called in two days, and already I was alarmed, beginning to suspect that he wasn't as steadfast as he'd seemed, beginning to raise my shields. And then he came to my talk on Friday, and this weekend happened.

Don't want to return to the dark, silent house. Like the dark, silent apartment I came back to when Felix walked out on me back in Grahamstown, the parting that set us on different paths for so many years. Groan at the memory. For a long time, it made me wary of getting involved with anyone.

Oh, Sal.

I know, I know. We were fighting. I was too possessive.

And I was a fool.

Shake myself back to the present. I'm grateful for friends here in Cape Town, and the far-away people, like Libby in Connecticut, and Felix's kids, Joanie and her half-brother, Trevor, and Joanie's adorable Freddie. But I miss them all. Heartache swelling, for them, and for Ethel, my tough, loving mother-in-law, who died just a few weeks ago.

And here comes the anger—at my ex-husband, Charles, who kept Ethel and me apart for so many years, until it was almost too late, and at her, for letting him do that. And anger at Humphrey, who turned up on my doorstep and broke down my defenses with that wonderful illusion that I had my beloved back.

You turned Humphrey away. He would have parked himself with you . . .

Yes, until his wife was ready to take him back!

Maybe. But it was your choice.

I hear him, but still feel the anger. And, of course, anger at Sam. Even anger at my mother and father, gone so many years. If Imma and Pops hadn't tried so hard to shield me from hurt, would I be this bereft each time I find myself alone again? Why didn't they make me tougher?

My fingers intertwine, as if one hand is wrestling the other, till shame stills them. How could people who lost everyone and everything *not* pass on a fear of abandonment?

Wipe my cheeks. Pull my shoulders back. Breathe deep, inhaling the astringent scent of the fynbos growing all around me. Threading through it is a cindery smell from recently burned vegetation. It's all very dry.

That reminds me there are other people up here, those we call bergies. They live on the slope, sheltering under the bushes and rock overhangs. Bob works with them, helping them feed and clothe their children. He has told me repeatedly not to come up here alone, though he does all the time. "They're good souls," he says, "but demon liquor can lead to bad things."

Do the bergies look at the houses below, sheltering the

Next Steps

privileged—people like me, mostly white but not all these days———with abundant food and clothes, and assume that we are all happy, blithely grateful for our good fortune?

Libby always says the best remedy for sadness is helping someone worse off. Maybe I can help the mountain people, but how? I don't have much money to spare, and I'm not about to offer my guest bedroom again. Somehow, I don't expect any of them would want free dance lessons.

Hug my jacket tighter. Too cold to stay seated and getting dark. Gingerly, I make my way down the steps to my cottage. Turn on lights, feed the cats, and heat up the remains of Sam's pie. The *Dirty Dancing* cassette is still in the player. Start it again from the point where he stopped it. Try to forget him and instead revel in Baby's glorious leap into Johnny's strong arms, and imagine doing it myself—if only there were arms to leap into.

~ 5 ~

Began asking questions the moment I woke up this gray morning.

Was I cold, like Felix said? Is that why Sam dumped me, and Charles did, and Humphrey did?

Charles, yes — he was a bastard. But Sam didn't dump you.

Ah, you're around. Good! I'd rather argue with you than with myself.

And neither did any of the others, or not without cause.

The phone rings. I answer and for a moment, doubt my ears. It's Charles, as if summoned by our discussion, calling from New York. I almost tell him that: "Oh, my deceased lover was just talking about you." Struggle to hear him. The line is scratchy, but more confusing, his delivery lacks its usual punch.

He says, "Is this a good time? You know I'm lousy at this time-difference business."

Yeah, I know that. Remember with a disgust that never

Next Steps

seems to fade how he woke me on a call from New York when I was at a conference in L.A., forgetting or not caring that it was dawn at my end, to confess that he had been sleeping with one of his students. "I needed to clear my conscience," he said, as if that proved his virtue.

All I say now is, "I'm awake. Why are you calling?"

"I've written a long email to you. But I felt I should give you a heads-up."

This new, softer tone disarms me. It reminds me that once upon a time, Charles was my mate, my partner. I assumed I was bonded to him for life, and to his family.

That warm, opinionated clan, led by his mother, Ethel, embraced me as one of their own. Can still picture the crowded get-togethers, always with too much food, always ending with her asking, "Do you have to leave already?" It was the salve I had longed for, to make up for the isolation of my little family of three. And it was the loss I should have anticipated when Charles dumped me seventeen years later in favor of his pregnant girlfriend and told them I had cheated on him. My "chosen family"—led again by Ethel—chose loyalty to him over their affection for me.

"What's it about?" I ask Charles.

"Well, first, I've been thinking and thinking. I want to accept your suggestion that some of the proceeds from your book go to a fund in my mother's name. I love the idea, and I want to help you get the book out into the world."

I am so stunned, no words surface. It's all there, tightly bound up in this moment—my reconnection with his mother last month in New York, and how she so kindly introduced me to Gail, the family friend who has become my agent for *Next Steps*. And Charles's fury when he found out.

Libby, of all people, suggested this strategy after Ethel died last month, to get Charles to drop his opposition to the book. I was shocked; she is normally so guileless, but I liked the idea because I loved Ethel, and I was happy to honor her. But I didn't think the strategy would work.

Finally manage to say, "That'd be wonderful. Thank you." But I have to add: "You do know that my coauthor on the book is Felix, my late partner?"

"Yeah, king of the campus and the guy who took your virginity," he snaps. "And the guy you got pregnant by on that trip to L.A." He stops and coughs once, as if to expel those thoughts. "Sorry. I didn't mean to get into that." His voice goes mellow again. "Ancient history. I want your book to succeed. Really, I do."

Torn between the usual urge to lash back at him, and astonishment at what he is saying. Just ask, "This is what you wrote about in your email?"

He coughs again. So unlike Charles to hesitate. "Er, yes, but I also have something else to ask you. This might come as a shock. I don't know if you'd be interested. Look, maybe this wasn't a good idea. Read my email and get back to me."

~ ~ ~ ~

Charles writes:
Sally, I am also working on a new book, about identity and displacement. In the course of my research with a Holocaust organization in New York, I have encountered a woman from Poland who helps

Next Steps

reunite survivors and their descendants. I hope you don't mind, but I told her your mother's maiden name. I couldn't remember the exact spelling, but she said it rang a bell. It's possible that she knows someone related to you. Would you mind sending me the spelling, and where her family lived?

What the hell is he up to? Almost pick up the phone to call him, but I'll end up shouting at him.

We have no surviving relatives. That is a hard fact I saw reinforced all through my childhood. Again and again, my parents tried to find survivors from their families back in Poland, anyone who might have made it through the war. They searched, not just for their sake, but for mine too. They so badly wanted me to have the kind of warm family connections they'd had.

Each time they heard of a possible lead, hope would flare. I'd watch them speculate about this cousin or that aunt, who just might, maybe, miraculously, have made it through. For weeks, they would watch the mail for the airmail envelope with its red and blue edge and some fancy insignia. Finally, it would arrive, and their faces would crumple with grief. Right name, wrong spelling. Right spelling, wrong age.

I came to hate those envelopes, to dread seeing their pain. I would do my best to block out the corresponding pain it triggered in me.

So, what is this about? I suspect Charles is hoping it will yield a poignant story he can cite in his next book. Once upon a time, I was awed by his academic prestige, but Professor Smith lost his luster in my eyes a long time ago. I don't want to be part of his research. After we split up, he wrote about me in a scholarly article about infidelity. That caused a rather memorable row and might explain his nervousness this morning. I want to tell him to get lost.

Work with him, Sal. Don't waste time on old anger.

You're back?

Don't make silly choices again.

For a ghost, you're being very judgmental.

Not judging, Sal. And not just talking about the way you let Charles keep you from Ethel, or the way you kept Sam at bay. With your parents . . .

My parents? I was devoted to them.

A shadow of guilt dims that declaration. Even as an adult, with all the new options offered by technology, I chose not to help them search. There was no point. A cruel fate had cut them off from their past, and I wanted them to accept that, to shut the door on the past, and be happy in the present.

You're not living entirely in the here and now either, are you?

I snort. If he was alive, with me, I would storm out of the room. Instead, I walk away from the computer. I want to tell Charles he is wasting my time and his own. But how can I refuse to cooperate when he is offering to help me with the book? Besides, if I don't, Felix will give me a hard time.

~ ~ ~ ~

I need air. Don a sun hat, socks and sneakers, and head out for a long walk along Main Road, out toward Fish Hoek, with its wide sweep of sand and sea.

Don't plan to turn back until I steady the seesawing in my

Next Steps

mind. The sun is hot on my bare arms, but the breeze counteracts it. Try to ignore the smell of diesel from the traffic and stench from a passing train. A hedge of honeysuckle and rose offers an antidote. Stop to inhale as deeply as I can.

A butterfly lands on a flower at my elbow. See it in my peripheral vision, wings slowly parting and meeting. Know if I move it will flit away. Trying not to think of Charles's bizarre message. How could there be any relatives? Turn to the butterfly. Glimpse the intricate black and yellow marking and a round blue spot on each wing before it disappears.

You have another chance to find kin. Don't blow it again.
Don't. Just don't.

Felix never said it, but I hear in his words a reminder of how I left Imma and Pops to go study in Boston. True, they urged me to go, to get away from the riots in Cape Town. But I could have come back. By the time I finished my master's degree, things in South Africa had calmed down. Instead, I married Charles and settled in New York. They blessed that choice too, though it left them even more isolated.

Children might have made things better. That thought cuts deeper, as always. Wanted so much to give them grandchildren. Their survivor friends all talked about their big families as "the ultimate revenge against Hitler." I provided no such comfort for Imma and Pops. I was the last in their line.

Wishes and secrets, secrets and wishes. Feel in my arms the baby they never knew about, conceived with Felix on that unforgettable trip to Los Angeles, and miscarried. Grateful they didn't know. And grateful too that they never knew how my marriage crumbled, in part because of that. They would have been heartbroken.

But what if all that secrecy cut you off from real closeness?

Ha! What about you, Felix? If you hadn't been so cautious, so self-protective, think how much more time we might have shared.

You think I don't regret it? Learn from our mistakes, Sal, please.

~ ~ ~ ~

This walk was supposed to get me out of my head. Turn my gaze to the sights in front of me. Focus on the woman coming toward me in a misshapen evening dress, glittering as she walks. Her triangular face is pinched with anger directed at the child she is dragging by the hand. He shuffles his feet, as if to keep on shoes that are too large. He has a Coke can in his hand, evidently empty. As they pass, I hear a fragment: "I told you not to drink so fast. Now what must I do?"

I look back and see the boy hunch his shoulders to ward off her scolding. Where are they going? Will there be a better chance of food there? The woman looks as if dressed for streetwalking, but surely the child would have prevented her from seeking customers. And at this hour? Or is this the only dress she owns?

If I had shoved a ten-rand note at her as she passed, at the café in Kalk Bay they could have bought milk or bread, or another soda. Felix would have. So would Sam. But I'm out of practice at spontaneous giving.

The woman's rasping voice pulls me back to the present. She shouts, "If they're hurting, take the damn things off." The child slides off his shoes. The mother grabs them and hurls

Next Steps

them over the railing to the rocks below. He cries out, but hobbles barefoot after her. The sidewalk must be scalding him.

I can't bear it. Yell out and run after them. They stop and stare at me, both with chins tucked in, wary. I pull off my sneakers, then my thick wool socks. Thrust the socks at the boy. He shrinks back, his hands clenched against his chest, but the woman grabs the socks and tells him to put them on. I watch them go, the blue feet scampering with at least one layer of protection.

Put my sneakers back on and lace them tighter. Start walking again. The breeze is stronger now, propelling me from behind.

~ ~ ~ ~

At my desk later, instead of working on the book, I start browsing the Internet, randomly reading this story and that. I don't want to see my email, in case Charles has written back. Have had enough of him for one day.

Up comes an article about *lyngchi*, a form of slow execution—death by a thousand cuts—refined in Japan. Not interested in the actual torture, which was outlawed long ago, but rather the notion that prisoners would torture themselves with fear of the pain they were anticipating. Imagination as a weapon. Is that what I'm doing? Felix would say yes.

Still fretting about that when, finally, I do open my email. Nothing from Charles. Up comes a much more welcome missive, a "How are you?" from Libby. She has been checking in with me like this, one way or another as our modes of communication have changed, since we met as students. Loving, gentle Libby doesn't think I'm cold, though she might agree that I torture myself.

Among the other emails is one from Estella with "PLEASE CALL ME" in the subject line, and one from Joanie. I click on Joanie's first, instantly anxious. Each time her name appears, my tinnitus grows louder: Is Freddie all right?

Her little one, my kind-of grandson, has some sort of congenital problem that interferes with digestion and development. But the doctors have him on a new regimen of medication and a diet that seems to be working.

Joanie insists that Freddie's turn for the better began with my dogged pursuit of information. I'm proud of what I accomplished, but it was with crucial help from Humphrey, whom she calls "Uncle Boet," and from our beloved Maria in Barcelona, that same Maria Soares I showed to the conference audience, dancing in her wheelchair. Sam would approve if I told him how we fitted the pieces of the puzzle together.

Joanie's last paragraph makes me smile.

> When are you coming to us again? You have to see how this boy is growing. He has a grip that could squish I don't know what! As you can see, my brain isn't quite back to normal yet, but we're getting there. We'll send you a ticket. What do you think? Come iIn a few months' time?

What do I think? It would be marvelous! Or maybe I can persuade them to come out here. It won't be beach weather, but Cape Town is always beautiful. Thus heartened, I carry my tea and laptop out onto the patio and scroll to see what Estella says.

Thanks again for coming on Sunday. It meant the

Next Steps

world to me. Looking forward to meeting up again. Is your American friend still with you? Can you ask him to phone me? He gave me his card, but in the rush to clean up after the concert, I lost it.

What on earth can she want with Sam? The irritation from Sunday flickers again, and I wonder how she'd feel if she'd heard his criticism of their shabby conditions. But that's unfair. I know he meant well. I saw them talking very intensely after the performance. He was serious; she was all smiles.

Are you jealous?

About Sam? For goodness' sake, no!

Ha!

Ha! back at you. I'm almost seventy; give me some credit.

Despite myself, I picture Sam in his gaudy T-shirt. See the freckles on his arms and the pitched tilt of his eyebrows when he was listening. I miss that intense attention. Not sexy like Felix, who drew a flutter from every woman who came near him, even in his seventies, or like his even more suave brother, the two of them with their feline grace. Just an ordinary guy I'm missing in ways I never expected.

I write to Estella that Sam has gone. Promise to look for his email address.

~ ~ ~ ~

I find Sam's card where I tossed it weeks ago, in a basket of knickknacks. Consider sending him a greeting, something about that dark chocolate, but don't. Consider writing an email to Estella with his info, but don't. Instead, pick up the phone.

She exclaims in delight when she hears my voice. Before I can make any subtle inquiries about her desire to be in touch with Sam, she burbles forth the answer. "I love your American friend! What a terrific guy." Huh? "Herman says he said he might be able to help us get funds to fix up the hall, that there are some foundations we can ask for a grant."

Contrite about my pettiness, I tell her she should come and have lunch with me one day. It's an amiable, empty suggestion, but Estella promptly asks if she can come this Saturday and bring Herman. Realize now that the suave, very straight-backed guy at the piano was Mr. Estella.

"He's got a crush on you," she giggles. "He has a very soft spot for white-haired ladies. Wants me to stop dying my hair, but I'm not ready to start looking like my mother."

I look maternal to her? I suppose I could. "I was a redhead," I tell her, "like my mother. She'd have a cadenza if she saw how I've let my hair go."

"I might do mine red next time," Estella says. "It'd be nice to add some oomph, especially for when I'm doing flamenco."

Flamenco? I didn't know that about her. A different part of my brain stirs. Maria in Barcelona, though paraplegic, is an amazing teacher of Spanish dance and of children with disabilities. She taught Felix to do flamenco back in his youth. She and Estella should meet, though goodness knows how.

An American would simply think, "How?" not "Goodness knows how."

When my friend, Mary, calls later, she who made the conference happen, I mention the call with Estella. Big mistake! I tried to tell her last week that I was relieved to have the whole thing behind me, and how I was going to rest, veg out for a while. That is not what she wants for me. Ever the team-

Next Steps

builder, she invites herself to Saturday lunch and asks if she can also bring Ama, the dynamic Nigerian PR wiz who handled publicity for the conference.

Why didn't I just tell Estella I was busy this weekend?

~ 6 ~

Though the group is small, Saturday lunch on the patio is one of the noisiest events I've ever hosted.

Mary, such a formal academic, is the very opposite in this setting. At one point, she leaps to her feet to illustrate a point, swirling her huge black and white scarf as she stamps her feet. Herman yells out, "Olé!"

Estella, taking a break from her own anecdotes, prods him to tell tales of his wild youth as a young dancer set free from apartheid, partying his way around the companies of Europe. He still has the peacock posture of a performer and is extraordinarily handsome.

"My toy boy," Estella calls him. Apparently, he's five years younger than her—same as the difference between Sam and me, though I've never given that gap a thought. She says, "Better than what he tried to call me—his 'sugar mama.'"

I doubt her "toy boy" wanted to hang out with a bunch of women today, but having come, he can't resist the spotlight his

Next Steps

wife gives him. He struts and flirts.

"He wasn't always so suave," Estella says. "You want to see how he looked when I met him?" She takes out a bulging leather wallet of photos, held closed with an elastic band. Opens it, flips past plastic sleeves till she finds a shot of a skinny, grinning teenager with a massive Afro. One of his top front teeth is missing, the gap giving him a devilish air. "I fell for that naughty boy, and I landed up with Mr. Charm," she sighs, but with a smile.

Ama, in a white denim jumpsuit that sets off her midnight skin and bleached-blonde hair, observes us all, her long legs folded under her, now and then tapping away on her phone—taking notes? The ultimate modern African woman. I feel very pale and wrinkled alongside her, but happy.

Relieved that they seem to like the food and the pineapple sangria I concocted from Felix's fabled recipe. Come to think of it, that—even with way lower octane—might have fueled this hilarity. He is gone, but still stirring trouble.

I go inside to make coffee, and bump into Herman, trying to find the bathroom. Not sure how one can get lost in a house this small, but I point the way and head back to the kitchen. When I came out, my neighbors, Roxie and Edith, have joined the party.

"We couldn't believe the racket coming from here," Edith says. "Curiosity got the better of us. You don't mind, do you?" I go inside to get more glasses and coffee cups. This time, Ama follows and asks me to wait a moment. She has been busy, I know from Mary, with follow-up articles about the conference and tie-ins with potential sponsors who make dance shoes and prosthetics. With a cryptic little smile, she says, "I have my eye on your new book. I think we could weave some very fruitful connections. When do you think it will come out?"

"Heaven knows," I say. "Within the next year or so—if I can ever finish it."

We chat a while about my contacts in the U.S. She has already been emailing Joanie, who helped her place a story about the conference in a newspaper in Seattle, the home city of one of our major speakers. I gather Ama and Joanie have also discussed some photo projects, using Joanie's pictures from her trips to South Africa.

When I return, Herman is back outside with a giggling Roxie in his arms, coaching her in a paso doble, twisting and turning in the confined space of the patio. She looks flustered and girlish. Grateful that Edith has her back to them, and has Estella deeply engrossed in some topic.

As they dip past me, I hear Herman mention his and Estella's struggle to reach CEOs of local companies, to raise funds. He tells her that "Sally's beau, that nice American," might be good for some dollars. Estella hears him too and casts me a raised-eyebrow apology. I shrug, not pleased but not about to intervene.

With the music still loud around us, she crouches with her mouth to my ear. "Ignore him," she says. "I do. What I really came to ask is, will you come teach with me? Just now and then, maybe once a week, or a month? Mainly to work with one kid in particular, my little Fausia."

The name tickles, and then I remember the tip-toeing child handing out programs, but not dancing herself. "You know,

Next Steps

her mother's here in Kalk Bay," Estella says. "They got kicked out of their house—there was some big drug trouble with the husband, now he's in jail—and she and the other kid ended up staying with the grandmother on the mountain. Fausia's too fragile to live like that; I couldn't let them take her. She's staying with us. I dropped her off now, to visit for a while with her mom and her brother. We'll go get her before we head home."

"What do you want me to do with her?"

"Find a way to get her moving. You can see how much she loves music, and she isn't nearly as disabled as some of my other kids, but she won't do anything with me. It's like something inside is frozen. Will you help?"

A headache winds around my skull and down my neck. What can I do with this child? It's been so long. I'm busy. I need to finish my book. Sort out my taxes. Suddenly impatient for everyone to leave, so I can lie down in a darkened room.

After the other four have gone, as Edith is departing with Roxie, she halts and says to me more gently than usual, "Sal, remember the last time we partied like this with Felix?"

I do remember. The sangria flowed, as did the dancing and laughter. The ache in my head swells. The wrongness of his absence jabs at me.

No need to hold back with Roxie and Edith; they've been with me through all the drama. In fact, as they loved to remind us, it was they who rescued Felix when he collapsed with his first aneurysm, and they who found Maria's phone number in Spain, which led to her emailing me to come be with him. "We're like your godmothers," Roxie used to say.

"The anniversary is coming up, isn't it?" she says now.

I tilt my head back. "I want to go to sleep and wake up a week later."

"Like that would change anything," Edith snorts. "You'll come to us for dinner that night. We'll party, as he would want us to do. Done, settled." Roxie nods.

I told you she's a softie, my ghost reminds me. This is soft? But yes, I know Edith's brusqueness is usually just a cover. She's also strong. I want to be like her.

You are, or you could be.

~ ~ ~ ~

On Monday morning, as I'm putting my garbage out, I see the woman from my Fish Hoek walk making her way up the street, still in that sparkly dress, lugging a backpack. The garbage truck rumbles up behind her, waiting for her to move out of the way, but she is oblivious, or doesn't care. The child is not with her.

I have masses of food left over from Saturday, stored in zipped plastic bags. Surely, she could use it. I run back inside, stuff them all in a shopping bag, and scramble back outside. She is just disappearing toward the steps that go up the mountain. I'm in flip flops, not the right shoes, but I hurry after her, calling out, "Hey, excuse me!"

She doesn't respond, so I keep going, following her. Skelm, my adventurer cat, follows me into the street, but gets distracted by a lizard. I'm pleased to note I'm getting fitter, but the shopping bag soon feels leaden. My quarry isn't all that nimble herself, but the distance between us lengthens.

Next Steps

She reaches Boyes Drive and crosses over, takes a path up through the bushes and disappears. She must be part of the encampment of bergies, the people living on the mountain. To follow or not to follow? It could be an unwelcome intrusion.

Bob's old green Morris is parked at the roadside, no mistaking it. If he is visiting with them, he will vouch for me. I make my way between the bushes, until I hear voices. Yes, that is Bob. I hear laughter and relax a little, though now I am panting heavily.

Just as I reach the cluster of men and women, Bob turns and sees me. "Sally? Good heavens, this is a surprise! Let me help you with that stuff, and introduce you." I make my way to him, stepping around the mounds of blankets, white shopping bags, and big, black garbage bags.

He takes me from one person to another, and each offers a handshake, some with a little knee-bend, very respectful—because I'm white or because I'm the minister's friend? The faces are guarded.

"Is your friend a social worker, Reverend Bob?" one man asks.

"No. Nothing like that. Sally is a wonderful dance teacher," he says. He turns to me. "But what brings you here?"

The woman I followed stares hard at me as she settles her bundle into a cluster of possessions. Still panting, I say to her, "I saw you the other day with a child, and then I saw you today, and I had all this extra food in my fridge . . ."

She takes the bag from me slowly and puts it down without looking inside. "You the sock lady?" So, she does remember. "You want them back?" I shake my head.

She has a faintly familiar look, something about her wide cheekbones and pointed chin. Could this be Fausia's mother?

One person has stayed seated, a skinny figure with gray hair sticking out from under her red headscarf. She says, "Come sit. You look like you ready to *vrek*, to die."

Gratefully, I squat next to her. Bob says, "Tannie Mavis, this is my very good friend. Sally, this is Mavis Joubert." She looks ancient, but I suppose she could be younger than me.

Her hooded eyes fasten on me, murky and unreadable. She clasps my hand with her rough, dry fingers, swaying a little, looking away now, yet somehow attentive.

Abruptly, she demands, "Who you grieving for?"

Bob answers for me: "Her husband, Felix. You remember him, Mavis, Felix Barnard?" I'm about to do my usual correction, "Not actually my husband," but shut up.

She frowns, and then a cackle escapes, crinkling her face even more. "Aagh, so you are Felix's *vrou*? Shame! Now *ja*, we miss him too, that crazy guy. How long is he gone?"

"Nearly a year."

I am taken aback. Why didn't he tell me about her? But Felix seldom said much about the people he met. He would go on forever about the ideas they shared, full of praise for their brilliance, but say very little about the speakers themselves. He had a notion—drilled into him by his mother? —that talking about people was gossip, laughed at my curiosity about his friends when I came to live with him, and left me to question them myself rather than divulge any background. He was the same about his family. It took until this past year, after he was gone, to learn all kinds of crucial facts about them, and about

Next Steps

him.

I could have pushed harder for answers. So much of what I remember from the past is based on false notions. I've been trying to reshape my memories in the light of new understanding.

"You are like the plants up here after a fire," Mavis says. "You got burnt to the ground, hey, Sally? But now I think you are starting to grow again. Your roots are strong."

"Not sure about that. I hope you're right," I say. "I am very glad to meet you. I hope you don't mind me barging in like this."

She shrugs and offers me one of the oatmeal raisin cookies brought here by the woman I followed. I recognize them from the café on Main Road, and remember hearing that the owners donate the prior day's baked goods to the poor. It feels odd to take one, but how can I refuse? We munch and chat, and then Bob says he must be going and suggests I get a ride with him. We both promise to come back soon.

"You and I must do some talking," Tannie Mavis says, and I agree gratefully, honored that she wants to. "And next time you come, can you bring me a bottle of Ribena? It's my favorite from when I was little, and my boy's when he was little. But that shop on Main Road doesn't have it anymore."

I loved it too. Weird to have this in common. My mother would pour me a glass when I arrived home from school, telling me how it was full of Vitamin C, and how it reminded her of her childhood in Poland, how they made juice from their own berries. Once upon a time, did Mavis have a mother who worried about her health?

Amazing that childhood choices survive in a setting like this, rocked by the elements, without privacy, sleeping on the ground. And yet, Mavis seems serene, possibly happier than I am. I want to know how she functions. She seems curious about me too.

~ 7 ~

Day #360 A.F. — After Felix. From Day #1 to, when, Day #60? —the idea of joining Felix beckoned to me.

The pain was so sharp, I couldn't imagine it ever fading. Still bad on some days, like today, but I don't consider exiting any more.

What has changed? Hard as it's been, some of the rethinking about our past has brought healing. I've learned how Felix's fears, not any lack of desire, kept him from me. Last year in New York, I discovered that Charles's mother didn't hate me after all, but misunderstood our breakup. On the other hand, some lessons—like about my own selfishness—make the past harder to contemplate.

Bob says he agrees with Edith and Roxie that we should have "an anniversary wake, or a *yahrtzeit* party," he says. "Isn't that what you do in the Jewish tradition?"

"Right word, wrong kind of party," I tell him. In Jewish homes, I don't remember anyone having more than a glass of wine in remembrance, and I have no desire to share even that. But then I remember my resolution to be more considerate of other people's needs. Felix's friends have also missed him sorely. I say, "That doesn't mean we can't have a get-together and get thoroughly plastered."

Earlier in the day I plan a different remembrance, a solo ride along the routes Felix and I loved to travel together on our motorbikes. Nervous about going for a long ride by myself, but can't think of anyone who would come with me.

With days to go, the gray mood seeps in deeper, as dank as sea fog. The energy from the conference has faded. Each plan I consider withers. My college pal Angie urged me to come visit her in Grahamstown. Other than a quick visit when she came for Felix's memorial/wake, we haven't had face-to-face time in ages. Being back where he and I met and fell in love could be wonderful, or it could be agonizing. Decide not to risk it.

The fact is I don't want to do anything that day or see anyone.

~ ~ ~ ~

Day #365

The doorbell rings very early, and rings and rings, drilling into my sleep. I half-open my eyes and see the time, 7 a.m., and register the date. Annoyance and worry topple me out of bed. Haul on Felix's robe and stagger to the door, expecting to see a meter reader. For a moment, so dozy I have no idea who the wizened little woman is, frowning up at me, though we have crossed paths and chatted at length.

"Tannie Mavis?"

Next Steps

"Ja, last time I looked in a mirror. Can you drive me to the doctor's place?"

I can't. My Volvo is at the garage for a tune-up. She says, "You got a motorbike? I remember Felix said so. He was *vies*, really pissed off with you for getting it, wasn't he? You can take me on the bike."

I sold that motorbike a few years ago, but I still have Felix's cherished Harley. She must have seen it parked at the side of the house.

The look on her face has shifted from irritation to sly glee. "They will get a shock, hey!"

"The surgery is open so early?" I ask.

"For me, yes."

Nothing about her suggests illness. I want to know why the hell she needs to see a doctor at this ungodly hour, but it seems too personal. Just ask for the address and tell her to come inside. I offer her coffee, but she shakes her head impatiently. She wants to get going.

Back in our youth, when Felix and I were together in Grahamstown, we argued often about how to help those in need. He was on a tight budget (by our standards), but he gave money to a select group of beggars who hovered on the edge of campus. He never gave to any one person more than once a week. "It's a system," he told me. "This way they know what to expect from me."

My own giving was more erratic, a juggle between impulsive generosity, embarrassment, and guilt. Compared to him, I felt mean.

No such feeling with Sam. I felt fine just as I am. Is it

maturity? Or the fact that we didn't become lovers? Or that he made me feel so appreciated? Or that I didn't care enough about what he thought? Dumb questions, given that he and I are history.

"Have you been on a bike before?" I ask Mavis. She says no. I tell her she has to wear a helmet, and a jacket, and jeans, and that I can lend them to her. She starts to argue, but I won't take her unless she wears protective clothing. She shrugs. When I come back into the living room with the garments, she is looking around at my books and photos, especially the ones of Felix. The cats approach her and she shoos them away, clearly not a cat lover. I direct her to the bathroom.

I dress while she does. When she emerges, she is transformed. We're close enough in size that the clothes fit quite well. I turn her to the full-length mirror in the hallway, and she squawks in amazement, "No, man, we look like sisters from another mother!"

The only passenger I've ever ridden with was my instructor, years ago. I tell Mavis that, and also that Felix would never let me or anyone else on his bike. I learned it was because of a terrible accident in his youth that cost his sister her life. With him so leery, there was no way I could take a passenger either. But Mavis is undeterred.

Why am I taking this risk? Because I can't say no to someone in urgent need of medical care, I tell Felix, though I haven't heard him ask. And I don't want to be that selfish white woman, refusing to share my privilege. I show her how to put the helmet on over her red head wrap.

The speed seems to terrify her at first. She clutches tight,

Next Steps

her arms wrapped around my waist. But it takes only a couple of wobbles till she learns to lean whichever way I do, as instructed, and a few miles for her to relax her hold. Soon we are moving in unison, we sisters from another mother.

I roll to a halt at the Wynberg address, a gracious Cape Dutch house with green shutters and a thatched roof, apparently both the doctor's home and surgery. We take off our helmets and, arm in arm, swagger like Hell's Angels up the path to the entrance. Without having said anything else, or learning anything more about each other, we have bonded.

There is a brass plaque next to the imposing oak door, listing the doctor's hours. I'm right: It doesn't open for another hour. Mavis bangs with her fist and rings the bell repeatedly, as she did at my place, until we hear footsteps and someone yelling, "Okay, okay, I'm coming."

A woman in a crisp green and white housecoat, apparently the housekeeper, lets us in. She seems to recognize Mavis but doesn't greet us. She ushers us past the reception area to an office and leaves us there. I offer to wait outside, but Mavis insists I stay with her. I sit down, but Mavis keeps strutting around, until a man walks in. He's Indian, I guess, with a serenely unreadable face. It's clear he has just finished dressing. His wet, black hair still has comb tracks, and he is tightening his tie. Mavis immediately seats herself, hands clasped in her lap, looking as docile as a child, but from the pucker of her chin it's clear she's suppressing a grin.

"To what do I owe the pleasure of this visit?" he asks. He glances my way with a querying lift of his eyebrows

"This my friend, Sally," Mavis says. "She's Felix's wife. She brought me on his motorbike."

"Ah, Felix!" He comes to shake my hand. "And that explains the unfamiliar garb, Mavis. Glad to meet you, Sally. And my condolences. Also a rider, huh?" He shakes his head in disapproval, and I mumble about my car being out of action and again offer to leave the room.

"Man, this isn't my doctor. This is her husband," Mavis exclaims. "I'm not here for sickness. He's a lawyer. I'm here for this." She reaches into her blouse, fishes around, and withdraws an envelope stuffed with banknotes. South African rands are more colorful than American dollars, but I can't tell what denominations she has there. Mr. Patel takes the money, and his smile goes from questioning to impressed.

"I told you I'd get it," Mavis says, her voice cracking. She looks on the verge of tears, but her smile matches his.

"They'd have accepted a check from whoever provided this," he says. "But wonderful. Well done. I'll take it to them. May I ask who . . . ?"

"No, I'm not allowed to tell." She tosses me an impish glance.

"You're a lucky woman, you know that?" Mavis tells me as we head out. She puts her helmet back on and walks ahead before I can ask what she means.

Early sunshine is sending hazy rays between the blue gum trees and across the glistening lawn. For a moment the lateral light blurs my view of the motorbike. I pause, feeling Felix's presence, not barring my way, but slowing my stride.

It's okay, I tell him, I will be careful. I am quite sure this expedition has something to do with him, though I can't

Next Steps

imagine what.

"Your friend Sam, is he coming back?" Mavis asks as she straddles the seat behind me. Sam, not Felix? So much for my intuition. I shake my helmeted head, press the ignition button, and swivel the throttle. It drowns out her next question and prevents me from voicing mine.

I drop Mavis off on Boyes Drive, just below where she and her group dwell. She hands me her helmet and says she'll bring back the jeans and jacket this afternoon. "No rush," I say. I don't want her to. I'd like to see her again, have a chance to ask questions, to understand more about her—but not so soon. I want to be alone.

As we hover there, the mother with the boy I gave my socks to approaches down the path through the bushes, with her kid. Suddenly, I remember Mavis's request for Ribena. Maybe this woman will go shopping for her. I reach into my pocket and find only a 50-rand note, hesitate, and hand it to Mavis. "For Ribena? Maybe she can get it for you."

The woman looks from me to her, but Mavis tucks the money into whatever undergarment she's wearing and waves her on her way. Mavis scowls at me. "Was hard enough hiding that other cash from them. She better not tell anyone . . . "

She steps away and then turns back to me. "So, Sam's gone? That's another man you've lost, huh?"

"Maybe I'm not so lucky after all?" I don't tell her about today being the anniversary of Loss #1.

"Aagh, rubbish," she snorts. "Two's just a chance. You lose three, and *ja*, I'd say you got a problem." And with that she marches off. No "thank you," just a wave of her hand.

Elaine Durbach

~ ~ ~ ~

For better or worse, the evening at Edith and Roxie's has turned out to be a wallow in all things Felix.

Right up to the last minute, I was ambivalent about coming. Worked for a while on my laptop, then gave that up. The wind was howling outside, and all I wanted was to curl up with the cats on the bed. Joanie and Trevor both called. So sweet and comforting, but I had to suck back the tears so we could talk. From the box under the bed, I pulled out Felix's journals, the marvelous record of his travels in his youth. Lay on my side, sniffing and dabbing, reading random passages from one volume after another.

I know every page. When he was around, he never offered, and I never dared ask if I could read them. After he died, I couldn't resist opening them. They were my time machine back to when he was alive, to when he was young, before we met. I've read them again and again. Some parts read differently in the light of what I've learned. Some change from day to day, like this one, from when he was in England:

> *Volunteered again at the seniors' home. Went with Suzie to show her I'm not just a sexy womanizer (ha ha). Truth is I've spent so little time with oldies, they shock me. They tell you all about all their ailments and shit! they have a lot of them. Getting old isn't for sissies, like one guy said. True. I can't imagine living like that, struggling to move and eat and shit. I don't want to get old ever.*

Needed to read this entry today, to be reminded of how

Next Steps

miserable he would have been if he'd faced that kind of old age.

Of course, he piped up as I thought that. *Enough. It's been a year. This is nonsense. Our friends are waiting for you.*

So, you are here?

Yes, but not in those old pages. Go!

I kept reading. With the books spread open across his side of the bed, I could almost see him. There was the part where he borrowed a motorcycle (almost like the one he bought here, that I still have) and rode through the Alps. And where he learned to meditate in India. And in Spain, when he worked in the bar in Moraira with Maria and her father, Jose (who died just recently, weeks after I met him, another sadness). I had had no idea why Felix went there; now I do, and probably know more than he did about his connection to Maria and Jose.

But my favorite part, as always, was the very end, the squeezed-in last entry from the day we met, registering for courses at Rhodes. Without that little snippet, I might never have known it was mutual from the very start.

Listened for more of my ghost. Hungry for more. Silence. But he had perked me up. If I paused to wash and change into something fancier, the impulse would fade, so I didn't change. Just reached for my precious pendant, the piece Felix made for me, wrapping silver wire around a teardrop-shaped globe of blue-green glass from a beach on the New Jersey shore.

Hanging alongside it on a hook by the bathroom mirror was the piece I made for him, a perfect abalone shell, like a small ear, suspended on a leather thong. Slipped them both over my neck, so they nestled together against my chest, like protection.

Have I always been this sentimental? Probably.

~ ~ ~ ~

Surrounded by friends, my mood has brightened. I tell them about my mystery mission in the morning, and we all, except Bob, try to guess what Mavis wanted the money for, why it was so urgent to hand it over to her lawyer. Bob just listens benignly. "I'm glad you got to know Mavis a little better," he says. "She has much to offer."

I know what he means. Despite my sadness today, I am glad I said yes, that we got to ride together.

Led by Roxie, we sing Felix's favorite songs, tell our favorite anecdotes about him, speculate about the parts of his life he didn't discuss. A few people ask about our book and when I'm going to finish it. Shrug and say, "Soon, soon." I listen for Felix, expecting to hear some sarcasm about their curiosity, or our maudlin reminiscing, but hear nothing. Perhaps the chatter is too loud.

~ ~ ~ ~

Back home, I open the windows wide before turning out my light, and let the curtains billow. I should put away his journals, but I like how the wind flutters the pages. It carries a faint smell of smoke, perhaps from a *braai* on the beach or one of the neighbors entertaining. Flop into bed still slightly drunk, too tired to take off the pendants around my neck.

So, Mr. Know-it-all, what now? I ask my ghost.

Listen, but hear nothing. Recall again Felix's impatience from earlier, but hey! I did what he told me to. I went to his anniversary wake and I'm glad.

Please don't leave me yet. Not ready to do without you.

Next Steps

Nothing. Just the moan of the wind.

Restless night, disturbed by all the emotions of the day, or the alcohol, or both. Sleep and wake and see the time. 1 o'clock, 2:30, 4:15.

Finally fall deeper asleep and sink into a dream: I look up and see the mountain shrouded in a hazy gray. A fierce glow rises above it, silhouetting the peak. Bob comes running in, calling out that the slope is on fire, and Sam wants to go help the people up there. "You have to stop him!" Bob yells. I see Sam running up the street, and shout to him, but I can't do it loud enough no matter how much I strain my voice. He can't hear me or won't. He's going up there, and it will be my fault if he never comes back.

Wake up quivering in the dawn light, still imagining I can smell smoke. Relieved that Sam is gone, and I can't harm him that way.

Then realize I'm not imagining it; the smell of smoke is real. It's prickling my throat, stinging my eyes. The room is thick with it. Start coughing. Make out Mergatroid and Skelm cowering by the door and reach for them, but they scoot away.

Choking, panic rising, I fumble for my phone to call the fire department, but even as I dial, I hear a jangle of sirens and a pounding at my front door. There's a crash, and then thudding footsteps and a voice calling out: "Ma'am, are you there? You've got to get out!"

~ 8 ~

Do we get what we need when we need it, or when we know how to ask for it?

Some people don't get what they need, I know, and go under, give up. But most of us muddle through, despite what seem like impossible problems, thanks to those little gestures of grace from … ?

Was the fire what I needed? I sure as hell didn't ask to have my home go up in flames that *yahrtzeit* night.

Staying with John Latimer, the old inventor who was Felix's lifelong mentor and a friend to both of us. His house is on the far side of the city, on the slope of a different mountain. Camps Bay is even more buffeted by wind than Kalk Bay, but we have a vast view of the western horizon instead of the east.

After the fire, various people offered accommodation. Bob, with his awful guest bed, insisted I camp with him the first few days, but the burn smell in the air made me nauseous. Mary

Next Steps

urged me to come stay with her, and I did for a while, but her husband clearly found my presence an intrusion. John needed company and help with daily chores.

He has a spacious house. For a few years, he lived in a retirement community, but I gather he was asked to leave because he insisted on doing experiments in his apartment. "They claimed the chemical fumes disturbed my fellow inmates," he told me. He has a housekeeper, a bossy Polish immigrant, Magdalena. She and I compare recipes and argue about whose mother had the best ones. I do the shopping and some of the cooking and take him places. With him, I feel useful. And safe—despite his experiments.

My Volvo is fine, thanks to its being at the mechanic that day. Grateful for that. At least I can get myself around; I don't have to rely on others for transport.

My motorbike—Felix's BMW—didn't survive. The ache of that loss comes in waves, like the loss of a friend. So much of our story was welded into it. Imagine the metal melting and hurt for it.

Many other things are gone too. I make lists on the backs of envelopes, or on napkins in cafés, each time I think of something else I'm without, but I lose the lists. Used to write lists in my journal, but the old one is out of reach, in the charred mess in the cottage, probably destroyed. I haven't had the heart to buy a new one. So much gone or ruined. Most of my clothes, my books, Felix's hats. Thank goodness I fell asleep with my pendants on.

But worst of all, the cats are gone, Mergatroid and Skelm, my loving, velvet companions. Frantically tried to find them as the firemen dragged me out, with Felix's robe wrapped around my shoulders, clutching my laptop. Called their names, sk-sksssing, but they didn't appear. No idea if they escaped—or if they didn't. Can't bear to contemplate that possibility.

Roxie has put up flyers around the neighborhood, asking people to keep an eye out for them. She's had a few calls with tips and has passed the phone numbers to me, but each time they have been the wrong cats.

Heartsick too about Mavis. Bob Halpert said when he went up the mountain the next day, some of the group were there, combing through the smoldering mess, looking for any possessions they could retrieve. He asked after her, but they had no idea where she was, if she had wandered off or been taken away by the ambulance that came with the fire engines.

"They think she died," Bob said, very quietly. I didn't want to hear that. "We will keep looking and asking."

It doesn't make sense to be so upset about someone I barely knew. But I was sure she and I had a friendship stretching into the future.

Keep recalling a conversation we had a few days after meeting. I was meandering through the farmers' market when I heard someone call out, "Hey, Sally whatsyourname!" and there she was, sitting on a bench under a tree, next to the guy selling home-baked sourdough loaves. "I'm watching out for sieves," she said. "He pays me with bread." Sieves? Realized she was minus her front teeth and having trouble saying "th." Sat down next to her, glad to shelter from the sun.

We talked about good bread and "crap" bread, and why some people get fat and others, like her and me, stay skinny. "I

Next Steps

wanted to be *lekker* fat," she said, patting her bony hips, "but I'm too speedy, they say." We talked about being "speedy" and worrying—or not worrying. On that we differed. I admitted to being a worrier; she said she wasn't one. I asked if she believed in God, if that's why she wasn't afraid.

"God? No way!' she squawked. People turned to stare, and one man shook his finger at her. "He's my maker, *ja*, obviously, but we got free will. No one tells me what to do; the only one what's responsible for me is me."

I asked her if she wished she could live indoors. '*Nee*," she said, "except if Kelvin, my boy, has a place for me. But bad stuff happens inside. Outside, if someone wants to *clap* you, you can run. In a house, they've got you. Outside, if there's a fire, you can run. Inside, people die. I don't like walls."

She told me she had a little girl who died as a baby. I didn't dare ask if it happened indoors or out. "But I have Kelvin and his kids," she said. "He does some damn stupid things, but he has a heart of gold, that boy."

She asked if I had children, and I found myself telling her how I miscarried the baby I conceived with Felix. I've told almost no one about that. Said I felt punished because I shouldn't have slept with him when he was married to someone else, and that the child would have been illegitimate. Mavis gave me an impatient "pfff!' The word was meaningless to her. And in that instant, it dissolved in me. My Leila was simply my Leila.

~ ~ ~ ~

Scared to hope Mavis survived, but find myself looking out for her. On a visit back to Kalk Bay, I spot a skinny figure with a red head wrap walking along Main Road, clad in grubby jeans and a leather jacket. I call out, "Tannie Mavis! Tannie!"

Too late, I realize it's a man. He spins around, his face puckered in anger. He yells, "Who's your *tannie?*"

I mutter, "*Jammer!* I'm so sorry!"

Bob hasn't mentioned her in weeks. Does he know something and is sparing me? But he did tell me a bit more about her money. He has a fund, apparently, to which his congregants and local businesses make donations. He gives it out where the need is most urgent. "Mavis's need was a bit beyond our means," he said, "but Sam sent us a very generous gift right after he got home, and he asked me to give her a portion." He wouldn't tell me what she wanted it for. "That was her secret, not mine."

I should go ask the Patels, the doctor and the lawyer, if they know anything about Mavis, but I've been busy, and they are probably too discreet to tell me anyway.

~ ~ ~ ~

Every few days I have had a nightmare about fire, the same one over and over. Not my fire, but a place of terrible despair, people enveloped in smoke and heat. The images have a familiarity I can't pin down. Feel the panic from inside the darkness, and grief from somewhere over the horizon. Someone—me? —is asking, "Is anything redeemable?"

What does redeemable even mean?

Where does the image of that dark place come from?

~ ~ ~ ~

The dream gets sharpened and halted by a blast of reality.

Next Steps

It comes in an email from Charles. "Do you know about Jedwabne?" he asks. I guess his contact in Poland must have mentioned something. "It's a village in Poland that used to have a Jewish community. Did any of your relatives live there?"

I have come across the name before, but can't recall where. "Used to have a Jewish population" plucks a chord. What became of them? In the far reaches of memory, I hear raised voices, my parents arguing, Polish words and Yiddish. It was the worst fight I ever witnessed between them, and it was my fault.

Imma never willingly spoke about her past. When I asked, she would begin reminiscing instead about the "miracle" of how she and my father, childhood sweethearts who grew up together, spotted each other in a displaced persons' camp. "I saw Frederik waiting in a line. His face was like a candle shining in that crowd," she told me. "I saw him—and I saw hope for the future."

So I asked my father what happened to his family. A historian by profession and passion, he was inclined to give me the facts. He told me how, after his parents were taken, he survived half-starved in a labor camp, and what he believed happened to his brother. My mother also had a brother, much older than her and, according to my father, a wonderful guy. When she refused to tell me, I asked Pops what became of my Uncle Salmon, the person they had named me after.

"Ah, *meydele*," he whispered, "Salmon and his wife were burned to death."

Was that in Jedwabne?

I can still hear his words: "The fire was set by his

neighbors."

That fact, more than their dying, triggered dreams that sent me into my parents' big bed night after night. All of a sudden, I became anxious about the people who lived next door, even their handsome son, the champion swimmer. My mother was furious, hence that fight. I stopped asking questions, and my father stopped volunteering information. They were always loving, but I think I absorbed that awful vulnerability into my bones.

~ ~ ~ ~

The cottage is a shell, parts of it pristine, others broken, shielded from the elements by pegged-down blue tarpaulins. All from a single flaming ember? Seems that one landed in the dry leaves of my bougainvillea and from there spread down to the motorbike and up onto the tiles of the roof, destroying the attic. My neighbors' houses were virtually unharmed, thank goodness.

Did you send it, Felix? To push me out into the world?
Is that how you feel? Maybe it's what you needed.
So glad to hear him, though we argue even more than before. He seems impatient with me, or am I just more raw?

I'm not allowed to enter the cottage, because they say it's dangerous, that they need to put up supports. When I peer through the living room window, I see an almost perfect stage set—except for the swathes of brown and black on the walls—where another life unfolded. I remember bits of the script, hear echoes of dialogue, but it hurts too much to hover. Hurry away, to meet Reverend Bob for coffee or to check in with Roxie and Edith, and always to meander for a while, calling out

Next Steps

"Sksssskelm! Mergatroid!" before driving back to Camps Bay.

My friends tell me I've been strong, that I've handled this whole trauma with admirable serenity. They seem not to notice how little I say about anything. When they ask how I'm doing, I say, "Fine, really."

In the mornings, before I dress in my new clothes, I put in time on my book, wrapped in Felix's robe. It smells of smoke; I know I should buy myself a new one, but I need so many other things. The smell helps me hear his voice, filling in details I'm having trouble recalling. His files are gone. All I have are the chapters I'd already written and saved, most of them already emailed to my agent, Gail. The book is nearing completion, so it wasn't the catastrophe it might have been. Crucial topics remain to be written, but Gail has suggested it's a good thing I'm limited in what I can add. "A slender book will do better than a tome," she keeps saying.

Felix's journals—ruined, gone. If I had put them away, back in their box under the bed, they might have survived. Another awful, wrenching loss. Felix wouldn't think so. Haven't heard him comment, but know he'd say it's good they're gone.

~ ~ ~ ~

In the afternoons, I take John down to the beachfront for a slow walk and a cup of tea at one of the open-air cafés. Later, we sit together on his porch, watching as the sun melts into the ocean,, he with a brandy, me with a glass of wine.

His memory betrays him. Words slip away, the names of service contractors, or brands he prefers to buy, even sometimes the names of colleagues he collaborated with over the years, developing the devices that kept him solvent. "Peter ... what's his name? Sally, you know who I mean." Quite often I do, people I remember Felix mentioning. But he doesn't forget a single detail of his inventions, or the steps involved in their development. I try to follow as he lovingly recaps those victories.

And, on his clear days, he seems to remember most of what Felix shared with him. We talk about him for hours. John loves telling me how Felix, alone and adrift in Cape Town, came to live with him. The teenager served as his assistant and started to study for a college degree. When John sent him to Europe to gather product samples, he studied by correspondence. I know; it was all recounted in those burned journals. We met when he came to Rhodes to finish the last credits and embark on his next venture.

The distant past fascinates John more than the present, but I love to remind him how, just a few months ago, he helped me solve a riddle central to Felix's identity—whether the awful man who expelled him from his home before he could finish high school was his actual father. "Felix wanted to believe he wasn't," John recalled with a chuckle. "He asked me to adopt him, but I couldn't do that legally."

"You were as good as a father to him," I said.

Felix's brother, Humphrey, also a man of science, reveres Dr. Latimer almost as much as Felix did, and it was he who suggested I contact the old man.

The brothers thought he was too married to his work to indulge in romance. I've learned otherwise. In the evenings, I play the piano and sometimes persuade John to sing old

Next Steps

favorites with me. It gets him reminiscing about the women in his life.

"There was this girl, this woman, very beautiful. Not pretty, not . . . it wasn't her skin or her eyes . . . just very beautiful. Posture like a queen, and a lot of chestnut hair, thick and shiny. I can still remember the smell of it." That was Georgina, who came from a very wealthy family, and married someone else. I think she's on husband number two or three now.

Then there was Jenny, and a singer called Vera whom he'd found exotic, and Beatrice who came and went in his life, hoping he would marry her, storming off in frustration—till they would cross paths somewhere and she'd fall for his charms again.

"Why didn't you marry Beatrice?" I asked.

"I didn't love her enough. Glad as I was to have her back in my life each time, I was just as relieved when she vanished. I could get on with my work, eating when I wanted, sleeping when I wanted, washing when I wanted."

That's how he lives these days, though I try to maintain some routine for him. A nurse comes by twice a week to check on his skin lesions, caused, I think, by the chemicals he worked with. On the days in between, I change the dressings. To my surprise, I've become quite comfortable doing it. It's the first time in my life that I've taken care of anyone this way. The closest other contact was with Freddie, when I visited Joanie and Eric just after his birth last year. In a way, I enjoy babying John, fussing over his well-being. It takes me out of myself.

~ ~ ~ ~

"I don't know what I'd have done without you," he said a few days ago.

"Likewise," I told him.

"But I will make do. I know you have to get back to your own home and your own life."

That I didn't particularly want to hear. It reminds me of the way he pushed Felix to go to Europe, ostensibly to purchase those items he couldn't find in South Africa. I've always assumed he was disappointed when Felix decided to carry on traveling rather than return home. He was away for years and came back fired up to finish his degree and get on with his career. It dawns on me now that John intended precisely that. I wonder if Felix knew.

I took our plates through to the kitchen, and when I came back, I bent and kissed the top of his head. He reached up to pat my arm and reminded me that his nephew is coming out from Britain now that his divorce has been finalized. John has invited him to stay. "He can look after me," he said.

There is enough space in this house for both the nephew and me. Is John pushing me out for my own good, or because he can only take a certain amount of female company? I can accept that, but what I can't admit to him is that I can't afford to make my home inhabitable.

Friends keep telling me that, as the owners, Joanie and Eric are responsible for most of the cost of fixing the house. But our deal was very specific: In return for a below-market rent, I handle maintenance and repairs—at least until the insurance comes through. Even when it does, though, will it be enough?

Joanie, meanwhile, has come up with a plan. She wants

Next Steps

them to come to Cape Town, so Eric can help with the finishing touches. Of course, I said yes. I'd love to see them. If the timing works, maybe they could be here for my birthday, as they were last year. That's a lovely prospect.

But where would they stay? Perhaps I can get a loan, so we can speed up the repairs. But without additional monthly income how would I repay it? I feel cornered. I don't want to delay their visit, and I don't know how to prepare for it.

Going around in circles. So much easier to stall them, and stay huddled in this sunny house of John's, if he will let me. Here I don't have to face fears of the future, or ghosts of the past.

Even me?

Hey, hi! No, not you. Thought you'd given up on me.

More like the other way around. You seem very comfortable around John.

You were happy living with him too.

True. But I was a kid. You have a life to lead. . .

I know, I know.

~ 9 ~

Friday evening, friends of John's, the Taylors, have invited us to dine at a posh restaurant on the beachfront. Husband and wife are philanthropists with a foundation they've created and are investors in some Latimer gadgets. I offered to drive him there and come back to pick him up later, not wanting to intrude. Also, my only suitable surviving garment is the silly pink dress from the conference. Pretty sure the conversation will go way over my head.

But John refused to go unless I came too. I think he feels more secure when I'm with him, to repeat a comment if he hasn't heard it, or to dab the inevitable spills of food or drink. Blasé as he tries to be, he clings to his dignity.

The restaurant is up a flight of stairs, a challenge for him but doable if we take our time. He has one hand on the railing and one on my arm. As we ascend, he whispers to me, "Remember I told you about Georgina, with the wonderful hair?" He looks almost boyish.

Next Steps

"This is her?"

"Yes. Now forget I said anything."

Georgina and her husband, Rupert, are waiting for us at a table by the window, on their feet and beaming in welcome. He is a tall, portly fellow, his tweed jacket straining across his belly. She is elegant, regal as John had said, with pale blond hair swept up in a lacquered chignon, not the chestnut of the past but still lovely. I feel him pull away and walk those last few steps with a straight back.

The food is excellent, as it should be, given the prices. The conversation is serious and every bit as intimidating as I feared. They are talking about finance and grants and tax advantages. If Sam was here, he'd be in his element; I definitely am not. If I weren't driving, I'd have a cocktail to ease my tension. Instead, I keep my mouth shut and follow as well as I can. That is, until they turn their focus on me and ask for answers.

"Sally, you've been involved with research, have you?" Rupert asks, peering at me. It's the first time our eyes have met. I have to fight not to look away.

"My late partner was," I say. "I've been a teacher all my life. But I suppose I have done research too."

"Okay. And you are comfortable speaking to different kinds of people?"

"I suppose so." I look at John, but he is staring down at his plate, smiling as he listens to them draw me in. I thought this discussion was going to be about an invention of his, not about my work. It was a trap, but for what?

Georgina picks up the thread: "You seem perfect. We need someone who can represent us in philanthropy circles and help us select people and organizations to give grants to. It can get very delicate and political, and we can't be in South Africa often enough to oversee everything ourselves. Would you consider taking it on?"

Suddenly aware of a faintly acrid smell. It's coming from me, from the dress.

"You'd be ideal, Sally," John says.

I am so willing to let the world go on about its business without me, why does everyone keep trying to drag me in? On the other hand, it sounds as if they do worthy work. Out of nowhere I hear strains of music in my head, melody for a dance of renewal— "The Rites of Spring"? Helping them with their benevolence could be energizing.

"I don't know," I say. "It sounds as if it involves complicated financial stuff. That is absolutely not my strength."

"You'd get whatever help you need. We have a first-rate CFO," Rupert says.

"And I have a home to repair, and a book to complete, and so many other things to consider. I'm sorry."

"It wouldn't be full-time," Georgina adds. "You could still do whatever else you're doing. We pay our people very well."

"I don't know," I repeat.

"No rush." She places her cool hand over mine, evidently not accepting that as a "no." "Take your time and think about it." Rupert passes me their business card. It's elegantly discreet, gray with gold lettering.

As we're walking back to our respective cars, Georgina threads her arm through mine and slows me down, letting the

Next Steps

men walk on ahead, Rupert with his hand under John's elbow.

"I have to ask," she whispers, "you and John——? I know he's still adamantly single, but . . . "

I give a snort-laugh, caught by surprise. "Oh no. Why would you think that? No, I met him through my late partner, Felix, who was his *protégé* way back. Felix adored him and so do I."

And then I turn the tables on her, feeling entitled now. "I gather he doted on you."

"Oh, it was mutual." She sighs. "He was the most fascinating man I'd ever met, and very debonair in those days. But I wanted children; he didn't. And I wanted to travel, and he'd done all of that. I was terribly hurt when he dumped me, but it was for the best. I was very happy with hubby number one. We had two kids. Sadly, he died way too young. And Rupert—well, I might not have rushed into it if he hadn't been quite so insistent. But he does take good care of me, and he handles our finances."

She stops and peers at me. "Felix? I remember John talking about him. Kicked out by his family as a teenager? I gathered he was the closest John ever came to having a son. He passed away very suddenly? I am so sorry for your loss."

She squeezes my arm. "But that makes you almost like a daughter-in-law? No wonder you seem so close. Now I don't feel as jealous."

~ ~ ~ ~

I liked that, her openness and the fact that she could be as silly as me. Who would have imagined that this glamorous woman ever got pushed aside by anyone? Equally impressive was that she forgave John, put that hurt aside, and built this long friendship.

Come to think of it, Felix pushed me aside back when we were young (though he insisted it was a two-way rejection), and I forgave him. That makes me feel even closer to Georgina. Not as sure about Rupert. He kept trying to assert his strength with John—aware, perhaps, that this man still holds a special place in his wife's heart?

Personalities aside, they would probably be fine to work with. Just scared that they are placing way too much trust in me, on the flimsy basis of John's recommendation. I don't think I can accept their offer. I didn't want to say that then, in front of him, so I'll wait a while and then write to them.

~ ~ ~ ~

Turns out, my home hasn't been as empty as I thought.

When I meet Frank, the contractor, at the cottage, he is wearing a yellow hardhat and insists I put one on. I head for the front door, but he steers me around the patio to the back entrance. The glass shattered in the fire and the door has been boarded up, but someone has cut off the padlock and it is slightly ajar. We push it open and step inside. The room, dark to begin with, is now even darker. I reach automatically for the light switch, but nothing happens, no electricity. When my eyes adjust to the gloom, I see a sheet of newspaper spread across the table, and a plate and mug resting upside down on it, and a stub of a candle on a saucer.

"Whoops! Careful. Looks like we've got an intruder," Frank says.

Is he still in here?—if it's a he. Could it be a woman? My

Next Steps

scalp tightens. Strain to hear any sound of human presence, if someone has scuttled into hiding. Could they attack us, resenting our intrusion? Frank is prowling around the room, picking up this and that, also seeking clues. "Whoever has been here, they're taking a big chance," he says, gesturing up at the blackened ceiling. "They could get killed. I'm going to take a quick look, check that they're not hiding inside, but you should get out."

"Don't go, please!" I whisper, but he disappears through to the living room. I stay where I am, rooted to the spot, listening. You can see an effort has been made to sweep the cinders and wood fragments to one side. The plate and mug look as if they've been rinsed and left to dry.

A pocket of rage erupts inside me. If I can't stay in my own home, how dare they? This is my Felix place, and this person has barged their way in and filled it with their presence. It's almost worse that the stuff looks carefully arrayed. The intruder isn't a *dronklap*, too soused to know where he or she is.

Anger drives out fear and I follow Frank.

Pad gingerly down the passage. Look into the guest room where he is tapping on the walls, and into the bathroom, which is more or less undamaged. Reach the bedroom and freeze in the doorway, initially unable to peer inside. When I do, what greets me is worse than I anticipated. The bed is a blackened, sunken mess. Fragments of charred paper are scattered across what were the blankets and pillows. When I look closer I see Felix's handwriting. I was reading his journals as I drifted off to sleep that night. If I'd put them away in their box under the bed, maybe . . .

Don't go there, I hear, but I can't stop myself. That precious record of my beloved before I met him, of the travels that turned him into a citizen of the world. That wealth of memories I thought Joanie and Trevor would cherish. Destroyed.

The two of them did dip into the journals when they visited after his passing, reading here and there, but both declined to take the books home with them.

"He didn't write them for us," Joanie said.

"He didn't write them for me either, but I find them very comforting to read," I told her.

"Then you keep them." She hugged me. "You need them more than we do. But don't bury yourself in them."

Drag my gaze away and up to the walls. Astonished! Above the bed, against the blackened plaster, I see the red sequined wall-hanging, the beautiful piece Felix brought back from one of his later trips to India. This past New Year's Eve, I impetuously wrapped it around my shoulders, like a shawl, to lift my spirits, and then hung it up again later. Still there, suspended by its brass rings, apparently whole. The embroidery glitters in the sunshine.

I climb up on the bed and carefully start unhooking the rings. As the cloth falls into my arms, Frank sees me. "Mrs. Paddington, what the hell are you doing?" He hustles me back to the kitchen and out. Pulls the plywood-covered door closed behind us and padlocks it. "I'm going to have my crew come in and start work in the next few days. Don't come back on your own." We agree to meet again next week, and he drives

Next Steps

off. I make my way up the street to visit Bob.

My mood has lifted. Still indignant that someone else has laid claim to my home, but my pulse has slowed to normal. Retrieving this one surviving treasure has allowed kinder thoughts to surface. How desperate do you have to be to shelter in a place that is so dangerous?

As I walk, I turn my toes out just a little, pull back my shoulder blades and inhale. The burn smell has gone, and I catch a whiff of honeysuckle. My love for this neighborhood rises. Out of the corner of my eye, I see an orange tail disappear. Swoop down in pursuit, trying to peer through a gate, but bushes block the view. But I know it wasn't striped as boldly as Skelm's.

~ 10 ~

Twice in the following weeks I cancel plans with the contractor. Once, because John had been having palpitations, and I wanted to take him to his doctor. The second time, I jar my gammy knee and decide I should ice it.

I keep telling Frank that I'm not sure how much work I can afford to have done. The insurance company, predictably, is stalling. His response each time is: "Don't worry, I promise I won't go ahead without giving you estimates."

But last time we spoke, he added, "I have a crew available at the moment. I can't promise you they will be down the road." I dare not cancel again.

Joanie has emailed, chatting about how homesick she is for Kalk Bay and how she's longing to see me. "How are the repairs coming along?" she asked. "Have they begun work? Contractors can be so unreliable." I feel guilty; it's me, not him, who is holding up the progress.

So, we do meet up, he with his van and his team, me with John, who has asked to come along for a drive. I suspect it is

Next Steps

also to ensure that I stick to the plan. I leave him sipping coffee in the café on the corner.

The workers have set up support beams in the kitchen, and they have lights wired to a generator, so the kitchen is bright. Everything else is as we left it, the newspaper and the cup and plate.

Evidently, the sinister occupant has not managed to get back inside. That lowers my anxiety a little, but it still gives me shivers to think a stranger has been there. Should I have told the police? They could take fingerprints from the cup. But what would I report? There was nothing of value to steal, except my peace of mind—and how much of that did I have anyway?

Peering around, I notice what was probably there before but overlooked, tucked away on a stool in the corner, a small pile of clothes. I approach and finger them cautiously. See jeans and a jacket—mine!

On the floor, under the stool, I see two grimy bowls, with a lump of crusted-over something at the bottom. For Mergatroid and Skelm? Dished out, but not eaten, like an "in case." Can't imagine Mavis caring about my beasts, but maybe she would, knowing that I liked them, even if she didn't.

I put up a hand to silence Frank, ask him to give me a minute. Push my way out onto the patio, torn between relief and hope and indignation. Did Bob know about this, even give Mavis permission? If so, why didn't he tell me? Why didn't he tell me she was alive?

The deck chairs are still on the patio, but so covered in a mix of cinders and twigs and leaves, I can't tell if the fabric is whole. I perch on the frame.

Realization thuds into place, certainty: If she was staying here, Bob would have told me. Like ash on the night of the fire, dryness grates in my throat. What of the clothes? Someone else from the group must have brought them back. That woman I followed up to their encampment. Was it her who broke into my home?

Remember glancing into the bathroom, seeing the toilet seat up. Not Mavis, or another woman.

My thoughts are toggling between people and cats and money and John Latimer. Frank has followed me outside. He gives me a quizzical look. "As I was about to say, I can give you a rough tally of what we need to do. Just the basic stuff, no frills, nothing extra," he says. "But I need an answer."

I know that he's being fair. If I had a reliable stream of income, I'd give him the go-ahead. The insurance money will cover some of it—eventually. I'm shivering, from the cold wind or tension or both. He goes back inside with his tape measure, and I make my way down to the café to join John.

Through the doorway I see two teenagers, a girl and a boy, sitting with the old man, listening to him with avid attention. I see the boy's hands flying as he responds. Instead of entering, With quivery knees, I sit down on a bench outside.

I don't know this self, this white-haired, jittery flake. Try to recall my old self, "Bunnington" as they used to call me, instead of Paddington, with my perfect posture and red hair scraped back with immaculate precision. What happened to her, that disciplined dancer? I feel formless these days. Maybe I should grow my hair long again so I can tie it up tight in a bun. Fake it till you make it, they say.

Next Steps

So, faking decisiveness, before I can chicken out again, I take out my phone and call the office number for the Taylors' foundation. They are away somewhere, but I leave a message with the secretary, the briskly efficient Miss Geldenhuys. "Please tell them," I say, "that if the job offer still stands, I would like to accept it, at least on a trial basis."

And then, of course, I hope that they are away for a long time, that she forgets to forward the message, and that I can still change my mind. What if I misunderstand what they ask of me, or mess up with their clients, or botch the administrative tasks? It feels like an invitation to catastrophe.

But still, it could be a solution, and that hope wafts through me like a sea breeze.

I waltz into the café and draw up a chair at John's table. The three of them keep right on talking. Listen quite happily to their smart, enthusiastic exchange, until there is a lull and John introduces me. Apparently, they are discussing ideas for a school science project—I have no idea how they found out what a resource he could be—and when they leave, they promise to let him know how they do.

John sits back, elated, basking in the afterglow of all that youthful energy. Then he asks, "So, when are you going to move back into your home? Did you give them a deadline?"

"They're making progress." I will fill him in on the details, but first there is one question I must ask. It comes out whinier than I intended. "Am I such a pain in the butt as a guest that you can't wait for me to get out?"

"Yes," he says, his crinkled visage utterly expressionless, except for one quivering crease just below the corner of his mouth. Despite myself, I start laughing. He gives in and grins too.

"Soon," I tell him. "Soon."

~ ~ ~ ~

Life can change so abruptly. By now I should know that. Still, it has come as a shock. One minute I was hibernating; now I'm zipping about like a pollen-drunk bee.

Georgina phoned right after Miss Geldenhuys gave them my message, full of encouragement. Rupert took over the call, unctuously welcoming me, and laying out again what they want done. "We'll give you an expense account," he added, a throwaway line. They had me signed up and on board by the end of that week.

In less than six weeks, I've gone from anxiously watching every penny like Scrooge, to being obsessed with abundance and all the responsibility it brings.

On the personal front, my salary, though modest compared to some listed on Charity Navigator, feels obscenely high. Plus, the insurance on the cottage has finally come through. No more excuse to avoid Frank. He and his subcontractors have been patient as I dither over the available choices, but I have given them the green light to get started on the repairs.

The job itself is every bit as challenging as I expected. The Taylors have given me the authority to bestow initial mini-grants, or "starter gifts," on worthy organizations of my choosing, simply by texting them a description, and filling out a form for their chief financial officer. Six months in, when we can vet how well our recipients have handled the money, they

Next Steps

will be able to apply for larger grants. For those, they will have to jump through hoops. The experts say you must assess applicants' staffing, methods, bookkeeping, track record, etcetera, etcetera. For now, thank goodness, Rupert and Georgina don't require any of that.

But each day has been hectic, jammed with new learning, new acquaintances, new questions. To find my bearings, I've been attending seminars, meeting with experts, and dutifully attending charity soirees to make the contacts I need. Panicky Paddington trying to cover all her bases, Angie would say. My social skills, rusted from disuse this past year, are slowly reactivating.

John, finding me in the living room way past midnight one night, still buried in a book, warned me that I'd damage my eyes. "I'd help you if I could, but I detest this stuff. Always did," he said. "That's why I preferred to get my funding from people I know and skip all that jargon and paperwork."

Of course, if Sam were here, if we were still friends, I'd be peppering him with questions. But he's not, and we aren't.

On the fun side—relatively speaking—I've been shopping, thanks to the expense account and at Georgina's insistence, so I can look presentable when I represent the foundation. "You can't turn up in a dress that still smells of smoke, can you?" she said. Bought two trouser suits, one black, one blue, plus three blouses to wear with them, and a pair of smart shoes. Not very exciting, perhaps, but a reminder that dressing the part helps you play the part. I look like a female presidential candidate!

But here comes the miserable part: having to refuse most applicants. I want to say yes to everyone.

After dithering and debating and middle-of-the-night agonizing, I have selected six groups. Done and dusted. Each one now has their own file on my desk. A reception is planned for next month when the Taylors are back in Cape Town, so they can present the checks. I can't wait. But how do I now smother the voice still asking, "What about so-and-so?"

For the first grant, I chose a home for battered women, a spotlessly clean, depressingly shabby residence full of traumatized people healing under the gentle ministration of a group of social workers and volunteers.

The second grant is going to a soup kitchen in Guguletu that offers pensioners one hearty meal a day, and a warm, safe place where they can congregate for a few hours. They sit on hard plastic chairs gathered around bridge tables, or lined up for seated exercise sessions, with golden-oldie tunes crackling in the background. I want them to get softer chairs, for a start, and perhaps a television.

The third recipient is a literacy program designed to help high school dropouts, so they have a chance of earning a livable wage. It also provides job placement, a tough challenge in this economy.

All three of the remaining grants involve children, their mental health, physical health, and creativity.

I think of myself as a decent person, but the people running these efforts are saints. They give so much of themselves. I've fallen in love with Hanie, the rotund powerhouse behind the women's home, and totally adore Edward, the hyperactive firecracker who runs the literacy program.

Those in the know have warned me to watch out for

Next Steps

charlatans. That's to be expected where money is involved, and my antennae have been on hyper-alert. But I think I'm a pretty astute judge of character—in this regard anyway. It's the one aspect where I feel confident.

I did consider giving a starter gift to Estella and Herman, but I couldn't see my way around the charge of personal favoritism. Tried to put them out of my mind, but their work is so beneficial, and they desperately need funding. Finally, called Georgina and Rupert, who were back in town for a lightning visit en route to the Seychelles. When I described Estella's students, Georgina said, "I respect your hesitation. Never mind that. I'll write them a check myself. And then they can apply for a bigger grant. Will you take my husband and me to see the children?"

That didn't happen—they had no time to visit a class—but Rupert asked Herman to come meet with him at the foundation offices. According to Estella, the two men got on very well. That surprised me; I couldn't imagine the peacock and the cockerel liking each other, but apparently, they found something in common.

The money from Georgina will be enough to cover rent on a better space, somewhere with a solid roof and smooth floor. When I called to tell them it was coming, I thought Estella was going to faint. She kept exclaiming, "Is this true? You really mean it?" Herman was his usual debonair self, even a little distracted, as though his mind was already racing ahead to bigger things. I remembered he was planning to get something like this when we met. He thanked me and handed the phone back to her. That was fine. I felt overly thanked already.

"No more money talk, okay?" I said to Estella. "Can we go back to just being two dance teachers?"

She laughed. "So, I can go back to nagging you about Fausia?"

~ ~ ~ ~

And go back to nagging, Estella did. She texted me this morning to say, "Sally, please. Fausia is really struggling."

So, I call her. Somehow, the fire on the mountain, the one that drove me out of my home, has deepened Fausia's problem.

Estella says, "She has totally shut down. Her grandmother seems to have disappeared, and her mother has gone off with a different bunch of bergies. Her father got out of jail, and he has come to us, trying to get Fausia back. But he doesn't have a proper home. I persuaded him to leave her with us till she gets stronger. Now she is angry with me. She blames me for keeping her from him, but she won't say anything. If she would just talk to me about it . . ."

"You can't let him take her!"

Hand this child over to a convict? The mere notion is nauseating. As much as people get locked up for nothing, some get released too easily— "the revolving door."

She agrees about the justice system, but not as it applies to Fausia's father. "I think Kelvin got scapegoated," she insists. "Someone paid his bail, but he needs a lawyer or he could land back behind bars for years. His wife is a total mess, especially now without her mother-in-law. Fausia needs her father to be okay."

Mother-in-law? I assumed the grandmother on the mountain was her mother's mother. "No," she says, "Mavis

Next Steps

was Kelvin's mother."

My Mavis? The question riffles through the layers of my mind.

Was? "She died?"

"Not sure. Maybe. He says he can't find what became of her. You knew her?" Estella asks.

"We were friends, sort of." My heart feels squeezed.

"The bergies say they think she was taken away in an ambulance. She might have been in the hospital, unconscious or mixed up, and no one could say who she was. You know, people like that don't have identity papers, not on them. All we've heard is that she never came back. Kelvin insists it was his fault, that because of him she had extra money on her. Her companions got hold of the money and blew it on booze, had a party . . ."

"She had money on her?"

Estella cuts in: "Sally, I think Kelvin stayed in your house, just for a bit. Sorry I didn't say anything before. I should have told you, but I didn't put two and two together. He said the people on the mountain gave him a bundle of clothes his mother left behind, that they were from this house. He brought them back, but no one was there. I think he might have hung around, hoping Mavis would show up. I told him about your cats being lost, and he said he would look out for them."

Images and questions are circling in my brain. That envelope of money Mavis was so excited to hand over to the lawyer, was that to get her son out of jail? The sinister squatter was him? But what money did she have after we'd been to the surgery?

I want to block it, but an image emerges, stark as a woodcut, of Mavis taking the fifty rand note from me and tucking it into her dress. Did that cash fuel the party that might have killed her?

If I'd gone to buy her Ribena instead of giving her the money, might she be alive? Might the fire on the mountain not have happened if I'd just been kinder?

I'm not a bitch, I try to tell my ghost.

He doesn't contradict me. I feel him at my shoulder, simply listening, leaving me to stray down this dark alley.

~ 11 ~

I've managed to slither past my birthday with minimal fuss, just phone calls from my Kalk Bay neighbors, and from Libby, of course. John didn't know and probably wouldn't have reacted anyway. Woke up with an image of my mother, determinedly auburn-haired, her blue eyes fierce. Much as she loved entertaining, she never invited guests to celebrate her birthday; it would have meant letting them know her age. I have no such qualms, but was glad to keep things low-key.

I am already four years older than she was when she died.

Was surprised not to hear from the Portland crew, until I found out what they were dealing with. Joanie called last night, contrite and sad. "Eric's leaving for Cape Town tomorrow," she said, "via a client in Johannesburg. But Freddie and I aren't coming with him. I'm so sorry." Turns out the little one has been ill again.

My heart sank. So disappointed, and then panic erupted. Joanie insisted Freddie was doing better. "But there was no way

Elaine Durbach

we could subject him to a flight," she added. "He's on antibiotics and being monitored by his pediatrician." Eric couldn't postpone; he has business meetings he needs to attend in person in South Africa, seeing the people with whom he is building a sustainable-materials consultancy.

I wanted to reach across the phone line to hug Joanie. "My mother has been popping in to help me," she said. Judging by the lack of venting, Deidre was within earshot.

She bought an apartment in Portland just a few months ago, with just such an emergency in mind. I'm glad she's nearby, even if Joanie isn't. Weird how that has changed. Still feel a pang of guilt when her name comes up, for sleeping with her husband. But I have come to appreciate her strengths.

Along with my guilt, there is envy—that she got to marry Felix as I never did, and to live with him for longer—though not nearly as happily as I did for the five years we finally had together. Most envious of all that she got to have this daughter with him, though I get to enjoy Joanie too. I should be grateful to Deidre for that.

Heartsore that Joanie and Freddie aren't coming. I'd been counting the days to having them with me, in person. "But I've sent you a substitute," she said, "Trevor." Can one's heart plunge and rise simultaneously?

Trevor has joined Eric's architectural firm. Apparently, he is coming along to be introduced to clients, and learn more of the ropes. Turns out, they are also debating whether he should stay on to help me complete the restoration of the cottage. Gave a whoop of delight when I heard that.

Quick flash of guilt toward Trevor's mother, the lovely

Next Steps

Nellie. I have no ambivalence toward her like I have to Deidre. She and I have been friends since our first encounter, teaming up over the years to get our wild boy back on track during his teens, and to get Felix to relax his over-anxious fathering. My gain, however, will be Nellie's pain. She'll miss him if he stays here in Cape Town.

~ ~ ~ ~

The guys fly in on a blustery, bright Sunday, full of tales of meetings and potential contracts. I love to see their collegiality. The first visible sign is their new beards. Not exactly matching—Eric's is dark and immaculately trimmed; Trevor's is patchy brown. But they create a physical similarity where before there was none.

Take them from the airport to the holiday apartment I've rented for them near the city center. Trevor approves enthusiastically; he's never been as close to the cool downtown music scene on Long Street and Loop Street and the quaint, funky restaurants. It's also within easy reach of me in Camps Bay.

They dump their bags, and we grab a quick lunch and head straight out to Kalk Bay.

On the way, I tell them about what's been happening with my new job. They are volubly impressed. I'm kind of impressed too. It's the first time I've had work talk to share with them. It's weird.

The cottage is less impressive. It isn't habitable yet. The bones have been shored up, together with the wiring and piping, but the surfaces aren't anywhere near completion. With the workers absent, it feels oddly quiet. I unlock the patio door and usher them in. The lighting is from bare light bulbs. Everything is dusty.

"I wish Dad was here," Trevor says, one hand trawling through his khaki-colored curls. His voice catches, and I feel my own throat constrict. He is tall, like his mother, but he folds into my hug like a child. He and Eric were here a year ago with Joanie, when the loss was still raw, but this home was as it had been all the times they had come out to visit. Now it's other.

"Did Felix care about sustainability?" Eric asks, running his hand across the dusty surface of the mantel. "He was passionate about so many things, but I can't remember him ever mentioning the environment. Am I forgetting?"

"I'm not forgetting, I don't think," I say, "but I can't recall him saying anything. He was fairly oblivious of his surroundings. But remember how he loved finding eccentric items to bring home?" They both nod, grinning. I listen for Felix, to see if he'll contradict me, but hear nothing. The kitchen table has upturned crates set around it. We sink onto them, and I hold my hands out. We three sit, linked, sharing the silence.

Finally, I start outlining the renovation plans. Eric is pleased with some of the decisions our contractor has made, and frustrated by others. I'm caught in the middle. I share his environmental concerns, but my budget biases me in favor of cheaper options. It helps, though, to really like the people you're arguing with. I know our decisions will be sound.

Over the next few days, Eric updates me on Freddie. Each time we sit down together, he passes me his phone to share

Next Steps

more photos and videos. I last saw the baby when he was just a few weeks old, in December. Now he is a curious person, wide-eyed and with a voice that lets his feelings be known. His features have become more defined, a dented chin like Eric's, and black curls and straight eyebrows, like fine, inked lines. Last year when I went out to see them, I was terrified of bonding with him, afraid of his frailty, and trying not to get too attached. Couldn't bear the thought of losing another chunk of my heart, but he got past all my shields.

Eric isn't usually this chatty, but it's his first stretch of time away from Freddie. I think the talking helps. "They're still not sure about his mobility and how strong his lower body will be," he explains. Maria, whom we now know shares the same syndrome, has been talking and texting with them and me, discussing ideas for later, when he is a little older "Some of her methods have already been helpful," Eric says. "Every day we see a little bit more progress."

Joanie calls Eric every day, sometimes twice. If I am with him, I get a word in too. Not like being face-to-face, but I love this more frequent connection. She gets to moan about her mother. "But you know how high-maintenance she is," she says. "I'm more exhausted when she leaves than when she arrives."

Day after day, she adds, "But if *you* were here . . ." Not sure why; I'm so unaccustomed to being around little kids, I really wasn't much help when I visited last year. But I was enormously impressed with how well she had taken to motherhood, and she basked in that admiration.

She is missing Eric, and he isn't due to return for another

few weeks. Still has the Johannesburg people to deal with, and a course in Switzerland to attend. "If *you* were here . . ." she repeats. I made the mistake of telling her that John is nudging me to move back to the cottage, though it's not inhabitable yet, that he's had enough of my company. "So, come!" she says, "even if it's just till the cottage is ready."

~ ~ ~ ~

Frustrated by my delays, Estella has brought Fausia to me, at John's.

Herman delivers them and comes in too, but he isn't feeling very well. Says he had a very late night and asks if I mind if he takes a nap. Direct him to my bedroom, draw the curtains, and put a rug over him.

"Goodness knows where he was last night," Estella says. "He's always up to something." He gets up about half an hour later and goes off to do some errand.

Estella is up to something of her own, in a good way. The connection I helped her make with Maria in Spain has flourished into a to-and-fro of questions and answers by email, followed by phone calls, and even a video so she could show Maria her students in action.

Estella says, "Maria says she might be coming out to see us. Can you believe it? I'm hoping we can be in our new space by then." She starts to say something about the grant money, but I hold up a finger. We agreed, no more thank yous.

I'd rather discuss her Maria news. When I visited Maria in Barcelona last December, en route back from Portland, I saw how severely handicapped she is. Wasn't that why she didn't come out to visit her beloved Felix when he fell sick? Instead,

Next Steps

she tracked me down through my publisher and begged me to come to Cape Town. And thereby she turned my whole life upside down—or right way up.

But this? The prospect of her visiting opens up all kinds of possibilities. If my cottage can be made accessible, I'd love to host her and Diego.

Trevor is with me at John's, taking a break from meetings. I've told him a bit about Fausia, and he hangs back, quietly observing. He is a superb natural dancer himself, as easy in his body as his father was, and I want to know what he makes of her. She seems fascinated by him, puzzled when I call him my "sort-of son"—because he's browner than me, or simply because she finds him handsome.

It's a freezing day, and the child has come bundled up in jeans and a jacket, but only because Estella insisted. "She doesn't seem to notice cold or heat."

Fausia walks as I remember from the time with Sam, lurching as if unsure of the ground below her. She greets me politely, again not looking directly at me. "Do you remember me from the concert at the hall?" I ask.

"*Ja*, I remember. Your man friend, he had a shirt with a big rainbow." I nod. "Miss Estella, she says you a dancer."

"I used to dance," I say.

"You can't anymore?" she asks. "You too old?"

Estella moves as if to hush her, but I hold up my hand. "Not too old, I don't think," I say. "I believe everybody can dance, even if just with their eyes." The child's own eyes go wide and then scrunch in confusion. "But I seem to have lost my ability to dance. I need help."

"You sick, like me?" She lays her hand over mine. I turn mine over so we are holding palm-to-palm.

"You're sick, Fausia? I'm so sorry to hear that. I'm not sick-sick, but my heart has been very sad." She nods, as if understanding. "But let's watch some dancing on the screen, and maybe we can get ideas to make us feel healthy."

Estella watches us with a lopsided, knowing smile. We haven't planned anything. I'm not even sure I can find what I have in mind online. Trevor tries, but isn't familiar with my machine, or John's internet and TV setup. He keeps trying. The child has squirmed back on her chair and is peering all around, taking in the details of the room. It must seem very large to her, and very empty. She stares at the paintings and John's antique gadgets, lost in thoughts of her own.

Finally, Trevor gives a victory whoop: We have a connection, and images. He hands me the laptop, and I find the video I have in mind, a wonderfully wild and exuberant performance by four dancers in South Korea. I sneak a look at Fausia. She is leaning forward, her mouth open and her hands making little feathery movements in time with the music. I imitate her, enlarging the movement with a little more deliberation, and letting it spread to engage my arms, elbows and shoulders. I see her look and her own movements increase just a tiny bit. My feet are tapping; hers aren't. But we are all swaying in our seats.

We watch three videos, and then I switch it off. Offer them refreshments. Fausia asks for tea, trying to sound grown up, I suspect, and I make some for all four of us. Estella comes through to the kitchen with me, leaving Trevor trying to get

Next Steps

Fausia to talk to him.

"Is she ill in some way?" I ask.

"Not according to our doctor." Estella hugs herself, frowning in thought. "Her feet were damaged—apparently burnt, I don't know how—but they're more or less healed. It's as if she doesn't trust the soles to be okay, as if she isn't feeling her body, and doesn't want to. She doesn't ever tell me she's hungry, or thirsty even. I had to force her to put on a jacket in this cold." I find myself mirroring her position, hugging myself, till the kettle boils and I shake myself into action.

I call to John, to ask if he'd like to join us for tea. He growls a "no." Trevor's eyes widen. "Sociable fellow, isn't he!" he says.

Brewing along with the tea leaves is a realization: I have to add another chapter to the book, one about invisible handicaps. Like Fausia's. Like my own. Oh, shoot! When Felix pushed me to do a more personal book, I never foresaw something like this.

Herman honks his horn a while later. As I walk outside with them, Fausia turns and flings her arms about my waist. "Can we come see you again?" she asks. "And see more videos?" Estella raises her eyebrows, echoing the question.

"Yes, for sure," I say. Like a climber embedding a piton higher in the rock face, I'm forced to carry on ascending.

When I turn back into the house, John is standing in the hallway. "You invited them to come again?" he asks. "I'm glad you all had a good time. Next time, you go to them."

I shrug off his grouchiness. There is something I'm more interested in hearing. I telephone Maria in Barcelona to hear her news for myself. Her husband, Diego, answers. It was he who told me, without preamble, that his wife had no legs. When I remind him of that, now he says, "She does have wings."

Metaphorically or literally—the wings of her visionary teaching, or access to the wings of an airplane? Either way, they have decided they want to come to Cape Town sometime early next year.

For all my insistence that I want nothing more to do with Mary's big conference, a light goes on: If the timing is right, she could be the keynote speaker for World Dance #2. Before I can stop myself, I make another call—to Mary.

"I'm not saying I want to be involved in the planning again, just that . . . well, Maria Flores would be an amazing 'get'!" She agrees.

Baby steps with Fausia. Given that John refuses to have them come to us, I have had no choice but to get in my car and go to Estella's.

The first time, I watched and helped a bit with the other children, but spent at least an hour with Fausia. I showed them the slides I shared at the conference back in January, of great dancers—fully mobile or limited—playing the fool, being animals and clowns, or just plain goofy. With the kids crowded around me to watch my laptop, I showed them videos of those same dancers in action. They shrieked in laughter and disbelief that grownups could dress up and cavort like that, let alone ones in wheelchairs or on crutches. Then Estella put on some of the music that had been featured in the videos and invited them to cavort too.

Next Steps

Fausia stayed at my side, proud of our connection, I think, but still not doing more than sway in place. But she was grinning as broadly as any of them.

On this second visit, I'm better prepared. Trevor has come with me. He helps me set up my laptop with a projector borrowed from Mary and a white sheet. Then he installs himself at the back of the room.

Almost immediately, he picks up on something I missed, perhaps because of my absorption in Fausia: One of the boys in the class is blind. He's a handsome child with deep-set milky eyes and he seems to be turning his head to look, like the others. But no, it's sound that is attracting him. A new plan pops into my mind.

YouTube offers up just what I want, a fabulous piece featuring Zulu dancers, with drums and thudding feet, and then a Spanish number with clicking castanets, and then some footage of Native American women from the Ojibwe tribe dancing in jingle dresses. I give the children a brief introduction before playing each video, pointing out what they have in common, not so much for the children who are watching as for this one who can only listen. He stands very straight, head tilted, his fingers spread wide against his thighs, and then begins moving this way and that, one step, one step, a stamp and swirl. Estella, hovering close beside me, sighs a deep "Oh my!" His body moves with total grace.

Fausia nods and smiles along with everyone else, but still won't do more than sway in place—until the jingle dress dance. Though she is watching, she too tilts her head, as if the tinkling of the silver cones is transporting her.

"Do you like those bells?" I whisper to her.

"Is like— is like—," she stammers. I have no idea where this is going. She turns to Estella. "Is like that *Heidi* book you were reading me, *né*? With the goats in the mountains, with their sweet milk."

Estella and I glance at each other, eyes glistening. I say, "When energy flows like this, it threads connections we can only follow and fan." She nods.

Was there a time when Fausia could move freely? I don't think she is like Maria or Freddie, with their congenital challenge. Not like Charles with his polio damage, or me with an injury to my knee that didn't heal quite right. But perhaps like me, she is tethered by a sad heart. Does she remember prancing like a little goat, or like Heidi herself?

The American writer Maya Angelou keeps rising in my mind, describing how she was mute for years after being raped, silenced by her fear of blurting out her attacker's name. Of course, it might be nothing like that in Fausia's case, and just a matter of dyspraxia of some kind. That would remove suspicion about her home life with her parents. On the other hand, trauma might be more easily healed than a brain dysfunction. If we can evoke pleasure . . .

I haven't felt this deeply moved by a student in years. And I haven't come this close to dancing.

~ 12 ~

Two weeks into their visit, Trevor, Eric, and I are strolling along Main Road to Muizenberg after visiting the cottage, going over ideas and enjoying the hazy sunshine of a windless winter morning. Tip my face up to the light, reveling in the sheer pleasure of being with these two guys, with their decency and smarts and creativity. At last, everything feels possible with Felix's funny little house.

The cellphone in my bag buzzes against my hip. Apologize and hold it cupped to my ear, trying to hear over the broken-rhythm rush of waves and passing cars.

It's Colin Bartlett, the accountant in the foundation office. We haven't spent much time together in person, but we talk frequently and email often, sorting through various issues. He is usually chatty, ready with a pun or a riddle. Not so today.

"Sally, what have you done?"

"Done? Regarding what?"

"You have made a mockery of the Taylor Foundation.

How could you think we would let you proceed in that manner?"

"What on earth do you mean? I've followed all the procedures Georgina and Rupert and you spelled out to me."

"Mr. and Mrs. Taylor would never have okayed what you've been doing! Foundation funds can't be sprayed around like a garden hose on goodness knows what, with no accountability!"

We're passing a bench, and I drop onto it. Trevor, puzzled, sits next to me. Eric stays standing, gazing out to sea. Hearing my tone, he lays a hand on my shoulder. My face feels stiff. Blood is drumming in my ears. On some level, this isn't a shock; it's the catastrophe I feared when I stepped into this job.

What made me think I could take on a new role at my age?

I manage to push out the words: "I don't know what you're talking about. I have represented the foundation as well as I possibly can. The people I've dealt with have been thrilled and grateful to the foundation. They can't wait to get their checks."

"Oh, oh, I bet they can't!" Bartlett sputters. "Well, there won't be any checks, and you're going to have to repay the money you've stolen, because that's what it is—stealing!"

This is such a bizarre exchange, initially I'm blank. Then anger surges up like lava. "You are wrong," I snarl at Bartlett. "You are so wrong, I've got a good mind to sue you for slander." Is that even possible? No idea, but I want to make him burn for whatever he is implying.

"If that is the case, come to the office. We must talk face to face," he says. "You're going to need a very good explanation. Be here tomorrow morning at nine."

Next Steps

I don't like being given orders, but I tell him I'll see him then and bash the button to disconnect. It was so much more satisfying when there was a receiver to bang down. The click doesn't do it.

I fold over, my head in my hands, groaning. Trevor puts his arm around me. Eric sits down on the other side. "It's okay, Sal," he says. "It's okay. Whatever the hell is happening, it's going to be okay."

I wish they didn't have to witness this catastrophe. I don't want it to mess up their visit.

Breathe, Sal.

Oh, Felix. I wish. . . .

Not even worth thinking what I wish. But I catch a hint of amusement from him. This is funny? Surely not. He knows what a Goody Two Shoes I've been all my life, terrified of being in the wrong. No one has ever accused me of taking something that wasn't mine.

Trevor pats my cheek. "Hey, Sal, calm down. What's happened? You're panting." It brings me back to the present. I stutter out a recitation of Bartlett's words. He and Eric listen, punctuating my words with "Whaaa?" and "No, that's crazy."

Has Bartlett already told Georgina and Rupert? And have they told John Latimer? Like an avalanche, the repercussions keep thumping down on me. If I'm fired, what about my repair people, all the decent, hard-working people I've been writing checks to? They will suddenly lose the income they expected. Are they going to think I've stiffed them?

And the grant recipients? What happens to the starter gift checks I've written for them? What of all their jubilant plans?

They will hate me.

The air has gone very still. No traffic, no train, just the waves sucking back, leaving dark tangles of seaweed, till it flows back in. Before a tsunami, that withdrawal keeps receding.

~ ~ ~ ~

Back at John's, alone again, I call Angie, in Grahamstown. She won't have any answers, but I need her brand of bracing reality check.

Straight away she picks up on my tone. "Bunnington, what have you done?" she demands. The old nickname, from my ballet-girl days, undoes me even further.

"Nothing. Nothing that I know of." I give her the *Reader's Digest* version of Bartlett's charges.

"Did you take great chunks of money for yourself?"

"Of course not!"

"Then why the sheepish tone?"

Start to deny it, but I know what she means. "I feel sleazy."

Angie softens. "That's just guilt-by-association nonsense, being close to a misdeed. I used to feel like that all the time at school—though, in my case, often I was the wrongdoer. Look, Sal, even if you did screw up somehow, you know it wasn't on purpose."

I do know that. She says, "So, put the whole thing to one side and get a good night's rest. But maybe tomorrow you should speak to a lawyer? Do you have one?"

I hate that suggestion, but Eric said it too. I do have a lawyer, my friend Rosemary, but surely I don't need her. She's away anyway, staying with her sick mother in Johannesburg. I can't lay this on her now.

Next Steps

Yet another stone in my stomach: What about Jacob, who used to tend our garden? He was planning to start work on the patio, clearing away all the debris from the fire and the construction so we could begin new plantings. We made a plan last time I saw him over at Edith and Roxie's. Told him Joanie and Eric and their baby were coming, and he clapped his hands with delight. I hugged him—to his surprise, sharing that joy. We were so happy to see each other again. And now I need to tell him Joanie and the baby haven't come—and that I can't pay him.

"Let Jacob start as you planned," Joanie says when we speak on the phone. Eric has told her what he knows, and she has called me to get the details. "Eric will pay him."

"That's not how things are meant to work between us. We have an agreement."

Joanie cuts me off when I begin to object. "Don't shut us out again, the way you did after Dad died."

"Joanie, you know that's bull! You know I just assumed you wanted me to sell the house, so you could have the money."

"Assume, assume!" she exclaims. "When are you going to learn to just come out and say what you want to say?"

"Good heavens, you sound just like your mother!" Immediately regret that, but she bursts out laughing.

"Ew, yeah, I heard it myself. Sorry! But I meant what I said."

Joanie has another suggestion, that Eric go with me to the meeting tomorrow. "At least you'll have company when you walk in."

He agrees at once. Just says, "Will you come get me?

Trevor will have the rental car."

~ ~ ~ ~

The foundation has its offices on the twenty-fifth floor of a giant tombstone of a building. Eric offers to wait outside, but I beg him to come in, even if he waits in the reception area. We take the elevator, and I tell the secretary we're both there to see Mr. Bartlett.

"He only mentioned that you were coming in," Miss Geldenhuys says, peering at me over her glasses.

"That has changed," I state, having just decided. "Do you want to warn him, or can we just go through?"

"I suppose you can go through." As we exit into the passage, I hear her on the intercom, murmuring something about "Mrs. Paddington and some guy."

Bartlett stands up as we walk in. He has been so jovial whenever we've met, his rigid expression makes his flabby face look unfamiliar. He stands with feet apart, arms straight down, fingers waggling, like a cowboy in an old movie, ready to go for his gun.

He says to Eric, "I'm Colin Bartlett, the chief financial officer. And you are . . . ?"

"Sally's son-in-law, Eric Alexander of Alexander and Partners," he says. "Do you have a problem with my being here?" I stifle a snort-laugh. It's almost true, just I wasn't married to his father-in-law, and the firm handles architectural design, not legal matters.

Bartlett looks utterly confused. "Er, no, I suppose not." I think the American accent has caught him off guard as much as the notion that I have a son-in-law who is a lawyer.

Next Steps

Eric says, "Sally has told me what you told her, but I'd appreciate it if you would lay out the facts of the situation, so I have the full picture." He casts me a supposedly appeasing look, for his we-men-understand-each-other implication. I roll my eyes and shrug, urging Bartlett to get on with it. For an ugly confrontation, this is almost fun.

"Sally, Ms. Paddington, your mother-in-law," he begins, evidently trying to cover all bases, "was entrusted with representing this foundation, and she appears to have embezzled a substantial sum of money. This might be a matter for the police."

~ ~ ~ ~

When we emerge, I am so drained, I can barely handle the one-block walk to the car. Without Eric alongside me, I think I would just slide to the ground. Even with our little charade, it has been exhausting hearing Bartlett's outrageous litany of my supposed crimes.

His words are still echoing in my head: "If it wasn't you, who did you give the foundation credit card to?" No one. I still have it. Took it out of my purse to show him.

I used the credit card when I bought the pants suit Georgina instructed me to get and when I took consultants out to lunch, as both of them said I should, and to fill up my car when I was driving to foundation appointments, as they had said I should.

"What about the flight to Johannesburg, and the lingerie shopping spree, and the nights at the five-star hotel at the Waterfront?"

"None of that was me," I hissed. Had to repeat it louder,

because neither he nor Eric could hear me.

"And the checkbook? If you didn't write those checks, who did?"

Again, scrabbled in my bag, this time till I found the checkbook. I've carried it with me since they gave it to me, but have barely used it. He waved it aside, but I dumped it on his desk. Gave him the credit card too. I won't be using them again and don't want them anywhere near me.

~ ~ ~ ~

Eric says, "You were so icy cool in there. Now you look ready to turn yourself over to the cops. Want me to drive?"

"Ballet training," I say, lifting my chin. "I'll be fine!" Turn on the ignition and watch the wipers smearing grayness back and forth. "I don't know what to think. If that money has been taken from the foundation, someone took it."

"But you didn't sign checks or go on shopping sprees, not so?"

"Not that I remember. Maybe I was hypnotized or drugged, or I had some kind of mental breakdown."

He wrinkles his nose, trying to get me to smile, to admit I'm talking nonsense. But I'm in a nightmare zone where nothing feels real—not the car, or the people walking by on the sidewalk, not my own hands in my lap. They're numb, as if they belong to someone else.

It isn't just a matter of stolen funds; it's funds from a nonprofit, with a hedge of regulations and safeguards to prevent exactly what they say I have done. Rich people get out of pickles like this; people like me land up behind bars.

"You've never been accused of doing anything wrong

Next Steps

before, have you?" Eric asks. Why would I be accused? I've been fastidiously law-abiding. If you keep to the straight and narrow, you don't land up accused of crimes. Even as that thought plays out, I know it's a naïve, stupid notion in a country where in the past so many innocent people were arrested and jailed. But my life hasn't been like that.

"Just being accused makes me feel guilty," I groan.

I turn automatically to the freeway, to head home to Kalk Bay instead of taking Eric back to his apartment and going to Camps Bay. Realize and apologize to him, miss the turnoff, and have to take a long route along local roads.

As we're driving slowly through Mowbray's congested streets, my old ballet school comes into view, the place I attended through my childhood and teens. It's a Victorian mansion with turrets and a deep, shadowy verandah, gray where it used to be lilac. I try to read the sign at the front gate—not a ballet school anymore, now some kind of institute, but it still looks like a venue for dreams.

A spasm ripples through me, a vague ache that somehow echoes this day's discomfort. I can't pinpoint the trigger, but tell Eric what that building was.

My parents enrolled me in dance classes there because they heard it was a healthy activity for young girls. That was their only goal. They remembered hearing about the greats of the Ballets Russes, but neither of them believed dancing held any such value for my future. They were clear their Sallinka wasn't going to be the next Pavlova.

"I wanted to prove them wrong," I tell Eric. "Much as I loved my parents, I was determined to escape their careful, cautious limits. I was going to be a ballerina. If I just tried hard enough, I would learn to leap and spin. That house was my happy place, until . . ."

"Until . . . ?"

No longer the aging woman in this car alongside her sort-of son-in-law, but rather a freckle-faced teenager in a black leotard, swinging the drawstring bag with her precious pink satin toe shoes, the badge of recently acquired seniority—and now, my shame.

Finally, back on the freeway. Usually, I enjoy the smooth swoop of De Waal Drive as it curves around the mountain, past the university and the sprawling mass of Groote Schuur Hospital, with the city off to the right and beyond it the bay, dotted with ships. This time, I register nothing of that vista.

I tell him, "We had taken part in a citywide competition that we were expected to win. I was supposed to be one of the school's stars, and I had been practicing extra hard. But on the day, I was so nervous, at a crucial moment I wobbled and bumped into one of the other girls and knocked her off balance. Instead of taking gold, we got bronze. The other girl was forgiving about it afterward, and so was the teacher, but I felt humiliated. I'd let everyone down. It shattered my image of who I was, of how great I was going to be."

Eric reaches out a hand to me, but I can't take it. "And I then I lied to my parents. I couldn't bear to admit the truth, that they were right, that I had aimed too high. I wasn't their perfect princess after all; I had screwed up—like I have with the foundation."

I turn off the freeway into the tree-lined streets near where

Next Steps

Eric and Trevor are staying. "Did you ever tell your parents?" Eric asks. That makes me jerk across the median. I straighten out, grateful that no other cars are nearby. Roll to a halt in front of their building.

"No." We sit still, hearing the click of the cooling engine. Wet oak leaves flutter down and stick to the windshield. It's so long since I have thought about any of this. "They didn't care about such contests, but they would have been upset that I was so upset. I just pretended everything had gone perfectly well."

"That's a heavy burden for a kid to carry."

"I tried not to think about it."

Eyebrows raised, he shakes his head at me. "You just went on with your life?"

"Yes. And really, it wasn't all bad." I try to sound perky. "I switched schools and began exploring different kinds of dance. And I met my pal Mary at the new place. We've been friends for over fifty years."

Eric leans over to kiss my cheek before getting out of the car. "I can just see you as a prima ballerina! But could you have had the amazing teaching career you've had?"

I shake my head, absorbing that thought. He adds, "Just know you are not alone this time. It wasn't your fault, and we'll make sure the Taylors know that."

I force a laugh. "I feel much better, knowing the firm of Alexander and Partners is taking care of me."

119

~ 13 ~

That evening, I call Joanie to fill her in on what happened at the meeting. The first thing she says is, "Call Sam. He'll sort this out for you. Laura says he's some kind of expert on corruption in nonprofits. Isn't that what this is? Someone's embezzling money and trying to pin it on you."

I bark, "No! No calls to Sam."

He and I haven't exchanged a word since he left. But Joanie told me months ago that Sam had contacted her and Eric and invited them to dinner at the house he shares with his younger daughter, Laura, and her husband. His older daughter, Jillian, was also there and all four of the grandchildren. It sounded as if everyone got on easily right away—as easily as I did with him initially. I suppose they had a starting point in their shared fondness for South Africa, and they seem to share political views, an even hotter than usual topic since last year's elections.

"Jillian is a teacher," Joanie told me then. "I haven't seen much of her. But the younger one is a pediatrician, specializing

Next Steps

in developmental issues." I knew that already from Sam. He'd spoken of his girls with such pride.

Joanie gives up on the Sam suggestion, but urges me to phone Georgina. "If you tell them what happened, this whole thing will be cleared up." I hope she's right.

Wait until late the next morning, and then place the call. The Taylors are at their home in London. Georgina answers with that bright, gracious tone I liked when we met the first time. "Ah, Sally, dear girl. How lovely to hear from you! How are you? Is everything all right?"

From her warmth I guess Bartlett hasn't said anything to them. Glad but puzzled, and a bit winded. I hadn't expected to explain everything from scratch. But it also means I can give my side without having to contradict what they have already heard.

"I'm well, but things are not okay," I say.

"Is John all right?"

"Yes, as far as I know, he's doing fine." Glad to stall for a moment. "He has a nephew visiting from England, and they seem to be doing a lot of 'guy' stuff, going to rugby matches and the like."

She laughs. "That side of John always caught me by surprise. He was such an intellectual, but he loved to show he could be one of the boys. But you said things are not okay? With the grants?"

I hear Eric and Trevor's car pull up outside. They have come to take me out for brunch. The housekeeper, Magdalena, lets them in, and they sit quietly listening to my side of the call.

Too stiff to think of a preamble, I state: "A huge amount

of money has been withdrawn from the account you set up for me, tens of thousands of rands. Bartlett is convinced that I've stolen it. He says he's reporting it to the police. I don't know if he has already. I told him I know nothing about it, but he doesn't believe me."

Silence. Georgina says nothing. I try to hear her, but all I can discern is my own panting. Finally, she says, "Do you know where the money went? Was it checks or cash withdrawals?"

"Both, according to Mr. Bartlett," I say. "If you need to bring in the police, I understand."

A long pause, and then very quietly she asks, "How else can we find out who took the money?"

"Yes, yes, of course. I'm sorry, I'm very flustered." It sounds hollow.

"Have you told John?" she asks.

I haven't mentioned it to him. Too shocked and scared—and again, because he seems to be out and busy all the time. When I did see him yesterday, they were rushing off to a beer tasting. "I will tell him," I say.

Georgina murmurs, "Excuse me a minute." It's faint but I hear her speak to someone. It seems Rupert has caught part of our conversation and she is filling him in. I can't make out what he says, but she comes back on the line, apologizes for keeping me waiting, and says, "My husband says we shouldn't contact the police, or not yet. He has spoken to Colin Bartlett and told him not to be too hasty."

One layer of tension loosens, but it feels odd to be preferring Rupert's response to Georgina's. She has gone silent again. To fill the chasm, I say: "I don't know if you remember

Next Steps

that I needed a lot of money to pay for the repairs to my house. That's why I was so grateful when you and Rupert offered me this job. But I would never ever steal from you, you must know that! Why would I take money that so obviously came from the foundation?"

"Well, people do that all the time, and deny it, claim that someone else embezzled the money."

I want to throw up. I tell her, "I will help any way I can to clear this up. I have to go now. Goodbye."

Eric has been listening. He leans forward now and says, cowboy-style, "Sal, I reckon you should get outta Dodge."

"Why? You think the sheriff is on my tail?"

"Why wait around to find out? It's odd that Rupert hadn't said anything to Georgina—or she might have been playing dumb—but you could get caught in a legal tangle. John's making it very clear he wants his space back. Joanie would be thrilled if you came; you know that. And with me away another few weeks, she'd be very glad to have the help with Freddie."

"Isn't it illegal to flee from legal proceedings?" Trying to draw in deep, relaxing breaths, but a sharp ache is poking through the base of my neck and down along my arm.

"Not if they haven't begun yet. It's not like you're disappearing. You can still be contacted, still communicate. You just won't be hanging around, waiting for the cops to turn up to arrest you."

"What about the cottage?"

"I'm here," Trevor says, giving me his duck-bill grin.

Eric adds, "Trevor can liaise with the contractors, and he can keep an eye on everything."

A pain below my shoulder twists tighter. I clutch at it and wince. My face feels stiff. Eric stares at me, and then asks, "Is 911 the emergency number here too?"

I croak out, "No!" but can't remember the right number. He finds it and I hear him dialing.

~ ~ ~ ~

"You like being the center of attention, being taken care of," Joanie teases. She is a fine one to talk: She has pulled a muscle, either from toting Freddie around the house or lugging her heavy camera equipment, and she is struggling. It's so bad, she has asked her mother to move in, to help her.

But right now, I'm the focus of her concern. Eric has her on his phone, which he has handed to me. She gets serious and naggy. "You can't go back to living alone if your heart is dicey. Come to us!"

"My heart is fine," I insist. "I am strong like an ox," and I flex my bicep even though she can't see me.

Eric insisted I go to the emergency room, not me. "I'm not taking any chances," he said. "My grandma died of a heart attack because no one recognized her symptoms. With a man, they would have."

I was examined, fussed over, cleared, and told to take it easy. Eric brought me back to John's, and Magdalena cooked up some chicken soup. "I got that recipe from you," she said. "Now, you be quiet and eat."

Maybe Joanie is right, that I'm hungry for pampering, like when I was a kid. Reminds me of my last ER visit, when I fell off a ladder last year and was disappointed that the doctor didn't insist on keeping me in the hospital. Embarrassed.

Next Steps

"Sorry, Sal. You're not really self-centered. I didn't mean it," she claims now. But there is a kernel of truth in her teasing. I'm feeling brittle, loath to be back in the cottage alone.

~ ~ ~ ~

For all my resistance, it looks as if I'll be delaying my return to solitude after all.

Eric was going to cancel his trip to Europe and instead head straight home to be with Joanie. But one of his most important clients, a developer in Germany, has his sights set on a rundown backstreet in Portland and is insisting Eric come to Berlin. He wants to show him a similar project he has there.

It means Joanie being dependent on her mother for two weeks longer. Neither woman is happy about that. Eric, alongside me, and Joanie, on the phone, simultaneously said, "Sal, can you help, please, and stay for a while?"

It's a replay of their plea last year, but that time it was only for a few days. This time, they're talking about months. No one has mentioned my legal pickle; they already know my attitude to that. Eric just said, "There is nothing you really have to be here for. Like we agreed, Trevor will monitor the repairs, and it'll give the builders a chance to finish up, so you will have a safe, comfortable home to return to." That does sound appealing.

When I tell him, John doesn't even pretend he'll miss me. "What an excellent idea!" he says. "Go fuss over your family."

Fausia, when I tell her I might be going away for a while, frowns and butts her head into my arm. "You coming back?" she asks, not looking up. I have a feeling so many people have disappeared out of her life, she doesn't trust anyone to reappear.

But I say, "I promise I'll be back."

Piling on persuasion, Eric says, "You can finish up the work on the book from Portland, and go to New York to meet with the publisher if you need to."

In all the other chaos, I forgot that my agent, Gail, has found a taker for the book, a small, indie publisher who specializes in the arts. I didn't take it seriously, I think, because she said there were still issues to iron out. Not ready to get my hopes up. But it is a chance. And Eric's right; it might help, being within reach for face-to-face meetings and at least closer to the same time zone for phone conversations.

~ ~ ~ ~

The night before I leave, I call Angie in Grahamstown, to let her know I'm going away. She applauds the decision. "Isn't Portland also where your pal Sam lives?" she asks. I give what I hope is a dismissive "Yup" and distract her with my other news, about the maybe-publisher for the book.

To my surprise, that topic gets her more excited. "You have to come here to do the South African launch!" she says. "You and Felix are both Rhodes alums. People here will get such a kick out of it." She has taken on a part-time gig doing publicity for our alma mater, and in true Angie style, is enrolling everyone she can. "I have the perfect event for you, the Health and the Arts symposium in January."

I panic. "It might not be ready in time. It might be no good."

I try to tell her how terrified I was at Mary's conference, but she ignores me. "I'm inking you in!"

Next Steps

Go to bed for the last time at John's around midnight, with virtually no hope of falling asleep. Angie's suggestion weaves in and out of other thoughts. It's so long since I was in Grahamstown, with all its memories of joy and pain. Being back could be amazing.

Two hours later, I get up and go to the kitchen. Don't like warm milk, but if I add some of John's brandy, will that knock me out?

John is sitting on a stool, his old face gaunt in the blue glow of a counter light. He pours the brandy for me, at least twice as much as I would have. Puts the bottle down and takes my hands in his. "I'm sorry that I got you mixed up with that Rupert character," he says. "I'm glad you're going away." I smile and shrug: I know. "No, not for my sake. You need to get away from this foundation mess." It's the first time he has mentioned it. "I don't know what's going on, but I do know I trust you, and I don't trust Rupert." Neither of us mentions Georgina.

"Be careful," he adds. "Bullies like him can be toxic. Stay away until it blows over."

I feel a little slithery, letting him suspect Rupert when I have no proof, but his faith in me means even more than all his months of long-suffering hospitality.

~ 14 ~

Joanie is there to meet me at the airport in Portland, our beautiful girl, looking fit again, her maternity weight all gone. No longer pale and exhausted as she was last year, but she has her arm in a sling—just to support her strained shoulder now and then, she explains. Her mother is alongside her, trying to handle the stroller and the baby.

Deidre, catching me by surprise, grabs me in a one-armed hug, squooshing Freddie between us. She mutters in my ear, "Thank God you're here!"

So happy to see their townhouse again, with its lush façade of trailing vegetation. Once inside, Freddie wails when his grandmother passes him over to me. He squirms in my embrace as he was squirming in hers, till I plonk him in his mother's arms.

"This is Sally," Joanie tells him, trying to ease his shyness.

To me she says, "My mother is 'Grandma.' We need a name for you." I've never had a grandparent myself, but my

Next Steps

mother would talk about her *bubbe*. That's too far a jump. I suggest *ouma*, the South African version. "Can you say Ouma Sally?" she urges Freddie. He calls her "Mama" and their two Siamese kittens, "kikkie." He turns his big brown eyes on me, solemn as a judge, and shakes his head.

But within a day, he has decided I'm okay. On day three, he reaches out to me to be picked up after his nap and relaxes with his bottle, snuggled in the crook of my arm. That sends warm syrup through my veins, but even when he bellows in distress, it gives me pleasure. The vitality it conveys wasn't there when I last saw him.

He still has metabolic issues that will have to be managed and monitored, but his rounded little limbs feel strong to me. There is none of the slackness he had as a newborn. On day five he says, "Sasa," and we all get very excited, though he doesn't do it again.

The kittens interest him more than any of us adults. They are a double package of cream and brown-tipped mischief. Deidre thinks they are an unnecessary nuisance and a source of germs. I am enchanted, though they make me long for my twosome. Freddie wants to be on the floor with them, and when he is, they pounce on his toes, making him giggle.

This whole household makes me happy, even Deidre.

Joanie is less happy with me than I am with her. "You look better," she says. "I love your hair. You look like a dandelion." She runs her palms over the fluff. "But you're still not your old self. You're jumpy in a way I've never seen you, not even last year when you'd just lost Dad. Are you worrying about that embezzlement nonsense?"

I shrug, and assure her that whatever is amiss, I'm ecstatic to be with them.

"Then you should stay. I'm not going to let you leave us," she tells me.

"Maybe I will stay!"

She laughs. "That would please a certain someone."

Pretty sure I know who she means, but certainly don't accept her assumption. I have no idea what he is up to or where he is, and I'm not about to start discussing him. Instead, I ask brightly, "So, you and Laura have become close friends?"

"She has been a wonderful help with Freddie," she says, taking the bait. "She's very warm and down to earth. She's only practicing part-time while her kids are little, but I've been able to call her with so many questions. On the other hand, she's just getting into photography as a hobby, and I can help her with that."

This all pleases me immensely. Joanie and Eric moved to Portland so soon before the baby, she has had little chance to make friends. Given all his medical issues, contact with anyone outside the family, even with the local mothers' group, has been sporadic.

"So, what happened between you and Laura's dad?" Joanie asks.

To my relief, Deidre, eager to get back to her home, interrupts to say her goodbyes. I eagerly offer to help carry her belongings to her car.

~ ~ ~ ~

"You could ask Sam to bail you out," Joanie says that evening, as she and I settle down to eat dinner. We were talking

Next Steps

about the cottage, and the cost of repairs, and—inevitably—the conversation looped back to the foundation mess.

We are in the living room, with plates balanced on our laps. She has made a spicy Cape Town-style curry, complete with sliced bananas and coconut and chutney. As usual, she has left chaos in the kitchen. The spicy sambals are laid out in an assortment of small, clay bowls on the coffee table.

"You mean literally, bail me out?" I ask.

"Oh my God, no! You're not going to jail!" Joanie squawks. Freddie, amusing himself on the rug, locks up with wide eyes. She drops her volume. "This isn't a jailing matter! I just mean, if you have to pay back that money, maybe he can help. He's rich. Or he can help you sort out the legal stuff. He has a law degree, you know."

"Yes, I know he's a lawyer, and an accountant, and an expert in fraud. But no, I don't need his help." With the plate of food in my hands, I can't react as forcefully as I want. But my appetite has vanished anyway, so I take it through to the kitchen. Return, hands freed and face feeling flushed.

She persists. "So, what about asking Sam to help you?"

I snap, "He's the last person I'd turn to," and then try to sound more measured. "Even if I would, and even if he had any desire to help me, I doubt he's got that kind of cash lying about. It's a lot of money—yes, enough to be a jailing matter."

A leaden silence fills the room. I'm ashamed. "Sorry," I say. "I didn't mean to get heavy. It's just that—well, Sam and I parted on such awkward terms. I'm humiliated enough by this whole mess, there's no way I'd risk more embarrassment. And as I said, this would take someone very rich to pay back that money."

Joanie doesn't say a word. Realizing that she might notice that I've put aside the food she cooked, I go back into the kitchen and retrieve my plate. Make an effort to eat. It's really very tasty, and I tell her that. We munch without talking. I wish I could think of something to say to distract her. I don't want her dwelling on what I just blurted out or on my predicament.

The lesser of two evils, I'd rather discuss matters of the heart than my finances. "Okay," I say, "you want to know what happened with Sam?"

Immediately, her expression brightens. She scoops her hair back off her shoulders, twists it into a knot and sticks a pencil in to hold it. She looks like a reporter ready to take notes. "So, what's the scoop?"

"Sam and I kept each other company for a couple of weeks in January," I say. "We went to all sorts of fun places and a couple of very posh restaurants I'd never considered going to before. I felt I was getting back into the swing of things. He was so easy to talk to and so enthusiastic about everything. And he's like your dad; he talks to everybody, regardless of how weird or bedraggled."

"That sounds lovely and just how his daughters describe him. He seems like a great guy. So, what went wrong?" She adds, "My mother was actually impressed with you, that you were dating him."

"Impressed? Why?"

"Because he has money. She said something like, 'That'll take care of her old age.'"

"Ugh! That's ridiculous."

Next Steps

Joanie laughs. "I knew that wasn't how you'd see it. But it must have been cool to enjoy a bit of the high life, no?"

I'm not cross with her, but I am cross. The whole notion of being a gold-digger turns my stomach. I stop myself just short of saying, "Trust your mother to see things that way." Instead, I make myself give her a real answer. That way, she will be armed with the truth if Deidre starts spouting nonsense again—or if Sam's daughters have any wrong ideas.

"We discussed the money thing right at the start," I say. "I wanted to split the tab the first time we ate out. But I wanted to go somewhere affordable, and he wanted to take me to a special French place he likes. We had a very awkward exchange, and then he suggested a plan, that we each choose the dates we were comfortable paying for."

"Sounds smart. How did that work out?"

"Great. He could take me to shows and fancy restaurants, but I had something else to offer—my car and my knowledge of Cape Town. I took him for scenic drives, and we went for picnics to places like Kirstenbosch, and to eat in funky little cafés in the townships that he'd never have known about. I loved having someone to do those things with, and he was so appreciative."

"Until?"

"Until he tried to take me in his arms, and I froze up. I don't know why it was such a big deal."

"Oh, God," Joanie groans. "He wanted to go to bed with you?"

"Well, not exactly. He wanted to dance with me."

Her mouth drops into an oval of astonishment. "I had a

right to say no, didn't I?" I demand.

"No, no, of course you did," she stammers, "if dancing together was such a big deal."

She picks up one of the kittens and speaks to me over her shoulder, half turned away. "According to Laura, he hasn't been interested in anyone since her mother died. I gather the marriage wasn't easy. She says her mother was moody, critical of herself and everyone else. Her dad seems to have been very wary of getting close to anyone. It was a big step for him, asking you out, getting involved that way."

"What way? We weren't involved." I sound defensive even to myself.

Suddenly gentle, she says, "You're not over Dad, are you?"

"And never will be."

"But that doesn't mean you can't love someone different. He wouldn't have wanted you to be alone forever."

Nearly tell her how her father has nudged me to get involved with Sam, but don't. I think she knows I talk to him, but admitting I take relationship advice from her departed papa—that might be pushing her too far.

This conversation was supposed to be an escape from the ugly money business, and I'm feeling guilty all over again. To my relief—and yet another cause for guilt—Freddie starts crying. She puts down the kitten and hurries to pick him up.

With Freddie in her arms, she pins me with a glare that could put her mother to shame. "Meanwhile, whatever went wrong between you and Sam, you need him now. He has said he's willing to help. I'm going to call Laura, and we'll set up a time for you guys to talk. Your choice: face to face, or on the

Next Steps

phone?

"Not face to face," I mutter.

"OK, on the phone. Done."

~ ~ ~ ~

Though it's a month after the actual day, Joanie has designated this Sunday as my belated birthday. She wakes me, barging in with Eric, who arrived back just the night before last. He is carrying his son, who initially seemed puzzled by this dark, neatly bearded man—but is now snuggling into his shoulder.

The kittens, who've been sleeping on my bed, leap off in alarm. The people fill my attic lair, Joanie with a huge bunch of flowers, and Freddie clutching the string of a silvery "Happy Birthday" balloon. They have me laughing and hugging, in tears as usual, with the little one watching wide-eyed.

With perfect timing, my phone rings, and it's Trevor, calling from Kalk Bay to wish me "happy fake-birthday" from the cottage. Apparently, he's been able to move in, though conditions aren't exactly luxurious. Such a pleasure to see his wonderful, golden face on the screen, and those topaz eyes just like his father's, scrunched in laughter. I turn the screen to show him his sister and brother-in-law and nephew, with their goodies.

He announces someone else is with him, eager to wish me happy birthday too. I expect to see Edith or Roxie, but he tilts the phone down—and I see a furry, gray-and-white-striped face looking in other directions despite his effort to get her attention. After all the false leads and miserable disappointments, this is my Mergatroid. No Skelm, but this is already the best birthday gift he could have given me. I swamp Trevor with where and who and how questions.

Joanie is impatient to get me dressed and started on the day. She tells Trevor to save the story of how the cat was found for another day. My heart is already so full, I can wait, but what's our rush?

"We're going to Jillian's for brunch, and she's on the far side of the city," Joanie says. "We didn't say it's your birthday celebration, but it seemed the perfect way to spend the day."

I've only met Sam's older daughter once, when she came by with Laura. She is more reserved than her sister, but also very nice. I'd rather stay home, but if I can't, this does seem like a pleasant, low-key alternative. Come to think of it, this is what I wanted, company but not the spotlight.

Their father, as far as I know, is back in South Africa on one of his missions. He and I had our conversation on the phone and have emailed back and forth since, always quite formally, just exchanging information about the Taylor catastrophe. I appreciate his matter-of-fact assumption of my innocence—I had feared he might have doubts about me, given our misunderstandings—so the process has only been mildly uncomfortable.

"We're dressing up," Joanie adds, as if it were an afterthought. "I'm so tired of mommy sweats." A not-so-subtle hint that I should make an effort too? The only dressy garment I have with me is the awful dress from the conference. Should have packed the (also smoky) red, sequined wall-hanging,

~ ~ ~ ~

So much for low-key. They've invited masses of people,

Next Steps

friends and family and neighbors. "We do this at least once every summer," Jillian tells me, and adds with a wink, "It seemed like a great day to do it."

Sam is there, though for a moment I don't recognize him. He's wearing a rather formal-looking blue, button-up shirt. I suspect Joanie knew he was back and chose not to mention that detail to me.

When we arrived, he gave her a hug—clearly they're already fond of each other—and he shook Eric's hand warmly. He shook mine too and wished me a belated happy birthday. He barely smiled and I felt my cheeks stiffen. Against all logic, I was hoping to see those dimples deepen and his face light up with the glow that used to greet me in Cape Town.

Now, I approach him again and thank him. "I don't know what I'd have done without you. I've been so worried."

He brushes aside my gratitude. "I'd do the same for anyone." I swallow that, before he adds, "And I haven't accomplished anything yet."

This clearly isn't the place for the subject, but I have to ask, "Do you have any idea who wrote those fake checks?"

"It's too soon to know for sure. How well do you know Georgina Taylor?"

Hold back a groan. I expected him to ask about Rupert, not her. "Not well, though I liked what I saw." I start to ask why, but one of his grandchildren, Jillian's eldest, I gather, lopes over. He drapes himself around his grandpa.

Sam puts his arm about the boy's waist and introduces him: "This is Leo, my professor, the person who first taught me the duties of a grandfather." He kisses Leo's cheek.

"Are you the barber responsible for the haircut your grandpa had when I met him last year?" I ask.

Sam laughs, but the boy scowls at me in disdain. "What do you take me for? Alex did that. He was four, and Grandpa let him do it."

I'm mortified by the mistake. If I don't make my apology stick, this wound won't quickly be forgiven. I go down on one knee, my dress spreading around me, and say, "Professor Leo, please accept my humble apology! I'm new to the business of grandparenting, and I have a lot to learn."

He grins grudgingly and puts out a hand to help me stand up. Then he grabs Sam's arm. "Right now, I need my grandpa to solve an argument in the playroom. But if I have time, I'll teach you some basic stuff. You gonna be around for a while?"

Sam casts me a quick glance. I just say, "No, probably just a few weeks. But it's really nice to meet you."

They disappear into the growing press of people. Rather than battle to make small talk with others, I edge my way to the kitchen, hoping to make myself useful.

Busy, knife in hand, cutting up fruit, when Deidre saunters in. I pretend I haven't noticed.

"Sally! So, here you are, being a model guest." Her voice, as ever, is at public-address volume. "Birthday wishes are in order, I gather. The big seven-oh?"

"Yes, fancy that! Hello, Deidre. What a lovely outfit!"

She does look good, and focusing on her clothes always lowers the tension between us. She has on a burnt-orange, linen kaftan that hugs her hips and dips low enough to show off her tanned cleavage. She has just returned from Hawaii. I heard her

Next Steps

regaling someone earlier with tales of sunsets on glorious beaches. "You really should go," she told them.

I feel so puny next to her. She carries herself like God's gift to men. I know large black women who do that, but very few white women who can. My Minnie Mouse pink outfit feels even sillier than before.

Using her nails like pincers, she steals a melon cube from the bottom of the pile I've just carefully stacked. Nearly slap her hand. To my surprise, she doesn't swan past to the bottles and glasses in the butler's pantry. Instead, she hovers at my elbow as I carry on slicing and placing.

She says, "So, I gather you've gotten to know our Sam Parker. Smart move."

"Smart move? What do you mean?"

"For once, you're being pragmatic. Joanie told me about that nasty business in South Africa. Could have landed you behind bars? I don't know what you did to get into that mess, but befriending Mr. Parker was a very smart move."

With the knife in one fist and a dishcloth in the other, I turn to face her, tempted to use one or the other. "I met Sam months before that. We were friends. And I didn't get him involved; Joanie and his daughter did. They told him what was happening, and he volunteered to help."

"Ahhh, you were friends already? As I said, smart move."

"Why?" That comes out much louder than I intended, but I'm matching her volume. One of the young servers extracting trays of mini quiches from the oven jerks around in surprise. My cheeks have grown hot.

"Aren't you poor as a proverbial church mouse now that

Felix is gone?" she asks, stealing a mini-quiche. "No harm in linking up with a wealthy American who can provide for you. I know Joanie would worry a whole lot less if you did."

One retort leaps to my tongue, and then another. I stifle both. Finally say the one thing I think will hush her: "There are plenty of rich South Africans if that was what I wanted."

Her eyebrows arch higher. "They would be interested in you?" She gives a little shrug. "Anyway, I doubt many could compete with Sam Parker."

A trickle of people are coming and going around us, but I ignore them and snarl at her, "I'm not interested in Sam Parker or his money." It's like a bushfire crackling inside me. I didn't realize how flammable the kindling was. "If you find him so alluring, why don't you go for him yourself?"

She tilts her head like a bird, considering me or my stupidity. "I might just do that."

We both walk back into the living room, her towering over me with a wine glass waving in one elegant hand, me trying not to drop the wobbling tray of fruit. A server takes it from me just in time, and I'm free to wheel away to the terrace.

Sam is standing out there, alone, looking out over the garden. A misty rain has draped the view in gray. Drops are beading on his hair. He turns when he hears my footsteps, looks at me with blank, dark eyes, and walks away without a word. Just how much of our conversation did he hear?

~ 15 ~

Joanie has been wearing her blonde hair scraped back in a ponytail day after day, where little hands can't grab it, and it can't trail into bath water or baby food. But she has finally relaxed. On this day, she has it flowing loose about her shoulders. She has her partner to share the tasks.

I should start thinking about heading home. Keep resolving to get practical tomorrow, and then tomorrow becomes yesterday, and nothing has been worked out. Trevor reports progress on the cottage, but with much still to be done. "I'd love to have you here, but don't rush, Sal. This is still a camping zone."

Bless him, when he has time, he has been going out to Estella's. He sent me a series of pictures of Fausia doing her pussycat hand-dance. "She is trying," he wrote. "But she keeps asking when you're coming back."

When I mention leaving to Joanie, and now Eric, they quote Trevor about the repairs. They insist I'm not in the way, that they love having me around, and that there's still so much they haven't shown me in this pleasant city. Laura has offered to introduce me to a dance center that has all kinds of different programs and might, she thinks, be interested in a talk on special-needs innovations.

I don't know where I belong.

To my relief, a week after his return, Eric takes Joanie and Freddie to a private zoo they have read about. They are excited about introducing him to wildlife. One day they want to take him to a game reserve in South Africa, like the one we all went to. They urge me to come with them now, but I beg off.

I want everyone out of the house, so I can discard this "everything's fine" mask. The moment I hear the front door click shut behind them, I huddle in a ball on the sofa. In the past, if I lay like this, within minutes I'd feel one light foot and then another, and two warm, furry bodies would settle alongside me, giving comfort or seeking it. I lie there, homesick, thinking of Mergatroid back home again in Kalk Bay. Joanie's kittens are fast asleep together in an armchair, like a yin-yang sign, beautiful but self-sufficient.

Sorry for yourself?

Yes, I'm sorry for myself. You have a problem with that?

Yes. I wish it wasn't so. I don't blame you for feeling torn.

This is a shock. Felix doesn't usually indulge my moods. I rely on him to buck me up.

Where do I belong, Felix?

No idea.

~ ~ ~ ~

This morning, finally have a face-to-face meeting with Sam

Next Steps

in his office.

Almost cancelled the appointment. His office, apparently, is in a converted house in a suburb I've never been to before. Rain has been bucketing down since dawn. Catch the wrong bus and have to double back. Wash up on his doorstep, too bedraggled and chilled to be nervous.

"Oh, you poor thing! I'm sorry. I should have come to you at Joanie's," Sam exclaims. He insists on microwaving a cup of hot chocolate for me and makes one for himself.

Then, though back in tie-dye, he is all business. Pulls out a chair for me in front of his desk and draws up another one alongside me. He sweeps aside the clutter of photos and knickknacks and puzzles to make room for a fat folder of notes. Very methodically, he begins to sketch his lines of inquiry, pointing out the names of those he enlisted to help him, and what they have done or where they have gone. None of it makes sense to me. All I can see is a blur of handwritten words, some circled, some underlined.

He says, "I've been trying to decipher if there are any connections between the people you were giving the grants to, and if or where they crossed paths with you—or with the Taylors—in some untoward way. I couldn't pinpoint anything definite.

"What has emerged are some rather shady chapters in Rupert Taylor's past." I straighten up in my seat. This is what I've been expecting to hear. Feel savvy—for a moment. "He probably shouldn't be in control of a foundation—though in this instance his hands seem to be clean."

Slump back. "Did you find the culprit?"

"Well, not really," he says. "I thought perhaps there'd been a misunderstanding about procedures—or a problem with their bookkeeping." He glances at me and looks away, chewing his bottom lip. He's holding something back, I'm sure. Want to shake him, to dislodge that caution.

"It does look as if Mrs. Taylor may have been involved." I groan. "You really liked her, didn't you? It seems, from what we've found, that she spends very lavishly, and she might have wanted to obscure who was doing that spending."

Bury my face in my hands. I picture John Latimer, his pink scalp showing through the carefully combed gray strands, his back straightening as he approached Georgina in the restaurant that first night. He will be so sad if it turns out that she was behind this.

"I can see Rupert being crooked," I say, "but I haven't suspected Georgina even for a moment. She was so enthusiastic about me coming to work with them, that was what gave me the confidence to accept their offer. Was that all just a sham?"

Sam picks up a Rubik's Cube and twists it this way and that. "I just don't know. It might have been a sham. Bringing someone on board who was unfamiliar with financial matters, and unlikely to track complicated cash flows . . . "

"A sucker like me?" I hate to sound so whiny. Try for a less personal question: "Why would people with their kind of money bother cheating their own foundation?"

"If they did," Sam says. "For some people, money's a drug. It has nothing to do with need. Getting more is a thrill, using whatever guts or ingenuity they can muster. For others—like Georgina, I suspect—spending is the addiction, perhaps to

Next Steps

make up for some other lack in their lives. And the funds in a foundation can be low-hanging fruit."

He goes back to his chair on the opposite side of the desk. "I have an apology to make: I try to keep a very low profile when I'm gathering facts, but one of my sources evidently reported our conversation to the Taylors. Rupert got very offended. Seems he doesn't like anyone looking too closely at his history."

"Where does that leave you—us?"

"Well, he's decided that we're in cahoots—which, I suppose, we are." He peers at me. "Do you mind?"

"No, not in the least."

"I'm sorry about involving you," I say. I gather up my bag and damp coat. Say, "Thanks again, Sam," and then giggle a bit hysterically. "Oops, that sounded almost like the line from *Casablanca*." He grins, the dimples reappearing. Is he remembering that Saturday evening back in the cottage when we watched it together and I dozed off on his shoulder? Want to say, "Can we play again, Sam?" But I don't.

On the bus home, feeling totally disoriented—about him and me, and the Taylors, and life. Trying to make sense of it all, reviewing every word and gesture, hoping for a flash of insight.

~ ~ ~ ~

As I arrive at the house, Joanie is emerging with Freddie in his stroller. I help her lower him down the steps. "Come with us," she says. "The sun is out—at least for a while, and you look like you could do with some fresh air."

We head for the neighborhood park. She dries off one of

the rubber bucket swings and slips Freddie into it, maneuvering his feet through the gaps. We talk as she pushes him. He swoops away, his legs tucked back, and returns to us, stretching them out in front of him. It looks like a skillful move for such a little guy, and he seems proud.

"I'm really torn about this," Joanie says. "On the one hand, it's nice to see my mother happy for once. I have no idea whether she and Sam are compatible, but she gets all coy when she talks about dating him."

"So why are you torn?" Trying to be airily indifferent.

"Because you and I both know that you and Sam are a better match. You made friends when you thought he was just some regular old accountant. She wouldn't have given him a second glance if he wasn't mega-wealthy."

My ignorance is embarrassing. "I learned so little about him," I say. "Basically, I enjoyed his company and never tried to draw him out."

"You didn't tell him much about yourself either," she remarks. "Laura said her father had no idea how recently Dad died, not until just before he left Cape Town. Why didn't you tell him?"

"So, how rich is he?" I ask, sidestepping her question. It's a crass topic, but not as awkward as trying to explain why I avoided discussing Felix, why I was afraid that Sam would feel sorry for me, and his sympathy would turn me to mush. I liked that he saw me as vibrant and positive, and didn't spot how brittle that façade was.

"How rich? Not like Bill Gates," Joanie says, "but up there. He worked as an accountant for this big family firm, and their

Next Steps

daughter set her cap for him. She told Laura he was the most genuine, gentle man she'd ever met, unlike the gold-diggers who usually pursued her. Only problem, I gather, was that she was used to her family's ambitiousness, and once they were settled, she found him too easygoing."

"A bit like your mom and dad?" I ask. "Wasn't Deidre frustrated with your dad's lack of drive?"

She tilts her head, thinking. "That makes me appreciate my mother a little more. At least, she's positive. Laura's mother sounded so critical—of herself and everyone else."

It turns out, Joanie tells me, Sam's wife was an only child, and when she died, he and the girls inherited everything. "Only fair, according to Laura, given that he'd been running things for years, and doing it very well, despite himself. He had expanded the business enormously. But she says he's always been more interested in the nonprofit aspects and his forensic work. But they have enough money to do anything they want. Can you imagine?"

"If your mother marries him, maybe you'll also be able to live like that," I say.

She has stilled the swing and lifted Freddie out. She glances sideways at me. "Ugh, I wouldn't want her to have any more leverage over us. And we're doing pretty well on our own. Though I might not refuse the odd Caribbean cruise, or a holiday pad in Paris. But hey, if you married him, you'd also dish it out, wouldn't you?"

"Dish!" Freddie says, drawing out the juicy "sh" sound. "Dishhhh!"

We both grin at him and join his "sh-shing." Joanie goes

serious again. "You don't mind Mom going out with him?"

"I have no right to mind." I wish that didn't sound so petulant. The hurt that comes up when I imagine those dimples deepening in response to Deidre's flirting, or those dark eyes focused on her with that special Sam attention, is totally ridiculous.

~ ~ ~ ~

Have woken up in a bad mood. Focus very deliberately on the bright blue showing through the skylight. At least the rain has gone. And then I remember last night.

Sam and Deidre—ugh! She popped in late last night, on her way home from a function they'd attended at City Hall. Hear again her gleeful chatter, gloating over his attentiveness. She was wearing a gold, ankle-length sheath. Still has her tan from Hawaii or whatever health spa she favors.

"The man's eyes were like saucers when he saw me. He said, 'You're wearing that to the ceremony?' When we walked in, every head turned. He went bright pink. I don't think he's accustomed to making that kind of entrance, but with me, he better get used to it."

Joanie said, "Mom, he's Sam Parker. You think you're the only glamour puss who's ever tried to get her claws into him?"

"Would seem so," she chuckled, not offended in the least. She went on to list all the estate agents and big honchos who swarmed around the two of them.

"Do you like him?" I asked.

She stared at me, puzzled by the question. Joanie repeated it: "Mom, do you even like him?"

"Well, of course I like him. Why wouldn't I?"

Next Steps

Of course? My throat went dry. "Do you plan to carry on seeing him?"

"Yes. I think I may as well." She swung her coat around her shoulders, ready to depart. "Unless he gets too boring, or annoying. He does go on about his causes. Wants me to bring the real estate people onboard with his fair-housing campaign, to pressure the legislature to boost the supply of low-income rentals, or something like that." She rolled her eyes and leaned in to brush cheeks with her daughter.

"Are you planning to do that?" Joanie asked. She cast a glance at me, either concerned that I would exclaim something rude, or to signal that she'd handle this. I stayed silent.

"Oh heavens, I don't know. I'm not about to pressure my clients, unless there's some serious tax benefit from it. But I suppose I could organize a party and rustle up some celebrities, get the mayor to speak, or our new congressman. It would be a good way to expand my circle here, and it should please Sam. Sally, you know him better than I do; what movie stars does he like? Isn't that Charlize Theron from South Africa? Maybe she'd appreciate whatever it is he does there."

She mentioned that Sam is going away again, to Europe this time, with one of his friends. How come he didn't mention that to me? I pictured him playing tourist and had a flash of nostalgia for our weeks of exploring Cape Town together. Glad, though it's totally silly, that he hasn't invited Deidre to go with him.

~ ~ ~ ~

Trying to concentrate on some book questions Gail has sent, when my phone rings. It's Sam. "I've just been on the phone with my investigator in Cape Town," he says. "We got some information you might want to hear."

"I'm listening," I say.

"Actually, I meant see rather than hear. Can I come by?" I say yes, but stiffen. If it was good news, he'd surely tell me straight away.

He arrives, toting his weathered old briefcase. We sit side by side on the couch, and he opens a file on the coffee table. He says, "Are you ready for this?"

Enough with the stalling. I thump both fists on the folder. "Sam, I just want to clear up what happened. Have you got your culprit?"

"I'm afraid we might have. And it seems that somehow you gave him access to the foundation bank account."

I go blank. No thoughts. No sight. No hearing. All my self-righteous anger at Rupert, or Bartlett, or even Georgina—all misplaced? I am the one who screwed up?

Sam slides aside a few pages in the file, exposing a blurred black and white print. "My contact got this for me," he says. "He said it's an old one of the guy who's been splashing cash around the nightclubs of Athlone. Do you know him?"

Pick up the picture and hold it at arm's length. See a skinny young guy, very erect, with a wild mop of hair and a gap-tooth grin. Something about the face clicks, but not the teeth and not that hair. Imagine the hair immaculately slicked back, and the teeth perfect—and know this is Herman.

"So, they were right about me. It was my fault," I whisper. "Rupert befriended him, but I let him into my home. I left him alone in my room. I told him and Estella all about the

Next Steps

foundation and how it works."

Sam shakes his head as if to dismiss all that, but he doesn't deny it. "He's your friend's husband? The one we met at that performance in the prefab hall? I thought I'd seen him somewhere, but I couldn't place him."

"The Taylors know it was him—and me?" Sam nods. "Why haven't they gone to the police?"

"This is what makes me question their motives. I don't know if they believe you deliberately aided in the theft" — and he ducks his head with an apologetic shrug — "or if you made some kind of mistake, why wouldn't they want to expose that, and this guy? But I gather that they'd like you to just disappear, perhaps because of his subsequent contact with Rupert."

"I did disappear. I left town, as if I was running away."

"Not the same. That was the smartest thing you could have done, to put some distance between you and them. But I'm pretty sure that you can relax, that they aren't planning to pursue any charges, or to take any other action."

He sits back and smiles at me. I want to smile back—I am relieved—but the other part of this whole mess still looms large and ugly, and now clearly my fault. "Sam, what about all those joyful people who thought they were in for a heaven-sent infusion of funds, so they could fulfill their wonderful plans? I lifted their hopes so high, and I let them down so badly. Do you think there's any chance the foundation will still give them that money?"

Sam is gathering up his papers and his jacket, apparently late for his next appointment. He puts his hand on my arm. "I'm so sorry, Sally, but I doubt it. Rupert seems to want to take their philanthropy in a different direction."

We give each other a quick goodbye hug, and I wish Sam a good trip. Close the front door behind him and stand there with my hand on the cold brass knob, thinking: No wonder he is intrigued by Deidre. She would never let people down so badly. Come to think of it, she wouldn't have gotten into such a mess in the first place.

~ 16 ~

The weeks are slipping by so fast, I lose track of how long I've been here. The first signs of fall are flaring on the trees. In Cape Town, they must be seeing signs of spring. It's less dramatic, given how mild the winter is, unless you go north into the countryside, where dry scrub erupts into spectacular carpets of flowers. Sam would love it.

I miss Kalk Bay, but walking the quiet streets of this neighborhood, up and down and across the hills, often with Freddie in his stroller, slows down the inner whir. Sam is still away, I gather. It's a relief to know he isn't nearby.

As I'm walking, I caress my glass pendant and Felix's shell. They connect me to other times. Sometimes, like Aladdin's lamp, that rubbing summons my ghost. But he has been speaking up less and less often, or I'm losing my ability to hear him.

I miss you, I say, and listen past the cars and the birds.
I'm here. Will always be.

The pleasure of that remembered voice warms me inside. Feel feistier.

So, tell me, does this wife of yours really care about Sam?

Ex-wife. More to the point, do you?

I don't answer. It's irritating when he answers a question with a question. Realize too late that I've been walking downhill for a while, and the way home is all uphill. But that voice still buoys me.

~ ~ ~ ~

Gail-the-agent says we could have a release date for the book within the next few months, though there are nitty-gritty issues to resolve. Ama, the Cape Town PR dynamo, now complicit buddies with Joanie, has been asking for updates, and the two of them tell me they are planning a pre-release social media strategy to precede a press event in New York and the launch party in Grahamstown.

With a raised-eyebrows look, Joanie mentions seeing a picture on Ama's Facebook page, of her with Trevor, arms around one another. If she and they are scheming together, I'm in very good hands. I'm squeezed between panic about all that still needs to be done, and impatience to have my baby out in the world.

The middle of the book is pretty much complete, polished and edited. But two looming gaps demand my attention, the first chapter and the last. I had hoped they were passable, but the editor described them as "thin"; I know she's right.

The first, which profiles Maria Soares, is based on Felix's notes and my observations. I saw her for myself last December, when I spent that one day with her in Barcelona. Our focus

Next Steps

wasn't on dancing; it was on genetics, and whether what ailed her might have some bearing on Freddie. That issue was so urgent, so crucial, nothing else mattered.

Can I jigsaw what I saw of her physical limits and emotional depth into Felix's portrayal of her fight for mobility? He designed her "flowerpot," the seat-and-legs set-up that allows her to stand and even walk short distances. What counts most and makes her a great teacher is her spirit, the power that lets her dance, and the delight she derives from upper-body expression. I have photos and wonderful quotes to prove that, but do I have the words? I need to email her some questions, and perhaps set up a phone interview.

The last chapter is more elusive. The end pages will be like the finale of my talk back in January, featuring funny photos of great performers, but before that comes text which needs to be a personal statement. Gail and the editor want a statement "with punch and pathos." What on earth can I say?

~ ~ ~ ~

Deidre has been as good as her word, of course. Despite being a relative newcomer in Portland, she has established a network of high-powered contacts. It sounds as if anyone who is anyone is coming to the cocktail party she has organized for Sam. He isn't due back until a few days before; apparently, he has had little input, but he hasn't objected either.

We are all invited, of course. Joanie said she wouldn't go, claimed she couldn't find a babysitter for Freddie. But Eric is curious to see what housing new policy they will highlight. He begged me to come with him. Given his desire to champion sustainable development in Portland, he should be making all the contacts he can. I agreed to go.

When he asked me, Joanie gave him a dirty look. He said, "Oh, sorry, Sally. Would it make you uncomfortable to see Deidre and Sam?" I insisted I'd have no problem seeing them together, so now I have to keep up that blitheness.

Joanie insisted I buy an evening dress. Was thinking I would wear my pink one and the Minnie shoes, but she was adamant. "My mother might win this little campaign of hers," she said, "but I'm not letting you hide your light in an outfit like that. We're going shopping." I don't care to compete, but we always have fun on our expeditions, so I grudgingly agreed. Personally, I think that if Sam really has been enjoying Deidre's company, that proves he wasn't ever serious about me. Surely, no man could fall for the two of us.

Oops, I forgot. One did fall for us both, way back. Felix claimed, even years after we'd parted in South Africa, that he still missed me and dreamed of us getting back together, but he did fall for Deidre long enough to get over his wariness of marriage, and to produce this stubborn daughter.

~ ~ ~ ~

I watch Deidre at the party. Eric has gone to get us drinks. She is in full sail, garbed in a billowy chiffon number with an off-the-shoulder, asymmetric neckline. By contrast, I feel even punier than usual, though Joanie insists my little black dress looks classy.

Her mother stops circulating long enough to perch on a high stool next to a barrel-chested man in a fringed suede jacket and bolo tie. It's the first time I've seen Deidre not in pants or a long dress, and her legs aren't nearly as good as I'd assumed.

Next Steps

You'd never know from the playful way she has them crossed, one gleaming purple stiletto swinging as she laughs at witticisms from her large companion. He keeps leaning close to whisper in her ear.

Look around for Sam. I saw him just a few moments ago, and he can't be far off, but I hope he doesn't come near, doesn't witness this flirting. It's probably just Deidre doing her PR thing, charming a potential donor, but would he know that?

Did Felix mind her flirting, back when he was married to her?

I remember trying to picture her from his description the time he and I bumped into each other in Los Angeles. He implied that getting married had been all Deidre's idea. She was impressed with a prosthetic device he'd designed, and eagerly took over marketing it. He was grateful, and for a while they made a good team.

"What changed?" I remember asking. Wanted to hear something bad about her, to justify the fact that I was holding hands with him, had kissed him, was yearning to get naked with him. But Felix never gossiped. He just said she was vastly more dynamic, and their priorities diverged. Turns out, hearing that was enough to lull my conscience long enough to fall into bed with him. It was a blissful night. But guilt seeped in the next morning. Felix insisted we weren't hurting anyone. He was irritated by my regrets, and possibly hurt that I felt that way.

Can't imagine Sam ever thinking that way, or being unfaithful, or being comfortable with Deidre flirting like this. I grab a glass of wine from a passing server and try to focus on the people around me, and not on that man in the past, or this one in the present.

Eric winds his way through the crowd. I've never seen him so elated. "Sorry, Sal. I got waylaid by a guy who wanted to know all about my Johannesburg connections. There are some amazing people here. You know I'm not a big fan of Deidre's methods, but it's like a Yellow Pages of Portland's movers and shakers!" He hands me a glass, not noticing I already have one, so I'm standing there with a drink in each hand.

Felix had no head for business. On that score, clearly Sam is Deidre's match. I know Felix didn't value wealth the way she did. Evidently, Sam has more money than she has ever had, but also doesn't care about it. What will happen when that gulf opens between these two? Will she drop him the way she dropped Felix?

I'm not jealous, really. I wouldn't want that lifestyle. If it's what she wants, more strength to her. I glimpsed enough in my brief time working with Georgina and Rupert's foundation. Can't imagine living day in and day out with abundance that others envy. So many people in need. So many worthy causes competing for your attention, appealing to your generosity. How does Sam sleep at night?

Come to think of it, Deidre might be the perfect partner for him. She's motivated enough and thick-skinned enough to get stuff done, and she does like to be seen as a benefactor.

But what of the quiet times, out of the public eye? I've tried, but I can't imagine her snuggling down with Sam to watch slapstick comedies, or being willing to taste his culinary experiments, or taking delight in what deepens those dimples. The pale liquid in my two glasses sloshes this way and that as

Next Steps

my anger rises. The noisy, crowded banquet room takes on the dimensions of a stage, with performers like combatants facing off with one another.

I don't want Deidre to hurt Sam.

~ 17 ~

Gail phones a few days later to set up a three-way conference call for the next day with the indie publisher who is doing the book. "Can you be awake by ten o'clock New York time, seven your time?" she asks. "I'm sorry it's so early, but these people are on a very tight schedule."

Of course, I can wake up early. Haven't for a long time, but I used to be up and exercising by six in my teaching days. And up for coffee by seven when Felix and I were together. Sam gets up early too. Remembering when he stayed with me last summer in Kalk Bay; he'd be showered, dressed, and reading before I staggered out to feed the cats.

Focus, woman! Toss aside the shawl I've been wearing and get up from the floor where I've been sitting alongside Freddie, helping him construct a tower of blocks. All of a sudden, the book has evolved from a scrappy manuscript to this product.

Finished the first chapter, featuring Maria, last week. I've written my last chapter too, the personal one. Sent it to Gail a

Next Steps

few days ago. She wasn't enthusiastic. She wrote back: "I would have suggested a more positive conclusion, but this is very honest. If it's what you want to say, fine." Yes, this is what I want to say, but I could probably make it more upbeat.

The kittens, adolescents now, are perpetually in search of trouble. One has crawled under my shawl and is batting at the other from its fringed edges. Freddie is trying to pile blocks on top of them both. My efforts to finish the book feel about as effective.

Apparently, the publishers would like to finalize the cover design and font choices and photographs. It's only two weeks since I chose my favorites from the array they sent me. I thought things moved very fast with my first book, but this is Gail-force, pun intended, though she plays down her part in the big push.

"They want something to display at Book Fest East in January," she says now on the phone. "It would be a phenomenal springboard. If we are all in agreement, we can have advance copies and some promotional material, like posters and bookmarks. You are planning to be in New York for that, aren't you? I'm going to set up a press event for you."

I reassure her that I plan to be in New York for a day or two on my way back to South Africa. Joanie and Eric come downstairs just in time to hear me say that. Joanie gives me a sad-faced grimace. Eric grabs the stroller, she hefts Freddie onto her hip, and they head for the door. She whispers a query; do I want to come with them to the park? I shake my head. We are in the home stretch; I want this thing done.

Continue pacing the moment they disappear, phone at my

ear, listening to Gail. Pause to point and flex my feet. "I know you said they do good work," I say to her. "I like the books I've seen. But are you sure they can do it the way we want?"

"Absolutely!" Her tone is as warm as ever, but I picture her tossing her honey blonde pageboy over the collar of her designer jacket. I'm silly to doubt her choice of this firm. Ethel, my even more perfectly groomed ex-mother-in-law, would never have recommended Gail if she didn't have high standards. But her style isn't my style, and I want to be sure my preferences prevail, with a feeling of immediacy rather than slickness.

Joanie, when they come back and I tell her my concerns, catches me by surprise. She suggests I ask her mother for help. "This is her strength, getting people to do what she wants, and she does know a lot about design."

Picturing Deidre, I know she's right. Delay till the evening, but then pick up my phone. It's a strange moment, so soon after my inner tiff with her, but suddenly I'm wishing I'd consulted her before. I would like her to be at my side for that call, to make sure I'm not bullied into anything against my will. She's an early riser—another point of compatibility with Sam. Maybe I'll ask her to come be with me.

That is, if she isn't staying over at Sam's. Rather than hear that from her, I text instead of dialing and ask her if she can come by tomorrow morning very early. Promptly regret doing that, but it's too late to retract.

She calls me a minute later and asks what I need.

"I'm sorry if I'm interrupting you and Sam . . ." I start to say. Thank goodness she can't see me; my face must be puce.

"Not interrupting. He isn't here. He never stays over. The

Next Steps

man is such a gentleman, I was beginning to wonder about his sexual orientation. So, what do you need me for?"

Swallow very hard, push aside all the things I want to snap at her. Instead, tell her about the conference call regarding the book. Tell her that I would appreciate her eye on my design choices, and to brainstorm with us on ideas for the launch. She listens in silence and then responds unusually quietly. She seems touched that I've asked for her help.

"We make a good team sometimes," she says. "See you tomorrow morning. I've got a key. I'll let myself in.'

~ ~ ~ ~

The discussion with Gail starts with a surprise: My ex is a last-minute addition to the call. "You don't mind, do you?" Gail asks. I really don't. Her family and my in-laws have been friends forever. In fact, it was Charles's mother, Ethel, who introduced me to Gail when I was in New York last year. In the past few months, he has become very involved in the whole project.

The kitchen phone is on speaker, and Deidre listens in silence, sitting by my side at the counter. Gail introduces Charles and me to the publishing company's lead design and production duo, and steps back. They lay out the choices, referring to the photographs we sent them. A border or no border around the images? Half page or full page? Then the cover: gloss or matt? The picture is settled. White type for the title or blue? Or yellow— "very trendy"? On and on.

Each time they try to cut corners or overrule me or bully me into a choice Deidre doesn't like, she thumps her fist on the counter, or wags a finger at me. I look up and see her mouthing, "NO WAY!" or "BULLSHIT!" And each time, I know she is right. I "ahem" and then restate what I want. When I don't insist, Charles steps in. On a couple of points, Deidre shrugs, and I'm ready to agree, not feeling it's worth the fight, but Charles won't let us cave. Eventually, on most things, the publisher's people give in to us. My teammates and I all end up applauding ourselves and the "magnificent" (their word) book we are bringing into the world.

I ring off at last, draw a deep breath, and turn to Deidre with probably the broadest smile she has ever seen from me. I start to move forward to give her a hug, but she is staring down at her hands.

"Do you have a minute?" she asks. Do I have a minute? I assure her I do and offer to make us coffee. She shakes her head. "Let's go out for some. Isn't there a place nearby? There's something I need to discuss with you, and I'd rather not do it here, with Joanie around. Plus, I control my temper better when I'm in public."

Control her temper? Without considering the choice, I lead her in the direction of my favorite 24-hour café, a place Trevor introduced me to. We are halfway there before she starts to speak. "I just need to say this. You really hurt Sam, and you should make it right."

I stop walking. "*I* hurt *him?* What do you mean?"

"Well, you know he and I have been spending time together. Yeah, yeah, I know you all thought I was just after his money. That's bullshit. I make enough of my own—though it would be fun to be that rich.

"But I was puzzled by his lack of interest. I know he finds

Next Steps

me fun, but that's it, nothing else. Finally, I asked him, point blank. He said, 'You're beautiful. Any man would be lucky to be with you. But I'm still getting over someone else.'"

We've reached the café. Without thinking, I sit down at our usual table, in the corner, facing across the room. I wish Trevor could be with us, and then change my mind. This is definitely not a discussion I would want him to hear.

Deidre scans the all-seasons décor, Santa Claus figures alongside Easter bunnies and plastic palm trees, her eyebrows sky-high. "Isn't there a real restaurant we could go to?"

"This is as real as it gets," I state. "You were saying, Sam said anyone would be lucky to be with you . . .?"

She glances at the chair as if it might be sticky and sits down reluctantly. The waitress looks up from her book and flaps two menus at me. I shake my head and call out, "Just two coffees."

"And two muffins," Deidre adds, "if they're fresh. Toasted, with butter and jelly." I urge her to carry on.

"Well, I asked Sam if that someone he was getting over was you. He turned red, the way he does, and nodded. He said he's finally closed the door on that 'mess-up.'"

My cheeks are probably as red as his get. Past and present, or recent past, are all entangled, the crossed lines, and the distant storm of what happened with Felix, her husband, my beloved. Did she tell Sam about that? Hoping desperately that she didn't.

"I told him about you and Felix," she contiues. Okay. "He asked if that's why we got divorced. But it wasn't. I told him Felix and I were already on the rocks by then. You were the only woman he cheated with, as far as I know. He was always so wrapped up in his work. But I'd been with a bunch of guys. I was bored."

In all my shame and regret, I've never considered what she might have been up to. In any case, my morality was my business, hers was hers. Whatever she did, I had no right to be with her husband. Still, it clears away a layer off very old guilt.

I have to ask: "Was Sam shocked—I mean, about me?"

"Yes, kind of. I told him I knew that you and Felix were in love, always had been, and it was the only time you slept with him while we were married. That's true, isn't it?"

I grunt, "Yes. How do you know all that?"

"For Christ's sake, Sally, Felix and I talked. He told me all about you in the end, when we split up, everything except about you getting pregnant. Joanie filled me in on that bit. But Sam is who matters now."

She gestures with impatience at the waitress and turns back to me. "I think that part hit him hard—how much you loved Felix. He said if he had understood how recently you had lost Felix, he would have kept his distance, but you never told him anything. I said you're uptight—and not just with him."

The muffins arrive, slightly burnt, and heavily buttered. Deidre takes a big bite and waves at me to do likewise. I break off a piece and nibble. "And now?" I ask.

"He didn't say it—he probably doesn't realize it—but it's clear you led him on," she says, her mouth lined with crumbs. "That was really fucking unfair."

She licks her lips and her fingers, and leans forward, her hands on her thighs, glaring at me. "You know what it's like

Next Steps

to be hurt. Joanie says that Charles of yours gave you a real run-around. How could you not understand what Sam felt? The man is as transparent as a jellyfish; you had to see how vulnerable he was."

Her words sink through me like stones. I have no reply. Instead, I blurt out, "So you've never had any romantic interest in Sam?"

Deidre accepts the switch of direction. "Not really. It was fun getting access to some of his big-shot buddies, but I wouldn't marry someone I don't love, and there really is no chemistry between us. Shoot, I've stayed single all these years, and I've had plenty of opportunities."

I nod. I've assumed she's dated plenty of people and have been curious why she hasn't remarried.

She says, "I know you think I'm a bitch. I am one; I don't pretend to be anything else. But you're like Little Miss Butter-Wouldn't-Melt-In-Her-Mouth. What's your excuse?"

There are many things I want to throw at her, but don't. Finally, I manage to mutter, "Thank you for helping with the book stuff."

"Yes, well, you're welcome." She reapplies her lipstick perfectly, without needing a mirror. "It was fun. I like your Charles. Good voice, and he was quite something on that conference call."

~ 18 ~

Is this how it feels to be in a boat in a storm, rising and falling?

Back at the house, pacing again, back and forth across the living room, hugging my shawl tight around me, I hear the beloved gravelly voice.

Calm down, Copper Girl.

Calm down?

What's going on? This isn't the Sally I know.

This is the Sally I've become without you.

That's defensive, to ward off a growing sensation I don't like. Of what? Stop pacing and stand still, heels together, toes out, shoulders back, arms hanging down. Breathe deep, feel the pulsing inside me, picture blankness. What am I trying to shut out? Not just Deidre.

So much is changing, falling away. The book is almost done; Freddie is thriving, and his parents no longer truly need my help. And Sam has closed the door.

Next Steps

The first two are good; I welcome them. The third . . . I collapse into a heap on the sofa. I want Sam to forgive me. I want him to be okay.

You thought Deidre was the one who would hurt him? Seriously . . .?

Huh?

Haul the shawl over my head, enclosing myself in a dim blue tent. Cornered. I know what he means. Remember him back in Cape Town, telling me that I was being a bitch to Sam. Couldn't see it in myself then, but I could see it in this other woman.

Felix, are you saying I'm like Deidre?

No answer is forthcoming. Typical! He does this, leads me up to a precipice and then fades away. Answers are coming at me, not just from this Sam tangle, but from others. Remember the young Argentinian conductor I was angry with because he dumped me—after I refused to meet his parents. How could I? They would have seen me as a man-eating older woman. And Felix himself, to whom I refused to say, "I love you," because he hadn't said it to me first, never knowing how deep his own wounds were.

And what of my parents? And friends? And colleagues?

Always so afraid of being hurt. And so blind to the hurt you inflict.

Am I hearing Felix's voice or my own? I can't tell, but the truth of those words squeezes me like a too-tight embrace. There is no escaping this. All my life, I've felt small and slight. Aware now, thin as I am, of being heavy—and strong.

In my head I hear a crescendo of music I can almost

identify and sense a gyre of bodies whirling, some in toe shoes, some seated in wheelchairs adorned like chariots. For the first time in forever the choreographer within is clamoring to record ideas, something about wielding power, like Joan of Arc with her sword, sharp enough to defend against evil, but where is the evil? Which way does the sword point?

"Where is a pen?" I yell at Joanie as she comes downstairs with Freddie. She is wide-eyed, frozen by the sight that must have greeted her, of this woman emerging from under a shawl, wild-haired, and now scrabbling on the counter in search of paper.

I ask her, "Do you think Sam will ever forgive me?"

She must be wondering "Why now?" Just casts me a look of concern and shrugs. I will have to find out for myself.

~ ~ ~ ~

If I was more religious, I would recently have observed Yom Kippur, the Day of Atonement. I didn't attend services but, as always, did fast, to honor my parents. And this year, I spent most of the day in my room, contemplating my past. Judaism teaches, if I remember correctly, that atoning is worthless without an attempt to correct what one has done wrong. Doesn't Alcoholics Anonymous also teach that? I have begun writing a list.

Top of that litany is Libby. I should have called her weeks ago. I should have stopped over on the East Coast and gone to stay with her in Greenwich before coming here. The only reason she didn't complain about that, she says, is because she is happy that I'm seeing my kind-of grandbaby, and that there's been contact with Sam.

Next Steps

She doesn't know him and has heard all my complaints about the way he withdrew back in Cape Town. But none of that has undone her initial impression—the fleeting glimpse when she met me at Kennedy Airport last December and saw him say goodbye to me. "He looked smitten," she remarked at the time. She was so happy about our friend-dates, what she insisted on calling his "courting" of me.

I love that she wants to see me happy. I want to see her happy too, and for the first time in all our long friendship, I sense she isn't. How long has this been going on, with me oblivious? We exchange emails about once a week. She hasn't gone into detail, but it seems Doug, the brilliant doctor, her rock, her stalwart authority on everything, has been showing signs of what might be dementia.

At 2.30, allowing for the three-hour time difference between Portland and Greenwich, and hoping to catch her before she starts cooking dinner, I dial their number. Doug answers. I greet him and tell him it's Sally, in case he doesn't recognize my voice or my accent. "Sally's not here. She's in South Africa. She hasn't been here in years," he bellows at me.

"No, Doug, this *is* Sally. And I'm in the States, calling from Portland, you know, my daughter-in-law's place, in Oregon. Can I speak to Libby?"

"Libby?" I hear the blank confusion, and a wave of horror washes over me. Can it be this bad? And then remember, he always called her Elizabeth. It was a gesture of affection, distinct from the informal form everyone else uses.

I try that: "Is Elizabeth home?"

The clouds clear. "She's at the store." He's still very loud.

"I don't know what's keeping her. She's been gone for hours." He's abrupt, embarrassed, I think, by his mix-up. "You're visiting with that sort-of daughter-in-law with the sick baby, aren't you? What are they doing with him?"

In the old days, even when I visited less than a year ago, I'd have welcomed the chance to update him and ask his medical opinion. Maybe he needs that familiar respect, so I say, "They have Freddie on a regimen that seems to be working. He's not walking yet, but he's still young for that, isn't he?"

Doug ahaas, and hmms, and asks for names of medications and where they're taking him for therapy. It's almost like before, until he repeats the question we've just been over. To my relief, Libby comes in, and he hands the phone to her.

She sounds tired, but overjoyed to hear my voice. I feel doubly guilty. And I only have a few minutes left to chat before I need to take over care of Freddie, so Joanie can talk with a client. Arrange to chat again later, after Doug has gone to sleep.

She says, "He insists I come to bed when he goes, but I can slip out once he falls asleep."

We do talk later. It leaves me aching for her and, yet again, feeling a glimmer of gratitude for the way Felix died. I cannot imagine how tormented he'd have been if he experienced a mental deterioration like Doug's. And he would have been a torment to live with.

"I keep remembering what Nancy Reagan said," Libby tells me. "How, when her husband died, she wasn't overwhelmed with grief because she'd lost him years before. I still have Doug, but not quite my Doug. I want him to go for more tests, to see a different specialist, but he refuses. Denies

Next Steps

he has any problems, though it's obvious to all of us."

"You'd think a doctor would want the best diagnosis he can get," I venture.

"And yet, that's precisely the problem. He doesn't want to see anyone he knows, and he claims the others are quacks. I think he just can't bear the idea of being incompetent."

"Come visit me," I say. "Get one of your kids to stay with Doug and take a break. I need to see you. You've never met Joanie and Eric. They'd love to meet you." I hear a hiccup—of swallowed tears? She has always had a hard time leaving her family, as if everything would spin out of control without her. She promises she will try. Just that betrays how exhausted she is. We finish with declarations of "Soon, soon!"

We are so different. But then our circumstances have always been different, before we met as students in Boston and since. When Libby's mother was doing her debutante duty, dancing with disabled veterans to boost their morale, my mother was recovering from starvation in a displaced persons' camp. Where my family celebrated the High Holidays with just the three of us, she took for granted Christmases with more people than she could name. Even away at college, Libby couldn't go anywhere without bumping into cousins I was sure I had none.

And yet, loss is loss. It's time to become a far better friend.

~ 19 ~

I have agreed to babysit Freddie while Joanie leads a photography workshop. I'm happy to be useful again. She's battling to regain professional momentum, as I was when I gave the talk at the conference back in January. It was too soon for me, but for her the timing seems perfect.

Much as I love seeing her eager and excited, I am nervous about being alone with this little guy for a whole day. I confessed that to her, while assuring her he and I will be fine. But perhaps we could have his old baby nurse come as backup.

"You don't need that bat," Joanie declared. "I've got a better idea. Laura is coming to my workshop. Why not double up with her nanny, so you can keep each other company?"

"Here or at her place?"

"Hers. You'll love their house, and they have a fabulous nursery. I'll call her and check, but I'm sure it'll be fine. Her Gregory is a year older, and Freddie worships him. They'll keep each other entertained."

Next Steps

So here we are, parked in their semi-circular drive, me carrying Freddie while Joanie totes his diaper bag and stroller. There are three cars parked along the curve, in the shade of four towering fir trees. How many can one couple drive? Oh, plus a nanny and a housekeeper.

The house itself looks like a giant's forest cabin, with a slope-edged slate roof and walls of dappled rock. I do love it. The big oak door swings open and Laura emerges, arms out to welcome us. I see her and Joanie exchange a look—of what? Amusement at my anxiety? We're ushered into the nursery, as lovely a room as Joanie said, all sunshine and color, and the two of them bid Freddie and me goodbye.

"Where's your nanny?" I call to Laura as she heads out.

"Coming in a minute," she says over her shoulder. "He's just changing a soggy diaper in Gregory's bedroom."

He? A male nanny? Didn't Joanie mention a lovely woman? Are these people really rich enough to have two nannies? Not that there's anything amiss with men taking care of children, it just used to be so rare in South Africa, and here.

I'm checking Freddie's diaper, which happens to be sodden too, pondering that question, when I hear an exclaimed "Sally!"

I see a child forging forward on his sturdy little legs, tugging the hand of his clearly unforewarned grandfather. The two of them are in matching tie-dye T-shirts and look so much alike, with their dimpled pink cheeks. At any other time, I'd have delighted in the sight; right now, I want to flee.

"I'm so sorry, Sam," I say. "I didn't realize you would here."

"I live here. We divided up the family home. I occupy the

west wing, the granny flat—or the grandpa flat," he says. "I love having them nearby, and they like having a resident babysitter."

"I can go, get a cab, take Freddie home."

He shakes his head hurriedly. "No, no need to do that. Laura mentioned I'd have company, but didn't say who. I think our girls conspired."

He follows Gregory, who has toddled over to where Freddie is lying on the changing table, and is clambering up onto the stool so he can see who is up there. Freddie lifts his head, equally curious. They stare straight-faced, still free of the pressure to smile. I have my hand at Gregory's back to make sure he doesn't fall, and Sam takes over from me so I can finish up with Freddie.

"Please stay," Sam says. "Greg clearly wants you to."

The kids are squawking at each other now and reaching out pudgy hands. We settle them on a puffy mat patterned with birds and animals. Each reaches for a toy of his choosing, Gregory to a ball, Freddie to a little wooden horse on wheels. It looks like a smaller version of the rocking horse his grandmother Deidre gave him last year. This one he can push and pull, and a bell jingles as it rolls. From the little I've seen of other babies, his movements are a bit wavery, but he makes up for that with determination.

Think of Fausia, locked in her body, just starting to unfreeze when I last saw her. It would be so good to have this kind of drive in her. Estella has sent me photos of her, standing alongside the other children as they dance, her arms held out.

"She is trying, but there's been some backsliding." Estella

Next Steps

wrote. "I wish you were here."

After their initial glee, the boys seem to be ignoring each other, absorbed in their own goals. "Parallel play," Sam says. "Apparently, it's one of the first forms of social behavior." I try to think of something suitable to say in response. Each word that rises feels loaded with risk. Sam looks equally awkward, but then he pipes up: "I like Joanie so much, and your SOS."

"My SOS?"

"Trevor—your sort-of stepson. He said that's what he calls himself, that he has a great mother, but also a second mother—you."

I want to cry, I love this so much. Shiver and draw my sweater closed, hugging that "SOS" to me. "I call them my sort-of stepkids, but this abbreviation is far better. But what would that make Joanie?"

"Your SOD? Oh, no, that doesn't work. She's a honey." He grins, the dimples deepening. It's the first time I've seen them in so long.

"I adore that boy—that man," I say.

"He's a fascinating person, interested in everything."

"A bit like you," I say, to my own surprise.

Sam's cheeks flush. "Very much like his father, I gather," he says.

That thought glows, sending warmth through me. Last year, when I met Humphrey, his resemblance to Felix was like balm, a miraculous antidote to the heartache of missing my beloved. But it turned out to be purely physical. They were very different people. What we have now is much more satisfying,

177

a connection built around shared family concerns. With Sam, there isn't the faintest physical resemblance to Felix, but on another level—of heart? spirit? —they have strong similarities. I know they would have liked each other immensely.

Almost reach out to touch Sam's shoulder as he interacts with the kids, not to caress it, just to experience his solidity, his warmth.

He asks, "Trevor's in Cape Town? Laura says he might be staying there. True?" I nod, glad for the rescue from my own thoughts.

"I've daydreamed that, but not actually had it confirmed by him," I say. My hopes have been raised by his suggestion, seconded by Eric, to expand the attic of the cottage into a spacious third bedroom. And now there is this hint that Ama and he might be an item . . .

"I'm not sure it would be best for him in the long-term," I say. "The country is so unsettled. But at least for a while, it would be wonderful."

"You know how I feel about Cape Town," Sam says. "I might be able to introduce him to some very good contacts." He glances at me and looks away.

I want to grab his chin and make him look at me. Instead, I exclaim, "You're in tie-dye again. You never told me why you like it so much."

He gives a mock sigh. "Okay, okay. This is the story: I used to wear the accountant uniform--button-down shirts and striped ties to work, golf shirts on weekends. My girls got on my case about it. They said I was stuck. It was true, I could feel how rigid I was becoming. I was boring myself!

Next Steps

"The girls gave me my first rainbow shirt for Hanukkah that year, and insisted I wear it to the office. I felt so good in it—alive! —I bought a bunch. I decided to make them my daily wear, to keep me mindful that not everything is linear and logical."

"So, you adopted a new uniform?" I poke my finger at his chest.

"True." He shrugs and the dimples go deeper. "I'm a creature of habit—even hippy ones."

"What did your wife think of them?"

"Oh, the shirts came only after she was gone. She would have been horrified. Margo had tried to become a hippy. That's why she took a fancy to me, thinking I was a free spirit and would teach her to be one."

"But . . .?"

"Her rebel phase didn't last long, especially once we had the kids. Strict standards were like morality for her. And look, she was right; without her I've become a total degenerate."

We are both grinning now. Before the feeling can fade, I grab my chance. "Can we talk? I really need to clear up some things with you."

"Please, let me go first," he says. "I need to explain . . . "

"You don't need to explain anything to me. It was all my fault."

He frowns. "Your fault? What was your fault?"

There are two rocking chairs set further back, but we have perched on two stumpy plastic stools on either side of the kids' play rug, with our knees high. There is no way to feel dignified or empowered. But trying to get up right now might halt this progress.

"Felix says I was a bitch to you."

"Felix? We never met."

"I know. But I have conversations with him." Thinking I should stop, but feel reckless. "I hear him. Less than I used to, but still pretty often. He's always right."

Sam doesn't look shocked or even puzzled. He just says, "About this, he isn't right. You were never a bitch with me, just wary. I was a fool. It never occurred to me that you'd lost him so recently, that you weren't ready for some idiot to fall in love with you."

I hear that "fall in love" with a little thud of pleasure—and fear that it is in the past tense. But I just say, "You don't think I'm cuckoo, talking to a ghost?"

"Not at all. I used to converse with Margo. Still do once in a while."

"Is she always right too?"

"She's who she was in life—worried, impatient, afraid I'll screw up or make a fool of myself. It sounds like you enjoy hearing Felix; I try not to listen to Margo." He grins at me. "She was—is—a bit like my mother. I tend to be more like my dad, a leap-in-and-take-your-chances kinda guy."

"Did she warn you about me?"

"Yeah, and for once, she was right. She told me not to rush in. But I wasn't going to be in Cape Town very long. I didn't want to waste time."

"I didn't mean to hurt you. I'm so sorry. You hurt me too."

He almost topples off the stool. "I hurt you? How?"

"By withdrawing the way you did."

Next Steps

"Isn't that what you wanted?"

I duck my head. Reach over to push Freddie's horse back to him. Look up and see Sam's black-lashed eyes riveted on me, and no sign of his dimples. I say, "I don't know what I wanted. I guess I wasn't ready for real intimacy. But I had thoroughly enjoyed being with you. We had fun, didn't we? You were so warm, so encouraging. And then you vanished. You were gone, just like so many other people in my life—gone."

"That's what it felt like? Oh, Sally, I didn't mean to. I just wanted to get out of your way. You seemed . . ."

"All of that from the fact that I didn't want to dance?"

"Or be hugged." He tips his head. "I told you about my shirts. What about you not dancing?"

I sigh, surrendering, though I have no idea what I'm going to say. "The hugging part, yes, that might have been a timing issue. The dancing part wasn't your fault. I wouldn't even dance with Felix. It's because I've felt shaky, from when my knee started giving me trouble. I was accustomed to dancing well, and suddenly there was this unreliable leg that I couldn't trust. I chose not to dance rather than do it clumsily."

"Joanie told me you danced with her and Trevor at Felix's memorial. I thought when she said that, that it was long ago, but it was just over a year ago . . .?"

"Yes, very briefly, with them on either side of me. It took all the determination I could summon, for their sake, and for Felix's. Since then, only in very rare moments, on my own. I know you think I'm a hypocrite, writing about disabled people dancing, giving speeches. I was even trying to teach a little girl before I came here, the child you saw with Estella. You must have been disgusted at my talk in Cape Town."

Sam rises from his stool. "Disgusted? Sally, how could you think that? I was mesmerized by your talk. You had me in tears."

I don't look up at him. "But you said nothing. You walked away. I thought you saw through me."

"What was there to see through? Your passion is so beautiful. I struggled with my wife to get her to pursue her interests and share her talent with others. For you, all that comes naturally. I love it!"

His voice dips. "But I'd crossed some line. I imposed too much on you. I was too pushy."

I'm standing now too. "No, never, not at all. Oh, Sam! It was just my damn dancing. And a fear of getting too close, and being left. My stupidity, my fear—not yours!"

"I think you are brave."

His honesty demands the same from me, that I demolish that illusion. If I danced this, the movements would be rusty-robot jerkiness to some discordant violin and wind instruments. "All that passion you credit me with? —It's a farce. I teach other people to express themselves, but all my life I've guarded what I express. I've kept my own truth hidden behind barricades. Your wife had the excuse of demanding parents. I didn't. My parents were adoring; I could do no wrong in their eyes. I'm just a coward."

He shakes his head vehemently, but I press on. "When other people don't treat me as gently as they did, I'm shocked. And the only way I know how to defend myself is by pretending I don't care, by turning away, by hiding."

Next Steps

"That's not what I see." He says it very gently, his thick eyebrows tilting up, almost touching above the bridge of his nose. Can't remember what I was trying to say. Mesmerized by the vertical channel in his upper lip and the slight rise in the middle of his lower lip, so that it curves down on either side with such sensuality, I . . . Lean in as he does, feel the warmth of his breath a moment before the gentle pressure of his lips. Not sure he was intending to kiss me or if we bumped, but now can't bear to pull back.

Something goes thunk. We spin around as Gregory and Freddie bash their respective vehicles into each other. Both laugh uproariously, pull back, and do it again.

I gasp, "Oh my heavens, we're worse than teenagers! Imagine if Joanie and Laura had walked in right then."

He grins. "I think they would have stood back and applauded. I think we're being played like puppets."

"Do you mind?"

He gives me a dark, twisty look. "I'm not sure." And then swoops up Gregory. "But right now, perhaps we should take these two to the kitchen for a snack and something to drink."

I pick up Freddie, and do a one-two, one-two little waltz with him. Sam does the same with his partner. We are back-to-back, almost dancing.

"I need a drink too," I mutter, and lead the way though I have no idea where the kitchen is. My body is thrumming, my skin tingling.

~ 20 ~

I don't know where things stand with Sam. I don't know where things stand with me. I say that to Libby when she comes to visit, pouring out a litany of all the ups and downs since I arrived in Portland.

She is sharing my room with the skylight, the two of us head-to-head in the twin beds Eric has ingeniously fitted in at right angles. The arrangement is exactly the way we had our beds in the room we shared as students in Boston a hundred years ago. Her first night we talk as we did then, for hours, without looking at each other, our heads an arm's length apart, until something is said that requires eye contact. Then up we come onto elbows and twist around.

"That was the first time you kissed?" she squeals. I hush her.

"Yes. If that was a real kiss. I told you, there was nothing in Cape Town, not even dancing."

"And?" Her question floats between us. We're like those

Next Steps

twenty-something students, except now we know so many more ways things can go wrong. We were scared then too, but weren't we more optimistic?

There is a long silence, and we both sink back onto our pillows. I hear Libby say very quietly, "Sal, if—I know this is jumping the gun—but if things develop between you and Sam, where would you live?"

"Gun jumped!" I squawk, and hush myself. 'He hasn't even asked me out on a date-date. I don't know if he will."

Suddenly, she's up on her elbow again and says, "I almost forgot. You'll never guess who I saw on the plane, or I think it was him—Charles! He was in Business Class, so I just saw him in the distance, but that same Roman profile, same thick hair, but maybe grayer than when we saw him last year."

"I hope it wasn't him," I say. "He said—or at least he implied—that he's in New York. If he's come here to Portland, what the hell is he up to?"

"You've been talking to him?"

Charles is the only guy I've ever married, and divorced—or rather, been divorced by. And perhaps the only person I have ever really hated. Libby knows that; she witnessed it all. I'm too tired now to tell her what has changed, and still a bit stunned myself. I just say, "We've been speaking almost every day this past week. I'll tell you about it tomorrow."

Lie awake in the dark thinking. For so many years, whenever I pictured Charles, I saw his black eyebrows rammed together, his lips pale with rage, berating me for cheating on him with Felix—though only once, compared to his own multiple and long-running infidelities, a fact I yelled back at him—and announcing that he wanted a divorce.

These past few weeks, another image has resurfaced, of him as the young idealist I first fell for in my early days in the city. See him alongside me, working at a soup kitchen that Christmas Eve, with his handsome, earnest face and the heavy limp that made my heart lurch along with him. I've thought of him as manipulative and myself as his pawn, but that guy, still a boy really, was as vulnerable as I was. He hated the limp more than I realized, and didn't yet know how many women would respond to him as warmly as I did.

The man calling me to discuss how to promote *Next Steps* sounds vulnerable in new ways I can't define. He asks questions tentatively and listens to my answers. He allows silences, instead of filling every pause with his own opinions.

~ ~ ~ ~

The Charles connection might never have happened were it not for Libby, and her suggestion that I get him involved with the book, or at least with the money we might raise with it as a way to honor his mother—and overcome his antagonism because of Felix's involvement. I remind her of that as we chat over breakfast the next morning.

"And it's not just about his desire to be a good son," I tell her. "I had completely forgotten that he has a real love of dance. Remember how he used to love to see me perform, and how he'd invite his colleagues and his family to come to my students' recitals? Something about this book has touched a chord in him. He's genuinely enthusiastic.

"Without his championing it, I doubt the publisher would have taken me on."

Next Steps

Libby is delighted because she wants to see my career relaunched, and also because she likes to see people getting along—even old enemies like Charles and me.

She tilts her head, smiling. "You sound almost tender. You're not falling for him again, are you, after all these years?"

"Oh, heavens, no! Not falling in love—but maybe, possibly, in like."

"I never thought I'd see this day," she says. "So, what do you talk about now when he calls?"

"Aside from the book, his mother. He misses her terribly. And dance, and how much he longed to be able to dance himself. I can't believe how oblivious I was. It never dawned on me. We always avoided the subject of his polio, but the other day we were discussing some of the stories I tell in the book, and he began talking about his childhood. He described what it felt like to return to school after his illness, no longer able to run and climb like the other kids. He'd been short for his age, and now he had a limp."

"Oh my God," Libby gasps. "Poor Charles. He seemed so self-assured; I'd never have guessed."

Her voice drops, though no one is within hearing. "But Doug didn't either. You know, he disliked Charles, thought he was arrogant, that he had a Napoleon complex. But in his practice, Doug treated so many children with issues like that, you'd think he'd have recognized the covering-up. Or maybe there was too much of the preening thing men do."

That makes me laugh. But the notion sifts deeper: How many of these confident, assertive men do we take at their word, falling for their bravado, and failing to see the scared children they are inside? Come to think of it, how many women are like that too?

~ ~ ~ ~

In bed that night, we resolve not to talk, so we can get to sleep earlier. But, inevitably, we start digging up ancient memories, then commenting on the sights we explored today, and how Freddie is doing, comparing him with her grandchildren at this age. She met Deidre this afternoon for the first time and insists she has a sensitive side. I might be developing a liking for the woman, but that makes me guffaw.

"I was just joking, to get your goat," Libby cackles. Sounding more like a New Yorker than the sweet Connecticut WASP she's always been, she adds, "It's enough with you befriending all these pain-in-the-neck people!"

I switch topics then, asking her for updates on her grandchildren, the brood who call me not Aunt Sally, but Dance Sally. This is her happy place, the area where all is sunny.

~ ~ ~ ~

It's only as I hear Libby's breathing sink into sleep rhythm that I remember that Charles called me earlier. I saw his name and let it go to message, and then promptly blocked out the fact. With the volume on my phone very low, I listen now. He says nothing about being in Portland, but does say he has something important to discuss with me. Is the devious professor on some mission of his own coincidentally, or—and my skin prickles before the thought has taken shape in my brain—is he hoping for some kind of reconciliation?

Staring up at the big skylight. Can't really make out any

Next Steps

stars; the clouds might be too dense. If he is no longer living with his wife, could he be lonely? Nostalgic for what we had? He thinks I'm single and possibly lonely too.

Oh, shoot! I may be single, but I'm definitely not emotionally available. How am I going to keep the peace with Charles? I don't want to sabotage the book, but I really don't want to lead him on.

Hopelessly wide awake. My head might be nestled on a pillow in Portland, but within it thoughts are journeying across decades and across this continent.

If I could be so blind with Sam, how much more callous might I have been with Charles? My parents, my mother in particular, were so insistent that I protect myself from men who might injure me, it never dawned on me that I might be the inflictor of hurt.

I did try to be a good partner to Charles. Other than that one night with Felix, when I got pregnant, I was loyal. Played the perfect academic wife, listening endlessly as he refined his theories, reading and rereading the manuscripts of his doctoral thesis and his subsequent books.

A snarky little voice interrupts: What about the way he virtually ignored my first book, *New Steps*? Felix had nothing to do with that one, other than praising it when I showed it to him. But Charles didn't even do that. I thought he was dismissing it because it wasn't intellectual enough, or that he was simply mean-spirited.

He and I haven't touched on any of that in our phone chats, but when I told him how I got into trouble with the foundation job, he brought up a complaint that caught me by surprise. He said, "Sally, you know and I know that you can be a bit of a pushover." I snorted at the irony of that, coming from him. "On the other hand, you don't fight fair. You were so determined to avoid conflict, I never knew what you were actually thinking."

That behavior sounds plain dishonest, and I know he's right. Of course, I didn't tell him at the time that his lack of interest in my book hurt my feelings. His recent openness has been bracing; I've welcomed it on the phone and in emails. But could I handle it face-to-face? Could I match it?

Almost roll over and wake Libby, but don't. She's snoring now, a sound so relaxed and innocent, it lulls me into sleepiness too. Finally, decide she must have been wrong, that it wasn't him on the plane, and he isn't about to show up on our doorstep.

~ 21 ~

And then Charles does show up.

On a wet morning a few days later, Libby and I clamber out of Joanie's car and then help her unload the little one, who has dozed off, and all his paraphernalia, still singing the lullaby we were entertaining him with on the way home.

We've come from a hike in a beautiful park, cut short by rain, followed by lunch with Sam and his daughters and his grandson Leo, my gallant guide to grandparenting. It was a warm, genial event, with very little chance, thank goodness, for Libby to do what she wanted—assess Sam and his intentions. But she has been chattering about him all the way home, about his warmth and his integrity.

"I was right from the moment I saw him at the airport last year," she insisted. "He is a doll, and he is gaga about you, Sal. This is your guy!"

I start up the stairs to the front door, lugging the folded-up stroller and an umbrella, and register on a step above me a briefcase, the rubber tip of a cane and a pair of shiny brown Oxfords, one with a thick, built-up sole. Look up, still singing, and see that so-familiar face, with gray hair, silver in the storm light. He's smiling down at me, till I reach the same step. Then he and I are almost the same height. Slender and dapper as ever.

Charles and Libby greet each other. I make a hasty, awkward introduction to Joanie, and she hustles us all into the house. She settles Freddie on a pad on the floor and starts offering tea or coffee to the adults.

As she turns to me, her eyes narrow. I know exactly what query she is transmitting: "Are we really making this bastard welcome?" I give a little nod. I've told her about the recent warming up, but that hasn't dented her aversion. She knows all my old stories. When I told her he might be in the city, she was appalled.

"Would you two like some privacy?" she asks grudgingly. "Libby and I can take our tea upstairs. If you don't mind, I'll leave Freddie right where he is."

Charles is crouching over the baby, gazing at him in wonder. I remember that look when he saw babies in the playground near our apartment, in the days when we were dreaming of having a child of our own. I have great respect for the fact that he eventually accepted his own sterility and let Dorothea use a sperm donor. He adores their son. I just wish he had been as flexible when I was his wife—or maybe I don't.

He stands with difficulty, pushing up on the arm of the sofa. Looks at me with eyebrows raised. "If it's okay with Sally, yes."

I want to signal, "No! Don't leave me alone with him," but

Next Steps

there's no way. I gesture to him to sit on the sofa, and I perch at the far end, cup in hand, bracing for what's coming.

I start to say, "I knew you were here. I thought maybe you . . ." and stop myself.

"Ah, Libby? Yes, I saw her at the airport, but didn't think she had seen me. I didn't want to say anything over the phone, and I had business out here, so I thought I might as well chance it in person. I'm sorry. I should have asked if it was all right to come, not just show up. I was afraid you might say no."

This is so typical of Charles—to ride roughshod over someone else's possible objections—but his wariness of being turned away is new. "Of course, I would have said you could come," I lie. "What didn't you want to discuss on the phone?"

He twists to face me. "Sally, you know how your parents struggled to find if anyone from their families survived the war?" This again? I nod, warily. "You were always so desperate to find relatives." He's wrong about that; I wished I had relatives, but I wanted my parents to stop searching. Their disappointment was so seering each time a possible clue led nowhere. But I don't contradict him.

"Well, I believe I may have found some cousins of yours."

The words mean nothing to me. I know he mentioned the possibility months ago, when I was still in Cape Town, but he seemed to have dropped the subject. Floundering now, trying to make sense of what he has said, I tell him I remember his parents were ardent supporters of the Jewish Federation in New York and its work with Holocaust survivors. But that was years ago.

"I got involved too," Charles says. "It connected with

research I was doing on identity and community. I was asked to speak at a couple of conferences, and it grew from there."

"And then?" Take a sip of tea. Did he say "cousins"? Relatives are something other people have. Mine were only by marriage to him, and he cut me off from all of them. My hands are shaking so much, I slop the tea. Plonk the cup down on the table and spill more. I have relatives?

"I still don't understand. Who are these cousins? My parents had no surviving siblings."

Charles reaches out and grasps my hand. It's a shock. We haven't touched each other since the night we broke up. His fingers are cold, but I clutch him back, to still my own trembling.

"Remember I asked you a few months ago if you'd heard of Jedwabne, in Poland?" Typical academic, he lets go and reaches into his briefcase for a book. I know the author's name, Jan Gross. I've read about him and his efforts to correct the historical record but haven't read his books. "I'll leave it with you, in case you want to read more," he says.

"You remember your mother had a brother who was much older than her? She might have remembered very little about him. He married a woman from Jedwabne."

"Uncle Salmon—he died in a fire," I whisper. "My father told me. That's all I know."

"Yes," Charles says. "Your uncle and his wife died in the barn massacre in 1941. Basically, most of the Jews in the village were killed, burned to death. Afterward, the Nazis were blamed, but townspeople helped them do it. The same kind of slaughter happened in other places too.

Next Steps

"On the other hand, some of the Jewish children were taken in by Christian neighbors who risked their lives and the lives of their own families. The kids were hidden until later and, in many cases, brought up as their own."

"My uncle had children?"

"Yes, two very young ones, a boy and a girl, Alek and Zofia. Alek died a few years ago, but Zofia is in her late seventies and still going strong. It's her and her children, a son and daughter, who have been looking for relatives."

Charles has slipped into his professorial lilt. It used to irritate me; now I'm too curious to react. "These people, your cousins, didn't know they were Jewish until years later, when they were adults. I gather they suspected the truth but didn't want to confront their adoptive parents, so they didn't start investigating until after the old folks had passed on. And then, it was hard to find out their real last name. And till they found that name, how were they to trace their real family?"

I can barely produce sound. "And some people, like my parents, changed their names. Did these people you found, did they want to find their relatives?"

"Very, very much. But they thought your side hadn't tried to find them, that you didn't want to. I told them that wasn't true of your parents." He spreads his hands on his thighs. "But it's complicated. There's been corruption in both directions, people trying to claim property with false identities. Or people who think all American Jews are rich. Your cousins were afraid that if they reached out without enough proof, they might be suspected of fraud."

"Did they know my parents were in South Africa?"

"Not at first, but when they had no luck with the U.S. or Israel or Argentina, they considered it. I got talking to a researcher at a meeting, and I mentioned that my wife's parents, ex-wife's"—he bobs his head, acknowledging the misspeak—"were Polish Jews who settled in Africa. She asked what their original name was. I couldn't remember, but I found it in some old documents of ours and sent it to her. She traced your mother's maiden name, and a few steps later, she made the match."

I'm still floundering. "They're for real? How can you tell? Do they speak English?"

"It seems so. The sister, Zofia, wrote to me directly. I gather she's a retired academic, and quite fluent in English. But they've been very hesitant. She asked if I'm sure you would want contact, and how come you haven't tried any outreach yourself. I didn't know what to tell them. Why haven't you?"

"Because I'm a bitch," I say. Too stunned to come up with anything else, and it seems to be the answer to everything these days.

"Yes, there's that," he says, with a smirk, lighter now that he's dropped his bombshell. I don't care; we both know he was more of a bastard. "But if you bring forward the sweet, kind Sally we all know and love, your cousins will be thrilled to meet you. Zofia says she and her kids, Peter and Marta, have made plans to visit South Africa in the summer. You will be back in Cape Town, won't you?"

Just then, as if summoned by the word "bitch," the front door flies open and Deidre swoops in. She freezes in astonishment, seeing me with this man, on the sofa.

Next Steps

Then she does an "Aha!" and says, "You must be Charles! I know that voice and I recognize you from Sally's description. Ah, yes, very handsome!" and she winks at me. I could whack her. "I'm Deidre, your ally from the phone call."

Charles grasps his cane, heaves himself to his feet, and reaches to shake her hand. She is taller than him, but stays just as coy. She shakes hands, and coos down at Freddie, waking him. They spout pleasantries about Portland and New York and exchange business cards, and she excuses herself to go upstairs to see Joanie.

It's the first time I've seen Charles use a cane. I point to it, inquiringly. "Old age," he says. He's never made much of his disability. "My joints are getting stiffer. But . . ." As he sinks back down again, his face lights up. "*Next Steps* has started me thinking. I need to exercise more, so why not do it to music? Do you think I can learn to dance at my age?"

This is what I've been thinking. "Absolutely!" I find myself beaming at him with more affection than in forever. "I know you'd be a natural!"

"I think so too." He beams back at me, and then gestures at the child sleeping by our feet. "This is Felix's grandson? He's a fine fellow!"

"He is a darling," I say, "with some big challenges ahead." Charles listens intently as I outline what we know of Freddie's issues.

"Another candidate for the methods you outline in the new book?" he asks. As if hearing that, Freddie rolls over and sits up. I lean down and help him stand, and go to lift him onto my lap, but that's not what he wants. He starts edging closer to Charles, slumps to the floor, but gamely gets himself up again and continues, apparently intrigued by the carved horsehead handle on the cane.

Charles turns back to me. He heaves a deep sigh. "About the book, I'm afraid I've got some bad news. That's the other reason I wanted to see you in person. I may have screwed things up completely. I pushed too hard. They want to back out of the contract."

I am still trying to absorb the cousin news. This is more than I can handle, this totally unfamiliar, contrite Charles, bringing unwelcome tidings. "Can you come back tomorrow?" I ask. "I don't want to hear another thing today. Tomorrow, I promise I'll give you my full attention."

~ 22 ~

Later, talking in bed with Libby, I tell her about the contract collapse, and then I relate the whole cousin story. That astounds her so much, she forgets there's bad news about the book. I do too. She is even more thrilled than me that, at this late date, I have found I have real, living relatives.

In the darkness, suddenly, sadness overwhelms me. The wave bears a flotsam of old hopes and hurt, jumbling them in with the new joy. Libby hears my distress and climbs around so she can hug me. Trying not to make noise that could alarm Joanie and Eric, I sob into her shoulder: "If only I helped with the search, perhaps we could have found these people in time for Imma and Pops to meet them."

The emotions are too jumbled to contain. Libby denies it, but it feels like yet another instance of selfishness, of me being so wrapped up in self-protection, others paid a price.

~ ~ ~ ~

Next morning, we're both glum. Libby is heading home,

via a few days with her daughter in Indiana.

"Are you going to be okay?" she asks, as she starts folding and stashing her clothes.

"Not really. I think it's very irresponsible of you to leave."

She laughs. I don't voice my own concern about her and what looms ahead. There is nothing I can do beyond this, trying to be a better friend, a shoulder when she needs it.

Libby says, "You know, I was worried that Charles had come to Portland with plans to win you back."

I groan. "Oh heavens, that's what I was thinking too."

"Maybe he still will try," she says, eyes wide. "After all that sharing yesterday, and he's coming back today?"

~ ~ ~ ~

Libby texts me that she has arrived home. I'm circumspect in case Doug happens to see my reply—I think they still have a shared account—so I just ask, "How are things back in the homestead?"

Her answer makes me very happy:

Same as before from D's side. From mine, very different. I don't know how, but being with you always gives me back my center. I don't feel I have to be Doug's center, or anyone else's—just mine. I practiced being that way even with the grandkids. I don't think they noticed a thing, but I came away a whole lot less exhausted than usual.

She, in turn, is curious about how matters transpired with Charles on his second visit. Had he made a move? The next moment, my phone rings. "I'm too impatient to handle typing," she says. "So, did he come on to you? Please tell me you stood your ground and didn't give in to those deep, dark eyes!"

"Well," I say, drawing out the suspense a little, "to start with, he was all business, telling me what went wrong with the publisher."

~ ~ ~ ~

Charles plunged right in: "You know how I insisted that we have color on every page? You were willing to negotiate, and your friend Deidre suggested that there might be a way to use black and white just as effectively, but I wanted color?"

I did remember, but not with any acrimony. I liked what he argued for and was glad when they gave in. Deidre said she was too, that it would make for a richer reader experience.

"Well, they didn't actually give in. They went back to their calculators and didn't like the numbers that came up. Gail called me that morning to say they complained that we were demanding too much, and they want to pull out of the deal. She was going to call you, but I said I was planning to see you in person, that I'd rather break the news face-to-face."

Libby has listened in silence. Now she sighs in sympathy. "Oh, how disappointing. What now?"

"We brainstormed," I tell her, "ideas on how we can rustle up funds to publish it ourselves. He suggested we get patrons involved, or one of those crowd-funding plans. I came up with a bunch of old contacts we might try. Kept thinking of more names, but I hate the idea of going hat-in-hand, begging. Felix would have too. Charles says he will put in as much money as he can."

Libby says, "I keep remembering how mean Charles was

about *New Steps*. It amazes me that he's being helpful this time."

"It was your idea to enlist his help," I remind her. "I'm still grateful. Actually, I think he's being good now, in part, because he feels bad about his behavior back then. But I found out what made him so nasty." She is agog to know.

I tell her I was terrified I'd ruin our new harmony, but I finally braced myself and asked, "When *New Steps* came out, when I was so excited about seeing it in print at last, I thought you'd be excited too, but you were—I don't know—ratty. You didn't seem happy about it at all. How come?"

Charles turned away from me, his elbows on his knees, his head hanging down. "Yeah, 'ratty' is a fitting word. I'm sorry about that. It was pathetic." He swiveled to face me. "I was angry, Sally, hurt. I always felt I had a special connection with your dancing, that it brought out the best in me. And you just cut me out."

"I cut you out?" That made no sense to me.

"You called yourself 'Sally Paddington,' not 'Sally Smith,' or 'Sally Paddington Smith.'"

"But I always used 'Paddington' professionally. It didn't mean anything!"

Charles bounced his good leg, a jittery action I'd never seen him do before. "I took it the wrong way. I was an idiot. I thought you were dismissing me. But it's ancient history. Can we shut the book on it, so to speak?"

Libby gasps and gives a little laugh. "Why didn't he just ask you to use both names? You would have, wouldn't you?"

If he'd asked, I suppose I would have, but only to keep the

Next Steps

peace. I'm really glad he didn't. It would have infuriated me to see "Smith" on that cover all through these years since our breakup. It's not as though he was calling himself "Charles Paddington Smith" or "Smith Paddington" in the books he wrote.

I didn't want conflict now either. Pictured the insecure young man I first went to bed with, and that insecure professor who wanted his name on a book cover, and—without staring at him—tried to take in this gray-haired man and understand how he might be feeling. The mood between us was positively tender. But I was scared stiff. Kept chattering, scared to stop in case Charles took that tenderness the wrong way.

If he reached out to me, I would have to make it clear I have no interest in him. No way would I give in just to please him. But I really didn't want to wound his ego, or to make him regret opening up to me.

All that agonizing—and in the end, he noticed the time and said he had to run. He gave me a hug and said, "We're going to find a solution for the book."

I tell Libby, "I offered to call him a cab, but he got this little smirk on his face again and said he didn't need one, that a certain someone was coming to get him, to go out for lunch and more book strategy talk. Guess who!"

There are two beats of silence and then Libby squeals, "No, don't tell me—Deidre? I *told* you they'd be a match! Typical Charles. Did you feel anything?"

"Yes—immense relief!" We're both laughing so hard, Joanie, hearing my side, comes upstairs to see what's going on.

"Oh, thank goodness for that," Libby exclaims. "Now you

can focus on Sam."

~ ~ ~ ~

One of my favorite parts of these Portland weeks is going with Joanie and Freddie to his physical therapy sessions. There are moments when he's grumpy or tired or simply has other ideas of what he wants to do, but the therapist is very good at engaging his interest.

This morning, she introduces him to a device like a tiny baby seesaw. "We designed it. It's a great leg strengthener," she tells us proudly.

She slides Freddie into a seat at one end, and pushes the far end down, so that he rises, not too fast or too far. His eyes go wide, alarmed. He holds out his arms to Joanie, wanting to be removed from this thing. Instead, we applaud, to encourage him. She lets him sink. His feet settle on the floor, and he pushes them down—and up he goes, with a squawk of surprise. His face lights up. He shouts, "'Gain!"

Joanie is beaming. I feel a warm wave of ouma pride, but more than that —grandfatherly pride. Felix is right here!

He's a little champ, isn't he?

Absolutely.

As Freddie and the therapist continue their playing, Joanie and I talk. I know she has been itching for an update on what has happened with Charles. Buoyed by Freddie's progress, I try to be as open. I tell her what Charles said about me not being that way.

"It's true," she says, giving me a sidelong look. "You are so careful with what you reveal." I want to defend myself, but nod instead. "But then so was Dad," she adds. That surprises

Next Steps

me. Wait to hear an indignant snort from her father, but there's silence. I hope he's not hovering.

"He never outright lied," she says. "And he always gave an honest answer if you asked a direct question. But there was all that stuff about his family that he kept hidden. If it wasn't for your detective work, we wouldn't have found out how he and Maria were related, and we'd have taken so much longer to find out what's wrong with Freddie. Even now, some days, it makes me angry with him."

I have complained too. My biggest frustration: That he would never say he loved me. I tell her that, but even as I say it, the other side flashes like a neon sign, and I have to confess: Because he didn't say it, I wouldn't either.

"That's sad," she says. "But you do know he loved you, don't you?"

"Now I do. And I tell him all the time how much I love him." Being very open now. "Is that crazy?"

"Yes," she says, "but not as crazy as not telling each other all those years. Does it help to say it now?"

"It does, a lot." A bit carried away, I add, "Talking of love, you know about your mother and Charles?"

Joanie rolls her eyes. "You know my mother. She never hides anything. When she divorced my dad, when I was seven, she told me their whole story. But how do you feel about this match-up, honestly?"

"I am one hundred percent delighted," I tell her. "They deserve each other. I just hope they keep it harmonious until my book is safely launched."

She laughs. "And you and Sam . . . ?"

Clench my fingers tight and feel my toes bunch too. This openness thing is so hard. But before I can say anything, Joanie turns gleeful. "You are blushing. Oh my gosh, are you going to stay in Portland? Are you going to live here? Please, please say yes to him!"

"Everyone keeps jumping the gun," I protest. "All we've had is a few weeks of very enjoyable hanging out together. I have no idea what he's feeling, or what he wants."

"And you? What do you want?"

"Slow down! Can we just take this one step at a time?" I'm not being evasive; I just don't know the answer. We sink into silence, watching Freddie back on the seesaw, kicking with gusto. I would so much love to be around to watch each stage of his progress, and to help with the inevitable challenges that lie ahead. I know Joanie would be delighted if I settled here. Libby would too. Perhaps, even Deidre.

On the other hand, in Cape Town I have Bob and John and Estella and Fausia, and now Trevor. And my cat. And the mountain. And my cousins are coming.

~ ~ ~ ~

Not everything there is alluring. In Cape Town, I will face the mess with the foundation. Thought it would all be over by now, settled and forgotten.

But, as Sam warned, my decision to keep the peace was a mistake: None of the grant money has reached those ecstatic, hopeful, would-be recipients. Every now and then, a plaintive email comes from one or another of them, asking if there is still a chance. I keep saying, "No promises, but I'm still trying."

I've asked Estella a few times, given that Herman kept

Next Steps

saying Rupert would make good on the promise to them, whether she has seen any sign of the money. She doesn't answer the question. Tells me at length what has been happening in her classes, and about Trevor coming to help her, and about Fausia's ups and downs. But nothing about the Taylor money.

Through the winter months, when it was too hard in her hall to keep out the leaks each time it rained, and then to keep out the cold, she persuaded a church to let her use their community room. "Because I come from a Muslim family, they regard it as interfaith outreach," she wrote. "That works just fine for both sides."

With Sam's encouragement, I asked my lawyer to send them a reminder of what they owe, and a request that they honor their promises. The blowback was quick: Their lawyer said that if I don't desist, they will regard it as harassment and take suitable steps to stop me.

Have I harassed them? If not, I should step up my efforts.

~ 23 ~

Deidre is hosting Thanksgiving for her own extended clan and Sam's. On her side, that includes Nellie, the mother of her daughter's half-brother, Trevor, and her partner, Bertrand—also known by us women as the Ebony Adonis. Charles has come back for this event and to spend the week with Deidre. She tells me with a heavily meaningful look that I can't interpret that they have business to see to.

For Nellie's sake and my own, I wish Trevor was here. But I'll see him soon in Cape Town. "I'm jealous!" she tells me, linking her arm through mine. "Please send him back."

"Or you could come and see him there. It's high time you guys visited South Africa." It's years since we've met in person, but we've always had this easy connection.

I see Deidre observe us and turn away. There's no cause for hard feelings between the two of them; Deidre dumped

Next Steps

Felix at least a year before he and Nellie met. Could she be envious? Or insecure? Is this sympathy I'm feeling for her? Or pity? She would be horrified.

Moments later that flicker is extinguished. The meal has been catered, "so none of us need to lift a finger." she says, "you included, Sally." When the servers bring in the turkey, the bird has already been dismembered. The men, more than the women, voice disappointment that there will be no carving. When I query the choice, Deidre rolls her eyes and clutches her throat. "I was attacked by a turkey when I was a kid, a huge damn thing. No way will I have a whole bird set in front of me intact!"

Typical of her, not to bow to tradition or anyone else's expectations. And true to that form, she has an agenda for this dinner that has nothing to do with anyone giving thanks—except, as it turns out, me.

She announces: "Charles and I have something we want to tell Sally. Will you all be quiet."

Charles takes over. "You folks know that, thanks to my pigheadedness, Sally's New York publisher dropped *Next Steps*." I murmur that it wasn't just him, that I was also involved, but he plunges ahead. "They left her high and dry. I know she has been trying to be very philosophical about it, saying something else will turn up. Well, Deidre and I agree that's bullshit. This book is ready to go, and it should come out now, not in three years or five years."

What choice was there but to be philosophical? I've been trying hard not to feel like a victim, and instead to recognize my own responsibility, as I'm trying to do in other areas of my life, personal and professional.

With the book, my fault is clear: I should have fought harder to get it done when Felix and I first agreed to team up more than a decade ago. I failed to do that—and so did he—thanks to ego and a desire to keep the peace between us. Now I should be practical and downsize my vision, think in terms of black and white photos instead of color, etcetera, and go for the possible rather than the perfect. I've told Gail to put it on a backburner.

Apparently, Charles and Deidre told her otherwise. They have Gail on the phone, to hear their news, hopefully after her Thanksgiving meal has ended. I assume they considered her opinion—but who knows with these two?

"We have found a new option for the book," Deidre says. She gestures grandly to Nellie and Bertrand. "Did you know this gorgeous man has started his own printing company? They will print *Next Steps*, and in record time, and will help with the distribution." Bertrand stands and takes a bow. Deidre continues: "We'll handle the marketing, together with Joanie and her pal in South Africa, Ama."

I start to object but she plows on. "Sally, relax. You can check for typos and make sure the captions match the photos. We'll handle everything else, together with Gail. Charles and I understand your vision for this book." She sticks out her chin. "In case you've forgotten, I knew your coauthor pretty well. I promoted his work in the past, and I can do it again."

Charles chimes in, "And I know you, Sally. I understand how you feel about dance. What's more, my mother made it very clear to me in her final days that I have a duty to help you.

Next Steps

I'd never dare go against Ethel's wishes."

So much for taking responsibility. My only option is to let go gracefully. I do so, with profuse giving of thanks

~ ~ ~ ~

Finally, alone with Sam, out on the roof garden of the condo. City lights shimmer around us, and the chatter from below is muted. It's chilly, but he has put his jacket around my shoulders. Being with him, just us two, has become a luxury I anticipate with longing. It seems we're never alone enough. Trying to just let things flow without diagnosing or labeling anything.

"You're okay with Charles and Deidre taking over?" he asks. I assure him that I am. Just impatient now to see the final product. I shiver, but simply because I'm still cold. He wraps his arms about me.

Needless to say, the physical barriers have fallen away. Not that we've taken things all the way—we don't have enough privacy for that—but we seem unable to keep our hands off each other. Touch, caress, cuddle, simply keep linked, like teenagers.

"Thank you," I say, kissing his cheek.

"For what?"

"For forgiving me."

"There was nothing to . . . "

I don't let him finish. "Yes, there was. I was a coward. I nearly wrecked everything, just to protect myself from hurt."

"But I would never hurt you."

"Not deliberately. But caring this much is dangerous. So much can go wrong. But I didn't appreciate the courage it took for you to open up again, to risk getting involved with me. I am grateful—so, so grateful."

Sam cups my face between his hands and kisses me lightly and caressingly. Feel the warmth of his breath, the slight roughness of his lips, and push forward, kissing him back, my arms tightening around him. The door to the terrace has opened and closed a few times, but we are oblivious, ignoring whoever else might have come out here.

Sam draws back, grasps my hands, and says to me very slowly and clearly: "Sally Paddington, will you marry me?"

There is a shriek behind us, and the next moment we're swamped by hugs.

~ 24 ~

After the festivities of the past few weeks—Freddie's first birthday, and Christmas, and New Year's—I am partied out. Pretty sure Sam is too. All good stuff, but exhausting. Add to that, jet lag from our departure this morning and flight across the country. My head is spinning.

What's more, tonight will be our first time sleeping together, literally, in one bed. Also, maybe, our first time the other way, not literally. I feel as if I should have a frilly negligee in my luggage, like a honeymoon bride. But given our fatigue, not assuming anything. Also, I'm not a bride.

A more sensible woman would be focusing a whole lot more on tomorrow's press event. While the romance side is full of hope, the book affair looks doomed. We already had to cancel participation in the East Coast Book Fest, and the last straw was dropped on us this morning, by Gail, in an email I wish I hadn't opened.

It popped up on my phone screen while I was taking a last photo of Freddie, as Sam and I said our goodbyes to everyone at the airport. Ignored it, focusing rather on our delicious baby and his clear-as-a-bell "Bye-bye, Sa SaS." That name, apparently, refers to both Sam and me, a package deal. Rubbed noses with him and he laughed, which meant I had to do it again. Telling myself I'll see him—and Joanie and Eric—soon. No idea if that's true or not.

As Sam and I finally settled into our seats on the plane, I read what Gail said. She was supposed to receive two cartons a week ago, full of handsome volumes ready to be handed out to guests and reporters tomorrow. Instead, the books arrived today, only just in time, with high-gloss covers instead of matt, with muddy color and warped, curling corners.

"They look awful, completely unacceptable," she wrote. "Too late to cancel, but we're going to have to wing it without giving away any copies."

"Is everything okay?" Sam asked. I showed him the photo Gail sent. "Call her," he said, so I did, as we waited for takeoff.

"I am beyond frustrated," she wailed. "I know how upset you must be too. It doesn't help for tomorrow here in New York, but Bertrand has apologized. He's distraught. He says they will ship a corrected batch to South Africa, free of charge, for your event at your alma mater next month."

One nugget of amusement penetrates my haze: the Big Apple is going to get upstaged by Grahamstown (population: approximately 140,000). People there might not as famous in the dance world or media, but they are very important to me personally, and they will love the notion of being the first

Next Steps

people to see the book.

~ ~ ~ ~

Sneak a sideways glance at my companion and meet his eyes. He is quietly observing me, his dimples deep. "You look so beautiful with the streetlights flickering over you," he says. I squeeze his hand in both of mine. I know he's nervous too.

Surely we're too old for sex to be an issue. Bubbles of anxiety keep rising. Other than that day belly-surfing at Muizenberg, we haven't seen each other's almost naked bodies. I've put on weight since then, staying with John, and then Joanie and Eric, and I'm even paler than before, almost blue-white. Will he notice, or care?

This is all running through my mind as the car stop-starts through rush-hour traffic from LaGuardia Airport to Brooklyn Heights, to my tiny apartment, recently vacated by my tenants. Gail, very kindly and still upset about the books, is driving us.

And there is the building and, down the six dark, mossy steps, my front door, half-way below street level. It's almost seven years since I left here. Back then, I was grateful for this one-room apartment, bought with money loaned, borrowed, and gifted. It was a haven after Charles and I split up, cramped as it was, a place to recover, to learn to be alone again.

It looks even smaller than before. The street has become busier and noisier, footsteps pattering by right outside the window. You can hear people moving overhead, and conversation from the apartment next door. We can hear young kids calling and squawking now where there used to be just a very passionate pair of newlyweds.

The loft bed, which I built myself, is the one thing that's

larger than I remember. Gail has lent us linens, but we struggle to get them around the mattress. Sam must be horrified, given the luxury he is accustomed to. But, as always, he seems unperturbed and game for whatever.

We could have stayed with Charles, who offered quite warmly. I was tempted, remembering the beautiful brownstone apartment he and I shared, till he mentioned that Deidre had flown in and would be staying there too. If I was a real writer, not just a dance documentarian, I'd have said yes, to gather material for a truly bizarre modern love story. What genre of fiction would that be? —"geriatric romance"? "love triangle squared?" Titles start popping into my brain: *When Exes Unite*, or *Brownstone Bedmates*, or *When Sally Met Deidre Who Met Charles?*

But Sam insisted we take advantage of the fact that I still own "a garden apartment" in this prime neighborhood in Brooklyn. "It will give you a chance to decide if you want to keep it," he said, "so that we have a pied-a-terre in New York." That "we" caught my ear. He has also been referring to his home in Portland as "ours."

"Ours." I love the sound of that bond between us. I love that our pleasure in being together is mutual and declared. No more games. Except that we haven't actually decided what our plans are for the future. I can't bear to think of giving up Cape Town, and I can't bear to think of giving up Sam. Just keep blocking out that whole tangled dilemma.

And meanwhile, here we are, back in my old stamping ground. Gail, who lives not too far away, in Park Slope, insists she will pick us up again tomorrow to take us to the press

Next Steps

conference and, from there, to Kennedy Airport, for the flight home to Cape Town. "This is what we do for our star clients," she says.

I think it's also by way of compensating for the printing fiasco. I was inclined to argue, not to impose on her, but I shut up. She's a grown-up; she can make her own choices.

Perhaps she's scared I'll change my mind, and duck and run tomorrow. Does she know how nervous I am? Have already considered the fact that no one will turn up. It's in the middle of the day, in the weird post-festive season lull. Or lots of people will come, but they will spot that Felix and I were totally unqualified to write this book.

If Sam and I vanish before the talk, Manhattan is sufficiently crowded, no one will find us. We can head straight to the airport.

When I voice all that to my companion, he grabs my head and crowns me with a kiss. "Okay, let's do that, if you still want to in the morning. But right now, it's bedtime."

~ ~ ~ ~

After all my angst about this moment, we are too exhausted to be self-conscious or lusty. Simply clamber up onto the loft and collapse. With some trial and error, we work out whose arm goes where and whose leg goes over whose. The room is just cold enough to make it pleasurable to snuggle into this precious warmth.

"Do you want to go over what you'll be saying tomorrow?" Sam says, despite already sounding groggy. I probably should, but won't. Just move closer and pass out.

~ ~ ~ ~

In the morning, Sam wakes before me. I open my eyes and see him lying propped up on his elbow, watching me. His hair is damp and standing on end. He must have showered already. He smells of Old Spice, a little like Felix used to.

"Was the shower okay?" I ask. "The hot water used to be very unreliable."

"It was an adventure," he says. "I got the hang of it after a while." With the back of his fingers he strokes the curve of my breast, to the dip of my waist, to my hip. It gives me a shiver and I squirm closer to him, pushing my hand up under his T-shirt. He slides off the shirt and then helps me take off mine.

After all the months of wanting to be with him in Portland, and finally able to kiss and caress in stolen moments, this freedom is intoxicatingly luxurious. I am purring.

A metallic banging startles us both. Sam sits up. "A visitor?" But I remember the sound; it's just the heat coming up through the pipes. Beyond that rhythmic thumping, through the wall we can hear the mom calling to her kids that they're late. Feet parade by the window to a thrum of voices and engines.

And here we are, just a few yards from them, naked in bed, with nowhere to rush to—or not yet. "This feels illicit," Sam whispers, "as if I snuck you into my dorm room."

"I was thinking the same thing, or like my parents could come back at any moment."

He gives an evil chuckle that makes me giggle, and that turns into a gasp and soon to exclamations loud enough to alarm the neighbors. Hopefully, they're too busy to notice, or if they do, they remember their own childless past.

Next Steps

"Do you think they'd be shocked if they saw us oldies indulging like this?" I ask Sam.

"Just envious," he says. "I can't believe how lucky I feel."

Lying in his arms, my pulse slowly returning to normal, I realize that Sam is the first lover I've ever been with in this apartment. I used to be too embarrassed to bring people back to my itty-bitty cave when they had grown-up places. I tell him this space is our first home, humble as it is.

"Then we have to keep it," he says. "Okay?"

~ ~ ~ ~

The whole day has passed in such a whir, nothing is clear beyond the afterglow in bed this morning. I've had a smile inside me throughout, even at the bookless book party.

On the way back to the airport, as much to reassure myself as to fill in the gaps, I ask Gail and Sam, "It wasn't a total disaster, was it?"

"Not at all. I think it was pretty successful," Gail says.

"Did we get there on time?" I really can't remember.

"No," Sam says. "We were late, and Charles was ticked off."

"Oy! Really? My fault?"

"Partly. You got chatting to the neighbors. They were so excited to see you again—or impressed by your vocal strength." He grins at me. "But Gail took the bullet for you. She told Charles she chose the wrong route, trying to avoid traffic on the Brooklyn Bridge."

Thank goodness, Charles is very fond of Gail, in a big-brotherly way. Still, I remember him going on and on about the "ridiculous" printer and how he'd never had to deal with such incompetence before. Deidre, who knows Bertrand better and fancies him, was more forgiving, but not much.

Now I can picture the room. Big, beautiful pictures of dancers from the book adorned the walls, the graceful ones and funny ones and poignant ones. I remember perching on a high stool and holding a mic. On a stand beside me was a large photo of my coauthor, a blow-up of the picture Maria had provided, of Felix in drag, in a flamenco dress and blonde wig, trying to look imperious and not break up laughing.

I love that photo. I guess Charles didn't mind it—because it's unsexy or because he's bedding Felix's ex-wife? Either way, by the time I started answering questions from the journalists, he was smiling benignly.

"It was a good turnout, wasn't it?" I ask.

Gail says, "Pretty good, and just as well it wasn't bigger. The *New York Times* ballet critic was there and writers from a bunch of other publications. I'll send you a list."

Sharing the mic was the doyenne of world dance teachers, Darcy Feldman, an old friend from my New York days. She spoke first, introducing the book and—this part I recall clearly—discussing how her own sense of what is possible has been transformed by *Next Steps.* She said she hopes to see an expanded project, with multimedia lessons and videos online. That hadn't occurred to me before, and I love the idea.

Then she asked me a bunch of questions. Throughout the process, there was a warmth at my shoulder so distinct I almost turned around to invite Felix to answer questions too.

~ ~ ~ ~

Finally, on the plane to South Africa. We settle into our

Next Steps

seats, me by the window, Sam in the middle, with an empty seat beside him on the aisle. It's the same arrangement as last year, when we met on the plane coming to New York. For the first time, I notice that as often as he flies, this guy doesn't like to see how high up he is. I love flying, being way up in the sky, so now I'm the calming influence—until Sam scares me with a totally unwelcome snippet of news.

"Rupert wants to meet with you the day after tomorrow," he says. "His lawyer emailed me this morning. It seemed better not to tell you before the press conference." I almost gag.

"He said they'd been trying to get hold of you, but weren't getting an answer on your home phone." He shakes his head in disgust.

That phone has been out of action all year. Clearly, they weren't trying very hard if they forgot to try my cell phone. Do they or don't they want to speak to me?

"We still have phone reception. It'll be midnight by them, but I can reply," Sam says. "What shall I tell him?"

No point in delaying. "Tell him sure!" I say. "Meeting at the foundation offices?"

"It'll be a teleconference, not in person. They're in Ibiza."

He expects that to lessen my tension? It should, but I've been trying to prepare for a confrontation with them. Not sure about Georgina—I dread facing her—but I've been reminding myself I can control my body language better than Rupert can. I remember him squirming and fidgeting when I first met them at that dinner in Camps Bay when they offered me the job. Had planned to wear my black power suit to any meeting, one of the outfits they paid for, just to annoy them.

On the phone, your voice is your only tool. Almost a year since I last spoke under duress, at the conference, and then my voice quavered. If I'm going to win what I want from them, I'll have to project solid confidence.

~ ~ ~ ~

Sam is even chattier than usual, to the flight attendants and the fellow across the aisle and the kid who comes wandering by. Within minutes, he knows that the mother, Bethany, is on her way to visit friends in South Africa.

"He's such a lovely man," she tells me when Sam goes to the bathroom. "He told me he's hoping to marry you. You're very lucky." It reminds me of Mavis, how she said the same thing all those months ago.

I know I'm lucky, but what do I do about it? We haven't mentioned the subject of marriage since that moment on Deidre's roof garden. Sometimes think I heard him wrong, that he asked something else altogether. When I try to think about it, my mind goes blank. Either he has taken my answer for granted—that I said yes—or he is being very, very careful to avoid a misstep like the one we had last summer.

After dinner Sam falls asleep, and soon—like the first time—his head rests on my shoulder. I didn't mind then, and now I like it. But I can't fall asleep. My brain is racing. Could take a sleeping pill, but don't like to when I'm surrounded by strangers.

How do I coordinate with Sam's travel back and forth? Do I coordinate with it? Is he assuming I'll come back with him when he returns to Portland? I can't leave Cape Town again so soon. I have the book launch party at Rhodes University next

Next Steps

month (which he is coming to), and I need to be in Cape Town in February to see my cousins. That phrase still echoes like a fraudulent boast, but that is when they said they are planning to visit.

Also, Mary has her second international dance conference, in March this time.

Aside from introducing her to Maria, and urging Maria to be one of the speakers, I've stayed on the sidelines. But I insisted that Maria and Diego stay with me when they come. I have to be in Cape Town then. But where will Sam be? I don't want to be apart from him.

Felix, are you here? You've been championing this guy all along. What should I do? Is it too much too soon?

. . .

Now, when I'm desperate for advice, you're absent?

~ 25 ~

Trevor, grinning from ear to ear, meets us at the airport, driving my trusty old Volvo. It makes me so happy to see him, shaggy beard and all. And to see the glorious Mother City, flaunting a navy-blue sky, cloudless except for the "tablecloth" draped over Table Mountain.

Trevor drops us off in front of the cottage while he parks the car. Look up and gasp. The shape of my home has changed. The peak of the roof is higher, and there is a dormer window above the plaster mermaid over the front door. At least she is familiar.

I'm struggling to unlock the door, with Sam waiting patiently behind me as I jiggle my key, when I remember there must be a new one. The door swings open. I see Father Bob, and behind him a chorus line of smiling, greeting friends.

Almost like the group embrace that welcomed me home a year ago, when I came back after seeing newborn Freddie, and meeting Sam. Then, I was dreading returning to the empty,

Next Steps

Felix-less house. No dread now. So much has happened in these twelve months. If anyone had told me that the tie-dye accountant I met on the outgoing flight would be at my side, my cherished companion, still in tie-dye . . .

Gorgeous Ama is there, with a smile as smug as Trevor's. Know in that moment that the two of them orchestrated this, and that they are lovers. See Estella and Mary and even old John Latimer, with a rueful look that tells me he had his arm twisted to join this raucous chorus.

"All hail, our famous author!" Ama yodels.

Hear, "Welcome home, Sister Sally!" and there, to my astonishment, is Humphrey, as handsome as ever. "Just in town on business," he adds in response to my gaping-mouthed query. "Dr. Latimer asked me to drive him here today." I hug them both, and everyone else within reach.

A brief hush falls as they spot Sam behind me. Then the noise level shoots up again. "Did you say yes?" yells Estella. I hear a chorus of "Did you?" and "What did she say?" as we're swept into the living room, into a party already in full swing.

"How did they know you proposed?" I ask Sam. He shrugs and shakes his head, but his dimples are deep, his brown eyes crinkled in laughter. It seems unlike him to broadcast such personal news, yet he is clearly fine with this reception.

"Someone must have told someone," he says.

I collar Ama. "Did Joanie call you?"

She gives me a wide-eyed, fake-innocent look. Can't really object. They were all so invested in this outcome. I love them for it, even as it adds to my confusion.

Much eating and toasting ensues, and catching up, and

making dates to meet up. Eventually, most people kiss, hug, and leave, and the inner core is left.

Trevor leads me from room to room to see the paint colors and he has chosen, and up to the extended attic. It's all fresh and unfamiliar, except for the red, sequined hanging, back on the wall above my bed. To his evident relief, I approve of it all. He assures me we can change whatever I don't like.

Fatigue comes in waves that recede and rise again. Sam looks euphoric and utterly undiminished, but reminds me he is more accustomed to this transatlantic travel and that he slept on the plane.

"Can we venture to discuss wedding plans?" Bob Halpert asks, settling next to me on the sofa with a cup of tea for me and one for himself.

I glance up at Sam, standing next to me, and he raises his eyebrows, yielding the question to me. I have no answer. Mergatroid has been weaving around my ankles, purring under my nose-to-tail caresses. She turns to extend the weave to Sam's jeaned legs, and he sidesteps, trying to avoid her. I pull her back to me.

Just then, another cat jumps through the living room window. For a moment, I don't believe my eyes. It is Skelm, his orange lordship, my handsome buddy, leaner than before but unmistakable. He surveys the gathering, and then swaggers over to me with his sinuous, stroke-inviting stride.

Ama says, "He just walked in a couple of days ago, as if he'd been here all along. I was dying to tell you, but Trevor wanted it to be a surprise."

Skelm leaps up on the sofa arm and reaches his nose up to

Next Steps

my face, just as he used to, rumbling louder than his mother.

"Aw, you're getting kisses," Estella says.

How can I leave these cats?

How can I leave these people?

~ ~ ~ ~

Estella and I withdraw to the kitchen so I can ask all my questions. She is bubbling over with impatience: 'When are you free? Can you come to us? The kids are rehearsing the show we're going to be putting on. It's a fundraiser for the new hall, and it has to be perfect." I ask what they're doing. She gives me a wide-eyed, I-dare-you-to-laugh look. "*West Side Story*, a kids' version. You have to come."

Keep thinking of the grant, how they should have been rehearsing in their own space by now, but neither of us mentions that. I consider saying something about the meeting tomorrow, but bite my tongue. No knowing if any good will come of it.

"And Fausia?" I ask at last. Estella has forwarded messages from me to the child and passed on brief, sweet replies, and twice she sent me videos of Fausia trying new moves "for Ms. Sally." Trevor has filled me in too. I have a bunch of new ideas to try with her, suggested by various teachers I've met or watched online—if I'm around to work with her. It's a while since they updated me, and I've been distracted with book stuff.

"Is Fausia still living with you?" I ask.

"No. She's back with her father. He has a flat a few blocks away from us, not a bad place. It's where she wants to be, and her little brother is with them. The mother has disappeared."

Probably a good thing, though Fausia might not agree.

"Who watches the kids after school when her father is at work?"

"Mavis is with them," Estella says,

Mavis?! Mavis is alive? I grab Estella's shoulders. "Why didn't you tell me? I was too scared to ask."

"I thought your friend Father Bob told you. Aagh, I'm sorry. No, yes, Tannie Mavis is doing okay, full of spit and vinegar again, though some days her mind is a bit off since the fire. She might not remember you. But I'll take you to see her."

Sit with my elbows on the kitchen table, shaking my head, trying to absorb it all. Happy about Fausia. Overjoyed about Mavis. I was so afraid she'd come to a tragic end, I can hardly take in this news. Resolve that when I go see her, I'm going to bring jeans and a jacket for her to keep, even though I don't have a motorbike to take her on. Maybe somebody in their community will give her a ride.

As we're walking back into the living room, I ask Estella about Herman. "Long, yucky story," she says, puckering her nose. "Not for today. I'll tell you another time. See you very soon?"

~ ~ ~ ~

The cats come running as I exit the bedroom in the morning, evidently with no hard feelings about being excluded all night. Trevor has already fed them, but that doesn't stop them trying for more. Strokes are invited too.

Remember Sam's question. Go looking for him, though there is no way I can discuss life decisions right now, with the meeting looming. He's watering the plants on the patio and doesn't even try to bring up the subject I know is on his mind.

Next Steps

Instead, he suggests that rather than sit around worrying, we go for a brisk walk and get breakfast at the corner café.

Inhale the salt smell as we open the front door. It grows stronger as we stride down to Main Road, synching our strides. Greet vaguely familiar faces along the way. When we walk into the café, the owners call out in surprise and give me a welcome-back hug. The pleasure of all this floats above the leaden layer of tension.

No appetite, and stoking my jitters with caffeine would be unwise. Order a muffin and decaf coffee. Sam, deep in eggs and toast, offhanded or trying to sound that way, says, "I know how upset you've been about the people who were expecting grants from the Taylor Foundation. If things don't turn out the way you hope today, we will find a way to make good on the mini-grants. Okay?"

"No. I mean, thank you." I reach across the table and lay my fingers on his cheek. "That is a wonderful offer, but it's not how this is meant to work out."

~ ~ ~ ~

We settle ourselves at the kitchen table, with the phone between us. At exactly the appointed time, the it rings. Sam picks up the receiver and switches to speakerphone.

One by one, everyone comes on the line: Rupert, apparently back in London, not Ibiza, and their lawyer, somebody Anderson; my lawyer, Rosemary, in Johannesburg, and somebody here in Cape Town, Bartlett's replacement, I assume. Would it have been better or worse in person? Straining to hear each speaker, still antsy that there is no body language to reveal their intentions.

Elaine Durbach

Anderson states why we have gathered, reiterating what was said in their last email. I say hello to Georgina, assuming she is at Rupert's side, and thinking she might have something to add. There's a moment of heavy silence before he snaps, "She's not here. I don't know where she is, and I don't care." His lawyer tries to hush him, but he goes on muttering about women being irrational. "You can't trust any of them," I hear him say.

Hope pokes through. If he and she aren't together now, perhaps they weren't in cahoots in this whole mess.

"You shouldn't have gone digging into what wasn't your business," he says. "If you'd stayed in your lane, we could have overlooked your incompetence." When I object to that, he says, "You don't know who you're messing with." That makes me laugh out loud, which stops him in his tracks.

"This is a laughing matter to you?" Anderson asks. He sounds as clipped as an automaton.

"No, I'm sorry," I say. "It's just that *I* don't know who *you* are messing with. I don't know who I am any more. All I know is that I'd never intentionally take money that wasn't mine."

"Are you suggesting that I or my wife stole that money?" Rupert growls. "Are you implying that we embezzled funds from our own foundation?"

"No." I say. "I screwed up, and I apologize for my carelessness." Sam presses his knee against mine under the table. "I understand that it was my fault that the account number fell into the wrong hands. Mr. Parker's investigation proved that." I shrug at him, and go on. "But you managed to halt the damage before it went all that far. And the people whom I promised the starter gifts to, they did nothing wrong. It would be wonderful if you would consider reinstating those grants."

"Oh, you were careless all right. And now you expect us to pay blooming well up? You damaged the reputation of the Taylor Foundation. Our checks were being dished out like cocaine."

"Rubbish!" I snort. I hear an "ahem" from Rosemary, and pause before going on. "I'm sorry, I don't see how I did any damage. Will you honor your commitment to the grant recipients?"

Anderson pipes up. "Mr. Taylor is not inclined to continue with those arrangements."

"Not continue? Why not? Those people, you promised to help them. You are the one damaging the foundation's reputation." Sam is looking down at his lap, but I can see his cheek creasing.

"You have a book coming out, don't you?" Rupert asks, his delivery suddenly slow and smooth.

"Yes. Why?"

"It would be awkward, wouldn't it, if the media coverage you're probably chasing included the fact that you misdirected funds intended for worthy causes?"

Rosemary cuts in, "That sounds like a threat."

"But I didn't misdirect funds!" I shout.

"Well, it could be said that you did," his lawyer intones, "or that you enabled Herman Fortuin to obtain that money."

Herman? The room goes darker, and I lurch back in fright. But it's just Trevor at the patio door. He stands there, his curls limned with gold, and gestures a "How is it going?" to Sam, who does a "so-so" hand motion. He comes in and stands behind me, his big, warm hands spread across my shoulders.

Rupert says, "Is it just dumb naivete or were you in cahoots with Fortuin and his buddies? You got our foundation mixed up with a criminal element. And now you demand that we honor grants to your friends?"

Sam speaks up for the first time. "I gather that you spent some time with Mr. Fortuin. Do you have proof that he wrote those checks? I looked into the possibility, but I couldn't find a sure link. I think it would take a police investigation to get concrete evidence. Are you planning to bring in the police?"

The line is quiet. I strain to hear and catch what might be a whispered exchange, and then Anderson comes back on. "We are not planning to contact the police, and we assume that you will not be doing so."

"What about the grants . . .?" I start to ask.

He interrupts, just says, "We are discontinuing this call," and the line goes silent, except for a buzzing sound.

I thank Rosemary, press the button to disconnect. It's not over, but for now I can breathe. Kiss Sam's hand and turn to hug Trevor. Stretch out my arms and legs like a starfish. Sad for Estella, frustrated, and very relieved.

~ 26 ~

Still a bit jetlagged later in the week when a letter arrives from Krakow from my cousin Zofia. She encloses color photos of herself and her kids and grandkids. They are not very clear, but I pour over them, trying to find a glimpse of familiarity. It looks as if the children have red hair, but I can't be sure.

She writes that they are having hassles getting visas and can't work out exactly when they can come. Her granddaughter is pregnant for the first time, and her daughter doesn't want to be away when the baby comes, so wants to come very soon—or not for a while.

Muddled. She is a generation ahead of me. They must have married and reproduced very young. Coming or not coming? Any day now, or postponed indefinitely? Sam and I are leaving for Grahamstown for the book launch in a week. I can't cancel that. This whole thing is too much like the old rollercoaster I watched my parents experience. Open my computer to write back, but have no idea what to say. Stare blankly at the screen.

Sam and Trevor walk in, looking smug. They won't tell me where they went or why. Puzzled, but pleased by their complicity. When we first arrived, Trevor was monosyllabic with Sam, almost rude. I think he resented the intrusion where his father once reigned. It's a relief to see a friendship budding between them, the same as it did with Joanie.

~ ~ ~ ~

On Sunday, an email comes from Zofia. She says she is arriving on Thursday, in four days, alone. "My children will come another time, after the baby is born. I am going to spend one week in Cape Town, and one week I am going to a game reserve. I understand if it is not convenient for you to meet with me. Don't worry. I am a good traveler by myself."

It's so sudden, and her tone is so abrupt, I read it aloud to Sam, to see what he makes of it. "Does she or doesn't she want to meet with me?" I ask him.

"I think she does, but isn't sure if you want to meet with her," he says.

I write back that I am very eager to meet her, but we will have only three days together before I have to head off to Grahamstown, and she will be gone before I get back.

After all the stress and distress, the face-to-face contact will be so brief. On the other hand, maybe it's a good thing. How wrong can we go in three days?

Zofia says she has booked a room in a house in an area called Saint James. "I know this is your holiday season, and I am lucky to find a place, but is it near to you?"

Next Steps

St. James is near, walking distance from the cottage. But there's yet another problem: I'm scheduled to do a radio interview about *Next Steps* right when she is due to arrive. Trevor, my sanity-restorer, says he'll meet her at the airport. I send her a picture of my mop-haired sort-of stepson, so she will know whom to look out for. We arrange to meet for dinner later, after she has had a chance to settle in.

~ ~ ~ ~

A pearly twilight has spread over the bay as Sam, Trevor, Ama, and I make our way down to Main Road and head for St. James. Strung tight as a violin. As we turn the corner, I slip on a cobblestone. Sam catches me before I go down, and I hop-hobble till I realize I'm not injured. In all my years here, I've never slipped on these stones. Sam keeps a firm hold on my arm after that, bracing me.

Perhaps this whole thing is a mistake. Why didn't I let sleeping dogs lie? Now, I've allowed this stranger to spend money she probably can't spare to fly out here—and for what?

Trevor, a few steps ahead of us, flings out his arms and does a sideways heel-click. He turns and says, "She's very nice. Do you remember when I got lost at the Museum of Natural History when I was little?" Of course, I do. It was the first time we met. A museum staffer spotted this little wanderer within minutes and brought him back to us, but it took Felix hours to get over the shock. I was a quivering wreck.

"Do you really remember, or just our talking about it later?" I ask.

"I remember it," he says, "but not as a trauma—I didn't know I'd been lost—but I liked the look on your face. You'd been all cool and friendly, but suddenly your heart was in your eyes. From that moment, I knew you were family. Zofia is family too."

He starts singing "We Are Family," and I join him, trying to loosen up. Sam is noting the house numbers. He hovers a questioning finger over a doorbell. I take a deep breath, check my hair in a car window, and nod. He presses, and we hear the summoning ding-dong deep inside. The latch clicks and the door creaks open.

"Sally?"

I turn, and look right into my mother's face.

~ ~ ~ ~

I can't stop staring at Zofia. In the photo, she was white-haired, like I am, but she has dyed her hair red, the way Imma did until she was too sick to go to a hairdresser. It's slightly orange at the roots, evidently done very recently, probably at home.

"I am a silly old woman," she tells me over dinner. "I should have stayed natural, like you."

"No," I insist. "For me, this was the very best thing you could ever have done."

As I grow more familiar with Zofia's face, I see the differences. She has a mole high on her cheekbone, and she pencils her eyebrows a little darker than Imma did. Also, she is older. My mother was in her late sixties when she died. But the determined chin and elegant cheekbones, bright blue eyes, and broad, satiny forehead—all that is Imma. I soak in the familiarity, bask in it, breathe it in.

I dig in my bag and bring out a photo of my mother to

Next Steps

prove my point. Trevor, however, keeps remarking on the resemblance between Zofia and me. Sam agrees. He takes a photo on his phone of the two of us side by side, and it is undeniable. I thought, aside from hair color, I looked more like my father than my mother. Now, for the first time, I recognize the truth.

We search for other resemblances. She loves music and slapstick comedy and walking. What isn't alike is our manner. Zofia is blunt. Not sure if it's a Polish cultural trait or simply how she is. Where I am circumspect, she wastes no time in getting to the point. If my parents hadn't emigrated, if I hadn't grown up in this Anglo milieu, would I be like her?

The chatter doesn't slow for a moment, or certainly not from her side. None of my worries materialize, including how I should entertain her. She suggests—and has already researched—various tourist excursions. Sam and Trevor will be working, but I happily agree to go everywhere with her.

~ ~ ~ ~

On day one, we visit Robben Island to see where Nelson Mandela was jailed, talking politics all the way, and then ascend Table Mountain in the cable car, so she can see the whole city.

We have a late lunch in the restaurant on the top of the mountain. After what we've seen in the morning, our talk focuses on the horrors of the past and complications in the present. A true academic, she showers me with facts about my country as well as her own. Our values are more or less aligned, though we differ in the degree to which we trust people in power.

Finally, I squeeze in a question that has niggled at me since

I learned about these cousins: "Who do you regard as your real parents, my uncle and aunt, or the people who brought you up?"

Without a moment's hesitation, she says, "The people I knew, the ones who loved me."

But then her face twists. She props her hands on the table, shoulders up about her ears. I shouldn't have probed. I want to rescind my words. But before I can apologize, she says, "This is very hard. Sally, you know you are Jewish . . . " I interrupt, muttering about not being very observant. "You don't need to be," she says. "You are who you are. For me and Alek, and others like us, we grew up thinking we are one thing, and then we find out we are another."

She sits back, very straight. "I always felt something was wrong, something out of place in me. When we found out who our real parents were, I thought, 'Maybe this is my true self.' For my brother it was not a spiritual matter. He said, 'I knew always what was wrong with me: I had a piece cut off that none of my friends were missing. Now I know why.'"

Zofia has dinner with us at the cottage and we talk more. Mergatroid keeps a distance, but Skelm takes an immediate interest in our guest. I'm about to steer him away, but Zofia lifts him onto her lap. The stroking and purring seem to help her keep going. "For me, this new religious identity was bringing up many questions. When I met Jews, they tell me I have a *Yiddishe neshama*. That's the right expression—a Jewish spirit? But what does it mean? I knew our Lord Jesus was a Jew, but he is still my Lord and, in the end, that makes me a Christian. Does that bother you?"

Next Steps

I'm winded. This never occurred to me, that I could have cousins who are not Jewish. On the other hand, if they were Orthodox Jews, they might have found me not Jewish enough. I reach across, lay my hands on her knees, palms up. "What is there to be bothered about? We're family." She covers my hands with hers and, without letting go of them, dives into other topics.

As Sam and I are settling down to sleep later, I say, "She dominates conversation almost as much as Charles used to."

"And still does," he adds with a grin. Come to think of it, my mother was like that too. Perhaps it's what drew me to Charles, a comfort factor I couldn't pinpoint.

~ ~ ~ ~

On day two, we drive my cousin out to Stellenbosch, to the winelands. Sam insists on treating us to lunch at an estate famous for its swarm of Indian Runner ducks, employed to keep the vines pest-free. Zofia, fascinated, interrogates their herder. Reverend Bob, utterly delighted that I have acquired family, comes with us.

It's a relief to have others present to engage Zofia. I enjoy her energy, but also find her exhausting. Her presence chips away at an old wall, the barrier that shielded me from my parents' pain. Though she was too young to remember, her whole life was reshaped by the war, and in her presence, their reality becomes more vivid for me than ever before. Trying to let it come through, not to stifle it.

~ ~ ~ ~

On day three of the visit, after dropping off Zofia at the National Gallery in the Gardens, Sam and I have a mission of our own: picking up the carton of books. More boxes are on their way to Grahamstown, but I must check these before we get there.

Scared to look. Wait until we get home, and then push aside the scrunched packing paper, and there it is: *Next Steps*, with a smooth, matt cover, and the gorgeous picture of Maria, bunny ears and all, laughing, her hands bunched in a paw pose. Mergatroid and Skelm weave around us, intrigued by the box, and I purr along with them. Inside my head, jubilantly show it to Felix. Send a thank you to Bertrand and an email with a photo to Gail and Charles and Deidre, and to Maria. Floating with relief.

Gift the first copy to Zofia, with the inscription: "*Thank you for taking the next steps that brought us together. Your loving cousin, Sally.*" She hugs it to her chest, her blue eyes full of tears. She's a weeper, like me.

"My children are going to love you all so much," she says. Inspired by her enthusiasm, apparently, they have begun making their own travel plans, with their in-laws and the new baby. Zofia gives me a sidelong grin: "You think I talk a lot? My daughter talks more than I do, and faster." I react with mock horror, only half joking.

For this last meal together, we've invited Edith and Roxie from next door, and Father Bob again. We eat out on the patio. As promised, it's a true South African meal, with lamb chops and mielies, corn, grilled on the braai. Edith has made her specialty, granadilla cheesecake, and Zofia has picked up her favorite local discovery, syrupy koeksisters. We have way too much food, she declares.

Next Steps

"But this is traditional in Jewish homes," I tell her.

"In Polish too," she says, and begins listing what she makes for which holidays.

While the others are finishing dessert and talking among themselves, Zofia draws me into the kitchen and starts washing dishes, despite my urging her to leave them. "There is much we have not talked about yet," she says as she runs the hot water.

She asks me about my marriage. "Charles Smith is a very handsome man, no? And he seemed very nice when we spoke. You divorced him, why?"

I'm taken aback, but fair enough, he was the person who connected us. We've already emailed him a photograph of us all together, with an effusive thank you. I take the shortest route through the topic: "Handsome, yes, but as a husband, not so good. These days, he and I are good friends." I tell her how helpful he has been with the book, after first being very antagonistic because of my coauthor.

Tell her then about that coauthor, my darling Felix, and how he pushed me to try to find family. She is puzzled when I mention my fear of opening old wounds. "That was stupid," she declares. "But I was stupid too. I thought always that the people who emigrated had an easy life, that the sadness was left behind. Of course, you have heartache too." It's another hand-squeeze moment.

Then she dives right in again. "So, before Charles there was Felix, Trevor's father, and now Sam?" I nod, worried that she is disapproving.

"What about you?" I ask.

"Oh, only one, from when we were young. That was

enough. I kicked him out when my children finished school. A lazy drunkard. But I like your Sam. He is a mensch. Are you going to marry him? You should."

I'm about to bark at her that I don't need a man, but bite my tongue. She goes on: "Don't be stupid, Sally. Don't lose this Sam!"

This cousin of mine is a pain in the neck. The man himself doesn't say much, but without asking, gives me a shoulder massage before we go sleep. I ask him, "Is this what it's like to have a sister?" He has a younger one whom he mentions with affection, but wryly. Perhaps this sibling business is more complicated than I've considered.

~ 27 ~

Our flight to Grahamstown is in the early afternoon. Sam and I, equally averse to last-minute rush, are packed and ready by mid-morning. What now? We invite Trevor and Ama to put aside their work and come have brunch at the corner café. We're making our way up the street afterward, when I see a familiar white car maneuvering into a parking space in front of the cottage. Estella gets out and spots us. She calls out, "Sorry to drop by uninvited, but guess who demanded to see you?"

The passenger door opens, and she helps an elderly woman climb out, a hunched figure with a red headscarf. The spryness is gone, and pale scars streak down one side of her face, but the wicked grin is unmistakable. I yell, "Mavis!" and run the rest of the way. Before she has even straightened up, I'm hugging her bony frame.

"We only have a few minutes," Estella says. "Tannie has a doctor's appointment in Wynberg. But I reckoned you wouldn't mind."

"Mind *se voet!*" Mavis squawks. "She's my sister. How can she mind? You thought I was dead, hey, Sally? Nee, man, *onkruid vergaan nie* — weeds don't die so easy."

A young boy is peering through the back passenger window. He turns his head when he sees me looking but peeps back to watch us. His pointy chin looks familiar. I kick off my moccasin and show him my sock. A grin breaks across his face and he sticks his foot into view. He knows who I am.

Then the other back door opens and Fausia emerges. She is noticeably taller, and her hair is immaculately braided. I stand back with my hands held out wide. She grins, chin dipped down, clearly aware how good she looks. Though she is still slender, her limbs have substance.

"You came back," she says. I nod, speechless. Mavis is edging toward the house. It's clear she needs to sit down. I usher them in and ensconce them in the living room. Sam puts on a kettle for tea and then joins us.

"How is it, living in a house?" I ask Mavis.

She scrunches her face, and the scars merge with her wrinkles. "Still don't like it, blooming cooking on a stove, all that electricity stuff. Still it scares me. But what choice I got? They won't let me go back to the mountain."

Fausia puts her arm around her grandmother and ducks her head into her shoulder. "You promised, Ouma, you will stay with us." Mavis gives me a shrug and pats the child.

Estella says, "Remember I mentioned I had a surprise for you?"

"Let me tell her," Fausia pleads, straightening up.

Next Steps

"No, me, I get to tell her," Mavis says. "This granddaughter of mine, she is going to be the star of a show!"

"Of *West Side Story*?" I ask.

"I am Maria," Fausia says. "I dance, and I sing a solo song."

"You are the star!" I turn to Mavis, shaking my head in astonishment. "Can you believe this? You must be so proud."

"*Ja*, I'm proud. God has been good to this crazy old bergie. And to you too, *nê?*" and she winks lewdly at Sam. He gives her a wink in reply, and she cackles.

"But . . . " Fausia tips her head at Estella. "You tell her."

"But what?" I demand.

Estella shakes her head. "No, this was your idea."

Fausia looks up at me through her lashes. "You got to dance with us."

I am totally confused. "We want you to dance with them," Estella says. "We want the grownups and kids together in the chorus. Trevor says he will dance with us." He nods, grinning. "Some of the parents have said yes. We need you also!" She and Fausia frown at me like conspirators.

"Will you dance, Miss Sally?" Fausia demands.

All of them are staring at me, even the little boy. Sam, standing behind them, has paused what he's doing and is listening. My stomach tightens. If I go back to Portland with him, I have a perfect excuse; I won't be here.

"I have to think," I tell them.

If I go back to Portland, I can just forget the whole foundation thing.

If I go back to Portland, I can postpone the get-together with the cousins.

If I go back to Portland . . .

For the first time since we got back, Felix bellows in my ear. I hear him so distinctly, I'm surprised no one else seems to notice: *Don't be a blooming fool.*

Huh? I thought this is what you wanted me to do. Anyway, it's my choice, not yours.

~ ~ ~ ~

I'm looking forward to being back in Grahamstown, but nervous about all aspects of this trip. Trying not to build up preconceptions, to remind myself that I'm not a girl needing to prove myself to my old profs—if any of them are still around—and I'm not that girl who was so desperately in love for the first time in her life.

But before Grahamstown, here is a chapter that could be just as scary: We have been picked up by Humphrey in Port Elizabeth. It's the closest airport. The university offered to have a car and driver available, but Felix's brother, who lives in the city, has insisted he will drive us the rest of the way.

Should I have told Sam about Humphrey and the nonsense between us? It didn't seem worth mentioning.

On the phone he said, "I want to check out this bloke if he's going to be my brother-in-law," and I acquiesced. What a fool!

I ask Sam to sit in the front passenger seat and let me stretch out in the back. It helps ease my stiff knee, but not my tension about these two men sizing up each other. Thinking to start on a safe topic, I tell Sam to describe my cousin Zofia to Humphrey. He does it diplomatically, while I add details, to convey what a whirlwind we've just been through.

Next Steps

But I can't control the whole trip. As we speed up on the open road, Humphrey says to Sam, "So, you're the new man in Sally's life?"

"Er, yes, I hope I am," Sam responds, staring straight ahead. Silence, with just the whir of the road. Then Sam says, "I hope you don't feel I'm trying to replace your brother."

Humphrey shoots him a glance. "Those are big shoes to fill. My brother was quite a guy."

"So I gather. And Sally has made it very clear how much she loved him, and still does. Of course, he's also very much a part of this book and the launch."

"And you're okay with all that?"

"Not entirely." I gulp, wondering what's coming next. "Would you be?"

Humphrey laughs. "No, probably not. But I'm a jealous kind of guy. I don't see Sally putting up with that."

"You two do know I'm right here?"

Sam grins at me over his shoulder, and says to Humphrey, "I reckon you're right about that. So, I'm behaving myself. But seriously, I'm widowed too. I believe it's possible to still love someone but have ample room in your heart for a totally new, different relationship. I hope Sally feels that way."

Humphrey nods. Without taking his eyes off the road, he says, "My big *boet* would like that. I'm really very glad for the two of you. So, when's the wedding?" Another gulp.

Sam says, "That's still to be decided. What about you, Humphrey? How long have you and your wife been married? You have four kids? They had to be quite a handful!"

I lie back and close my eyes. Almost two years since his

passing, and still Felix is making his presence felt, laughing at us—or with us.

~ ~ ~ ~

Come Thursday, we have one day left till the book launch on Friday. Angie and her colleagues have been keeping us so busy, I've had little opportunity for reminiscing or nostalgia.

They have housed us in a quaint guest cottage just off the campus, simple but more luxurious than any accommodation I had here in the past. It has rough white walls, reed ceilings, and polished wooden floors covered with Persian rugs. Local art adorns the walls. When I tell Sam how much I like the atmosphere, he says, "We could do this in our place." I like that, though I have no idea which place he means.

The kitchen is stocked with all the food we could want, but we've barely had time to make tea each morning before someone arrives to whisk us out. They've taken us on walking tours of the campus and car tours of the city. Much is familiar and still picturesque, and much is not, either sadly deteriorated or slickly upgraded. It's a microcosm of current South Africa, except perhaps for the donkeys that meander about the streets.

The population looks older because most of the students are still away for the summer vacation. Among the permanent residents, however, are a surprising number of people who were students when I was, and who settled in town or nearby. Angie has reached out to all those we knew. Each gathering has begun with astonished recognition or cautious guesses, followed by hugs, and "How have you been?" Then we are onto "You remember So-and-So?" It is so much fun. Even the old catastrophes, like drunken brawls or raucous clashes with dorm

Next Steps

wardens or the security police, have morphed into fond memories. The memories get more outrageous as the bottles are drained.

I'm worried, though, about Sam. Predictably, he has been friendly but inclined to listen rather than talk. He has simply gone along with Angie's plans, interested in the sights, chatting to local people when he gets a chance. But he seems withdrawn. Is he? I'm too distracted to read him clearly.

Angie recognizes without my saying anything that I need time for the past. On this morning, with that brusque certainty that brooks no disagreement, she suggests that her husband, Gerry, take Sam on a guys-only, all-day tour of their own.

He agrees at once. They're going, he announces, to a new research facility on campus, to an industrial park, a rugby match, and then a pub, probably accompanied by a bunch of friends from the match. "Don't expect us home early or sober," he tells us.

That gives Angie and me enough time to meander through the places she knows I want to see, to caress my Felix memories. I'm longing to do it, and petrified. I know the clock can't be turned back, but that doesn't prevent a hollow longing for those days. I listen for Felix, but hear nothing. His silence feels like impatience.

We wander along the deeply shaded paths of the Botanical Gardens and around the austere dorm building where she and I became friends. The next stop is the house where Felix lodged, still gracious and oak-shaded, though the garden has become one big parking space. I gather the family's old rooms are occupied by students now. From the back gate I can see the door Felix used, that I stormed out of the first time we tried, unsuccessfully, to have sex. Remember blithely sweeping in one Sunday, hoping to surprise him, and finding blonde glamour-girl what's-her-name showering in his bathroom.

Why only the bad memories?

Oh, hi, you. Because I'm too scared to think of the good ones? We had so many, didn't we?

We did, a long time ago.

The student union, posh and much expanded, is not familiar. Neither is the big, impressive theater complex on the crest of the hill, where the launch will take place tomorrow. But Angie offers to drive from there to the reservoir where we used to go skinny-dipping. She waits in the car, making some excuse about avoiding sunburn, so I can sit alone overlooking the water. In the sunshine it looks blandly innocent, but I begin to see the dark blue night sky and the gleam of moonlight on the ripples. Beyond the bird twitters and the distant whine of a plane, I hear giggles and splashing, and the sudden silence of an embrace, with just the song of frogs surrounding us.

As we drive back into town, I can still feel his presence, that restless twenty-five-year-old, full of passion for his career path, for me, for friends—and occasionally for other lovers. I mention that to Angie, knowing how vividly she recalls our fights. "Do the memories still hurt?" she asks.

"The scars twinge now and then, but way less," I tell her. "I know Felix so much better than I did then. I love him better than I did. I was so insecure."

"Ah, you've changed?" she asks, eyebrows raised.

"Sure," I say blithely. "Can't you tell?"

Next Steps

We stop at a craft market, so I can pick up gifts for my Cape Town crew. On impulse, I buy a tie-dye tie for Sam as rainbow bright as his T-shirts and purchase a batiked kimono for myself.

Angie chooses a meandering route back to the guest cottage. We're chatting, and I don't anticipate the jolt that hits as she turns down one jacaranda-shaded street. The apartment buildings that line it are starkly functional, what used to pass as modern. And the ugliest is where Felix and I lived the year after I graduated and moved out of the dorm. With my ears ringing, I ask Angie to pull over.

At first, small as it was, we loved that apartment. It was our playground, a first try at adulthood. We cooked, and made love, and made plans for our future. But he was studying, and I was working. Gradually, money hassles and the conflicting pull of our different schedules and different expectations began to intrude. I wanted to know where he was after class when he wasn't home, and he resented my questions. I thought he was evasive; he thought I was judging him. I knew he was applying for various jobs around the country, but he had no idea where the best offer would come from, so I couldn't make plans to move with him. He accused me of not wanting to.

And then came that nightmare evening when I returned after being out all day, to find his motorcycle, his clothes, his books—all gone. He left nothing but a note on a page he had torn out of a calendar.

From the past, I hear my own wail as I realized that he had left me.

I expect tears to surface, but for once my eyes stay dry. One idea after the other is tumbling, unlocking, leading into unfamiliar alternatives. Could it be that my adult dread of being abandoned isn't a vestige of my parents' childhood trauma after all, but an imprint from my own first loss, blamed on Felix and never fully examined or resolved?

Angie, seeing my strange expression, demands to know what I'm thinking. Tell her—and she remembers that episode—and I start talking faster, because as I describe them, the old facts are dissolving. I am not the child, or the young graduate; I am this white-haired woman with the benefit of life lessons, and they are reshaping memories I have clutched for so long.

"What of Felix?" she asks.

That flirtatious guy who broke my heart, I finally understand, was coping with deep hurts of his own. My criticisms were especially bitter for him, coming from the partner who he'd thought loved him better than anyone before.

"We hurt each other because we knew no better," I tell Angie.

But you do now.

Perhaps. I hope I do.

~ ~ ~ ~

In the morning, Sam and I are both checking our emails when simultaneously we turn and look at each other. I was asleep when he came in last night and don't yet know how his day was, or how he is doing this morning. Somewhat hungover, I suspect.

"I got an email from Anderson, Rupert's lawyer," I tell him. "I'm scared to read it."

Next Steps

"I got it too," he says. "Shall I?" He reads: "Mrs. Taylor expressed her desire that the so-called starter gifts be paid as previously defined. Mr. Taylor has generously agreed."

Just like that, my wish is granted. The whole horrible mess is over. I fling my arms around Sam. "Well done," he says, cringing slightly as if his own voice is too loud.

"Well done, us!" I declare. He isn't as euphoric as I am, but then he was never as worried. I almost want to dance. "What a great way to start this day!"

"Yes, it is," he says, and then adds, staring out the window, "You don't mind if I skip the luncheon, do you? Gerry got me a pass to his health club. I could do with a workout and a sauna."

~ ~ ~ ~

The book event is at midday, beginning with brunch. I could have requested car service but opt to walk. Vaguely disturbed by Sam's absence, but glad in a way. It's been weeks since I've had any time alone. The climb up the hill to the center is steep, and I get tired, but between joy about the grants and tension about what's ahead, the fatigue feels kind of good.

~ ~ ~ ~

Angie is mistress of ceremonies, a role she was born to perform. She welcomes me in, asks about Sam, and then ushers me into the throng. The room is packed with friends, and with strangers interested in books and dance and health. Among the faculty members, amazingly, I spot a few from our time, people who taught Felix and me. They were the young bucks then; now they are old, frail, and venerable. The warmth of their greetings is deepened with sympathy about Felix. I'm taken aback by how many regarded him as a friend, young as he was.

My reading will be the last item on the program. No sign yet of Sam, but we have a while to go. The buffet is followed by a couple of brief speeches and an award to the retiring head of a language institute. Then comes a performance by a local band playing a medley of South African songs, borrowing from and blending different traditions.

Still no Sam. In the past, I would have gotten angry, but all I feel now is concern. Where is he? Humphrey's voice echoes in my head, asking Sam if he can handle my ongoing love for Felix. He answered graciously, but does it still hold true?

As the band is playing, a Xhosa woman approaches me, magnificent in a white traditional skirt with bands of black braid and an array of beads around her neck and wrists. She smiles shyly, with an expectant air. "Don't you know me?" she asks.

In that moment, I do: Cecelia! She was one of the students in my township class, a slip of a girl with striking grace even then. She is taller than me now and buxom, but I manage to wrap my arms about her.

"I am trying to teach like you do, children with trouble," she says. "I am doing many dances with them. I want you to see them." I tell her I wish I could. It's frustrating to be leaving right after the event. I remember the suggestion in New York of a multimedia version of the material in the book, and tell her. It could be the perfect aid for a teacher like this.

Cecelia turns away with a wide, sweeping gesture. The band starts playing a new South African song that has its own elaborate steps. I've seen videos of all sorts of groups doing

Next Steps

them. Children flood out from behind a screen, at least twenty of them, prancing and shuffling, some limping or lurching, with all shades of complexion—as my classes never were—all radiating excitement, doing their own version. Among them are two with crutches and one in a wheelchair. They remind me of Estella's kids, just more smartly dressed and better rehearsed, and impressively confident. I wish she could be here to see this and meet Cecelia. Perhaps if they come to Cape Town . . .

As Angie steps up to the mic to introduce me, Sam slips into the seat beside me, smart in his navy-blue blazer and new tie-dye tie. I reach out to him, but Angie, with a flourish, calls me forward, and I have to pull away.

"In New York, a few weeks back," I tell this audience, "I was horrified to discover my book would not be ready to hand out to the Big Apple press corps. It was an author's nightmare. But, I must tell you, it gives me immense pleasure to present it here for the first time, today, to you all." As I hoped, they respond with cheers and loud applause. Tears well up.

I was going to read from the opening chapter, but as I stand there with the book in my hands, eyes blurred, I change my mind. Turn to the last chapter instead. Struggle to keep the book open on the right page, then close it. No more fear. This is the moment I have traveled this long journey to reach. Clutch the beach-glass pendant at my breast, Felix's gift to me, and feel his presence. But this is my message.

"I am able-bodied, thanks to good genes," I say. "Apart from a gammy knee and some old-age aches, I have stayed fit physically. But I have allowed myself to become lame emotionally. I think many of us do that, letting self-consciousness disconnect our natural sense of harmony. I plan to change that."

I look out into the audience, not with fear as I did last January, back in Cape Town, that they might be bored or distracted, but with delight at this chance to share what is so precious to me.

"You know what one of our greatest gifts is? Gravity!" Laughter erupts across the room. "When we trust how firmly we're held by the earth, life gives us the next gift: our own heartbeat. These two forces work for all of us, and with those two, we can all dance, no matter what our physical impairments. Those wonderful young dancers proved that didn't they?"

For a moment, I am lonely. My ghost is silent. My blithe notion applies only to the living.

Sorry, Felix.

I hear him chuckle. *Without gravity or a heartbeat, there's another kind of freedom. You'll see one day—but not for a long time.*

"Let me tell you about a little girl," I tell the crowd. "When I met her, she couldn't dance because she had been so hurt, physically and emotionally. She couldn't feel the ground under her feet, or the rhythm within her. Now, she is starring in *West Side Story.*" I let that sink in. "It's on a very small stage, but one day, she might star on this stage, in this magnificent space."

Warm waves of applause bathe me. The band starts playing again. As others rise from their seats and begin moving to the music, my foot starts tapping. I want to dance.

Next Steps

"Time to sign books," Sam says and points to the table where a long line of people is forming.

~ 28 ~

Back in my own bed in Kalk Bay, sun beams just starting to sparkle on the red wall-hanging. It's very early, but I'm wide awake, listening to gulls. No thud and sigh of waves; the sea must be calm. Without turning to look at him, I know Sam is also awake. I say, "Good morning, you."

"Good morning, Sally." He turns on his side to face me and with two fingers strokes a strand of hair away from my cheek. Something in his tone suggests weariness. It isn't the elated greeting I've heard each day of these past few weeks, the invitation to join him in his Sam world of eager exploration.

"You're not coming back to Portland with me, are you?" he says.

"No, I'm not."

I stiffen. Had no idea that answer was going to emerge. Brace for his reaction. Can't bear to hurt him. And deeply, clearly, don't want to lose him. Vertigo pushes my head into the pillow.

Next Steps

"Does it have anything to do with being back in Grahamstown, with your feelings for Felix?" His voice is hoarse. "His second *yarzheit* is coming up, isn't it?"

"Yes, but definitely no," I say. "If anything, it helped clarify how much I love you. It's just taken me till now to know my own truth." Fumble for words, yet my answer is simple. "I'm not coming back—yet. I have too much to do here. I like Portland, but you're away half the time. I can't be waiting around for you when there is so much here. Can you understand that?"

His head is down. My tinnitus fills the silence Then he looks up and smiles at me. "I hear you. And I do understand."

I sit up, cross-legged, and kiss his nose. For the first time, he hasn't risen before me to shower and shave. His hair is rumpled, and his chin is bristly. I get the feeling he has been deep in thought for hours, waiting for me to open my eyes.

"What I was dreading has happened; you've turned me down," he says. "You don't want to marry me, do you? And yet here we are, and the world hasn't ended." I've come to recognize how the curve in his lower lip becomes more accentuated when he is trying to contain his emotions "I'm not deluded, am I?"

I nod, and then snuggle back into the crook of his arm. Usually, I need to face someone to say momentous things, to be sure they are hearing me, but with this man I trust his listening. He rests his head on top of mine, his hard spread across my hip. I stroke the muscle in his arm, moving up over the bicep, cupping the curve of his shoulder. Each inch of him pleases me.

"You're not deluded. I am in love with you," I tell him. "I want to be your partner. But, for now, this will be my home base. And I know I can't ask you to come live here full-time."

"So where does that leave us?" His question is bracketed by silence, and then the sound of plaintive meows and a scratching at the door. I ignore the cats.

We are so lucky. That realization rides the sunshine brightening the room. Unlike for my parents and all the generations before us, geographic distance need not strain our bond; we have the whole world within reach. I tell him, "It leaves us with a long-distance love affair, a committed, transatlantic romance."

I'm not sure exactly what those words involve, but the practicalities are crystallizing. "When we're apart, thanks to technology, we can still have daily contact. And we can have lots of in-person visits, here and in Portland." I feel small up and down movements of his head. "And when we get too old to travel, we will reshape the arrangement. Deal?"

There is silence for three or four beats. "Deal," he says slowly. "I can live with that, so long as you promise I can have you in my arms often."

"I want that too." I turn and hug Sam tight, then disengage and stand up. Toss Felix's robe to him and put on the batik kimono I bought in Grahamstown. "Ready for tea?"

He nods and stands up alongside me. I stick my arm out straight, lay my other hand on his shoulder and toss back my head. "Ready to dance?"

His eyebrows arch.

"You want to dance, together, with me?"

Next Steps

"Is there any other way to tango?" He gives a whoop of delight and pulls me to him. This might be more of a Texas two-step than a tango, but together, arms pointed forward, we barrel down the passage.

"We could have danced down the aisle at our wedding," he says. "Imagine!"

We swirl around the kitchen table, switching on the kettle, and the stove in passing.

"We should still have a really good party," I say. "An unwedding party."

You can serve my sangria. You still remember how I made it? I hear Felix's voice, clear as can be.

Indeed, I do, Tiger Man. Indeed, we will. Though maybe not as strong, so people can stay upright.

Sam twirls me into a dip so deep, he can't heave me out of it, and we tumble onto the floor and sit there, panting and laughing like kids.

So much for staying upright, Felix snorts, but I hear a note of self-satisfaction. He is pleased with what he has wrought. I am too.

I clamber to my feet. Reach out a hand and pull Sam to his feet, and back into my arms.

The End

About the Author

Elaine Durbach was born in Zimbabwe and grew up in Zambia, Lesotho and South Africa.

She earned a Journalism degree at Rhodes University in Grahamstown and began her journalism career in Cape Town. As a student she was awarded the inaugural Cape Times Scholarship, and as a reporter, won a World Press Institute Fellowship, which brought her to the United States.

She returned to New York as a correspondent for the South African Morning Group, and then freelanced, working periodically for the United Nations. After moving to New Jersey, for 17 years she wrote for the *New Jersey Jewish News*. Along the way, she won another three press awards

Elaine wrote two non-fiction books, *With Mixed* Feelings and *South Africa, the Wild Realms* (both published by Don Nelson).

She wrote her first novel, *Roundabout*, in 2019. A sequel, *LAF – Life After Felix*, followed in 2022. *Next Steps* is the final book in her Sally Paddington series. All three are self-published. She has three other novels in progress.

Elaine lives in Maplewood, NJ, with her husband Marshall Norstein and their son Gabe. When not writing fiction, she edits other people's writing, makes jewelry, draws, and explores her neighborhood, photographing flowers with her cellphone.

Be In Touch

If you would like to schedule an interview, set up a book talk, or ask a question or share your views, you can do so via the contact form on the author's website:

www.ElaineDurbach.com.

You are also welcome to send a message or respond to posts on Facebook on the Elaine Durbach Author Page.

If you enjoyed this book, please share your opinion in reviews (e.g. on Amazon, Goodreads, etc, or online) and with friends and family. If so inclined, ask your local library or bookstore if they have it.

~ ~

Printed in Great Britain
by Amazon